INNOCENCE
ON
TRIAL

RICK BOWERS

Published and distributed by Book Baby
In association with Script Star Media
Print ISBN: 978-1-54395-867-6
eBook ISBN: 978-1-54395-868-3

To Wynn, Neva, Helen, and Luke, with Joy.

In the time it took to write this novel, 409 men and woman were exonerated of serious crimes in the U.S.

Innocence on Trial is dedicated to them, and all of the imprisoned innocent.

1

Eden, New York
July 2, 2008
3:17 AM

ERIN LAMBERT PLACED TWO HANDS ON THE PRECAST CONCRETE BARrier of the pedestrian bridge that arched over the Genesee River.

Erin had no doubt that the forty-foot drop would end her pain. The violent crush of flesh and bone on rock and water would break the grip of the street-grade OxyContin, acid-laced weed, cheap vodka, and uncaring men who had ruined it all. The plunge would also erase the shame of dancing nude for leeches and losers. Erin wondered whether her sister strippers at the Bottoms Up Gentleman's Club would hold a wake for her using her stage name, "Breeze."

"My life is fucked," she thought, watching the water swirled below. "Totally fucked."

At that moment, Erin heard the unwelcome sound of salvation coming in the form of tires on gravel. The engine stopped, the door opened, and footsteps snapped dried twigs and leaves. Tree frogs and cicadas screeched an alarm.

"Go away." Erin didn't bother to look back to see who'd crashed her pity party. "Just leave me alone. Get it? Go."

No response.

"For Christ's sake." She raised her voice even louder, her cry riding the jagged rocks that studded the shallows upriver. "What part of 'get lost' don't you understand?"

Still no response.

Erin turned to confront the intruder. She saw the dark outline of a man moving toward her. His shadowy presence stepped onto the footbridge, taking long strides. In his black sweatshirt, slacks, gloves, and boots, the figure blended into the night like the reflection of the black oaks on the dark water. His eyes, however, cut through the darkness, glowing in the moonlight like those of a predator closing in on his prey.

As the man approached, Erin opened her eyes so wide, her lids ached, straining to see if she could identify him. In the hazy moonlight, she could make out his face. The guy's rigid bone structure and cold, deep-set eyes sent panic racing up and down her spine. In the dim light of the starry sky, she moved her gaze to his hands. The man twirled a steel pipe in his right hand and swung a coil of rope in his left. Her heart pounded, and her brain raced; fear paralyzed her arms and legs.

"No!" she screamed. "Why?"

He kept coming, picking up his pace.

"I'm sorry," she gasped. "I am. I'm so sorry."

Her hunter laughed. His cold, deep voice said, "Too late now."

Her blood froze over.

Although she'd contemplated death just moments before, Erin Lambert now wanted to go on living. "Don't hurt me," she gasped, registering the noose hanging at the end of the rope.

She felt like one of those chiseled ice sculptures at a winter festival. Closing her eyes, she embraced the darkness, blacking out what she hoped was just a bad dream. When her eyes opened, however, there was no doubt that this was real. The intruder raised his right arm above his head and brought the tire iron down hard. The dull clunk echoed off the granite rock face.

White-hot pain cascaded over the right side of Erin's face, circled her skull, and spread through her head, neck, and shoulders. Her knees buckled. Her eyes rolled. She dropped the vodka jug she'd been slurping from and heard it shatter at her feet. She crumpled into a heap on the shards before curling herself into a ball at the base of the barrier. She felt another surge of pain as the black tire iron cracked against the other side of her skull. Now, she lay still, feigning death.

"Wait." Her mind raced. "What's this?" Hope flickered. Erin spotted the vodka jug's handle, still intact, and grabbed it, thrusting the jagged edge into the leg of her assailant. She heard a scream, followed by silence.

"Now go."

No chance. The man's muscular arms lifted her up and propped her against the barrier. His skilled and practiced hands dropped the noose over her head and snapped the slipknot tight. He pulled hard, squeezing the rope into her neck, cutting off her air supply.

The man in black stepped back and wrapped the other end of the rope around a steel bar protruding from the concrete. Then, he lifted her limp body onto the top of the wall.

"No!" Erin sucked in a lungful of air, summoning the strength to scream. "Please, no!"

She saw him smile and heard him snicker.

She felt his hands rest on her upper body.

She watched him step back and set his feet.

She felt him push.

Erin experienced an instant of weightlessness as she plunged into the abyss.

The rope unfurled and snapped tight.

The cicadas and tree frogs went silent.

2

2019

THE CRUMBLING RAMPARTS. THE SPIRAL GUARD TOWERS. THE THIR-ty-foot concrete wall.

Squinting into the sun on a cloudless summer morning, Laura Tobias scanned the century-old, two-thousand-man, maximum security prison. The Attica Correctional Facility in remote western New York looked like a medieval fortress rising from a barren moonscape.

Attica, a rogues' gallery of serial killers, gang leaders, pedophiles, and madmen.

Attica, a state-run torture chamber for the depraved, deranged, detested, and diabolical.

Attica, a monument to misery, misnamed a "correctional facility."

Attica, the scene of the infamous 1971 prison riot and takeover, and the merciless police siege that left thirty-nine inmates and hostages dead. Adding to the death toll were three inmates and one guard killed earlier in the revolt.

Laura imagined what the scene must have been like on that fall morning, close to a half-century ago. The morning that six-hundred armed state troopers reclaimed the D-Block exercise yard the cons called "Central Park."

She could almost see the armored choppers raining tear gas on prisoners as they retreated under a hail of gunfire, and the police sharpshooters picking off the inmate ringleaders. She could almost hear the automatic weapons fire and the booming shotgun blasts tearing up convicts and hostages as the amplified command, *"Surrender and you will not be harmed!"* rolled over the living and the dead. She imagined state troopers firing at the cons, who wore football helmets and fought back with shivs, crude Molotov cocktails, and homemade spears.

Laura crossed the asphalt parking lot and approached the prison entrance, which was flanked by the flags of the United States and the State of New York. She passed a granite marker bearing the names of the eleven guards killed in the '71 siege. Laura pictured the dead prisoners and hostages lined up on the pavement, as they had been after the '71 assault. The hardtop under her black ankle boots had once glittered with a thin sheet of crimson, and the humid air had once been beaded with red droplets.

Fuck Attica.

Laura Tobias was a woman of high ideals and personal secrets.

The young lawyer looked up at the words, "Attica Correctional Facility," etched in concrete above the arched entrance. Cracks in the grim façade cascaded in all directions like random slash wounds. Her gaze rose to the imposing turret and towering spire that made the place look like a castle. Disneyland for the doomed.

Laura hated Attica. Dungeons like this, and the hopeless souls locked inside them, were among the reasons she'd become an exoneration law-yer in the first place. Torture chambers like Attica, and the miserable men locked inside them, were among the reasons she'd never stop fighting for the wronged innocents.

Never.

Laura knew what to expect inside the classic, old-style "Big House": the mess hall rigged with automatic tear gas sprinklers; the howls of lunatics emanating from the Segregated Housing Unit the cons called "the Box"; the long, linear cell blocks linked by intersecting catwalks and tunnels; the stench of human waste and Lysol; the caged rage and choked fury. She also knew that inside those walls, beyond the guard towers and razor wire, beyond the spotlights and fences, beyond the guards and ghosts, she would find an innocent man.

3

LAURA STEPPED DOWN A RAZOR-STRAIGHT WALKWAY TO THE BRICK Administration Building. She passed through a metal detector, then a lobby with shifting shadows, barred windows, and portraits of former prison administrators. She could almost feel the stares of the dead white men in the frames as she continued down the corridor, reaching an office door with a sign that read, "Registration—All Attorneys Sign In Here."

The young lawyer entered the office, stepped to the service counter, and addressed the corrections officer on duty. "Laura Tobias. I'm with the Council Against Wrongful Convictions." She set her briefcase on the counter and opened it, extracting her Certificate of Good Standing from the New York State Office of Court Administration, and her business card from the Council Against Wrongful Convictions. She slid them to the CO.

The short-haired, stocky, middle-aged guard examined the certificate and card before sliding them back to her. He picked up a clipboard and ran his finger down a list of names. He found hers with a rigid scowl. "What else is in the briefcase?"

Laura turned the open case toward him for the requisite contraband search, saying, "I have a one-hour, non-contact visit with inmate Edward Thomas Nash. Lawyer-Client Interview Room Two." She told him Nash's inmate number, 00088417.

The guard snapped like a pit bull whose kill switch had just gone off, "I know that. It's right in front of me." He slid her a sign-in sheet and took a step back.

"Thank you, Officer…?"

"Cox." The CO tapped the name badge above the pocket of his starched shirt. "Jim Cox."

"Thank you, Officer Cox."

Cox's demeanor screamed ex-military. No surprise there. Laura expected most of the guards to be cut from that particular block of granite. After all, honorably discharged military personnel were given hiring preference for jobs with the New York State Department of Corrections and Supervisory Services. In rural backwaters like the town of Attica, those DOCSS jobs were one of the few remaining routes to a middle-class lifestyle.

The CO's sneer seemed to be standard operating procedure. Prison staff always gave the impression they were dedicated to blocking lawyer-client visits. Laura's request to meet her client had been delayed for weeks due to lost paperwork, sudden rule changes, bad communication, and incompetence. To put an end to the foot-dragging, she'd threatened a formal complaint. The whole rigmarole had made her more determined to see it through.

Even if she had to break into prison to do so.

Laura scribbled her name on the sign-in sheet and slid it back to Cox. She posed for a security photo and awaited instructions. After he collected her driver's license, car keys, and wallet for safekeeping, Cox fiddled to get the photo into the plastic sleeve of the visitor's badge. As he dallied, Laura studied a poster on the wall behind the CO:

DRESS CODE FOR FEMALE VISITORS:
No short skirts.
No halter tops.
No tight sweaters.
No hats or headbands.
No jewelry or watches.
No green clothing of any kind.

Laura hoped her thrift-store black jacket, long-sleeved, white cotton shirt, loose-cut black slacks, and black ankle boots would pass muster. Most of the time, her light brown hair hung loose to her shoulders and swayed with her steps. Today, it was washed, conditioned, moussed, and combed into neat conformity—the conservative look.

Handing her the badge, Cox barked another command: "Take a seat on the bench against the wall. A block CO will be down to escort you to the visitation center." Cox made no comment on her attire; his silence amounted to her passing muster on the prison dress code. Laura slid the sign-in sheet back to Cox, who sneered, turned his back, and walked to a file cabinet, ignoring her as he slipped papers into folders.

Thank you for your excellent service, Officer Cox.

Laura took a seat on the wooden bench and snapped open her brief-case. She'd never been in the place before, and she'd planned to read a report on Attica before her visit, but actual casework had gotten in the way. Figuring she was in for a wait, she pulled out the spiral-bound booklet bearing the logo of the Corrections Association of New York—an independent organization authorized by the state legislature to inspect and report on conditions of the state's major penal institutions. She scanned the title: *"Violence and Abuse of People Incarcerated at Attica C.F."* Reading the description put a lump in her throat:

> *Attica Correctional Facility continues to operate as a real and symbolic epicenter of state violence and abuse in New York State prisons. The history of the 1971 Attica rebellion, and the state's violent suppression of that rebellion, still infuse Attica's walls and operations.*
>
> *Staff brutality, racism, and abuses of power remain pervasive at Attica, creating an overall environment of abuse and violence. Incarcerated persons reported frequent staff assaults, including punches, kicks, beating with batons, choking, smashing people's heads against walls, and abusive searches.*

"Laura Tobias!" The block CO spat out her name like it was spiked with poison.

"Here," she shot back. "I'm Laura Tobias."

"Follow me." The CO blurted the words through a tight smile. "You're taking the Tour."

4

LAURA HUSTLED HER PAPERS BACK INTO HER BRIEFCASE AND JUMPED UP from the bench.

"Move it," the CO snarled with a mix of aggravation and arrogance. "Let's go."

He smiled, shot a knowing look to Cox, and turned back to Laura.

"You get the VIP tour," he said. "Right this way."

"Tour?" She posed the question with a tilt of her head. "What kind of tour?"

The CO smirked. "It's just a short stroll through the cells, over the catwalk, and past the yards. The Grand Tour."

More bullshit, Laura thought. It was probably just a tactic used to intimidate overly aggressive lawyers. The guards probably shared a laugh over giving an attorney "the Tour."

Laura locked eyes with him and said, "Let's go."

She read the name tag on the CO's shirt: Mathew Brady. She made him out to be twenty-one, twenty-two at the most. Probably too young to be a vet. Must have gotten the job through family connections. His complexion was baby-smooth and pink as a peach, like a razor had never touched his delicate skin. In an odd contradiction, his barrel chest and iron frame had undoubtedly been forged by thousands of bench presses, and cases of steroids. Brady wore a black stab vest over his rock-hard body. He kept his head high and his stare inscrutable, and marched like the soldier he never was.

Brady led her through the Administration Building Annex. She could see the entrance to A-Block at the end of the hall. The checkpoint was a steel door, rigged with an electronic operating system and guarded by a pair of officers. Lined up behind Officer Brady, Laura waited for an electric buzzer, passed through the metal detector, and emerged into the infamous prison.

"Ugh." She gagged on the rancid stench. "Shit!"

Brady looked back with a half-smile, half-sneer. "Water shortage. No running water. It'll be back up tonight."

Choking back bile, Laura resisted the urge to stop and demand the interview be held in the proper room. Instead, she kept moving forward, refusing to respond to the guard's obvious intimidation ploy.

"Don't stop for any reason," he snapped back at her. "Don't speak to any inmate. Don't respond to the catcalls."

Catcalls? Give me a break. Catcalls are the least of my worries.

Laura followed Brady into A-Block. She could make out her reflection on the polished concrete floor and feel the stares of caged residents in the long row of cells, which looked to be maybe eight feet wide and ten feet deep. The ceilings were high, maybe twelve feet. Each cell was bounded on three sides by cracked and filthy concrete walls. The front of each cell, facing the corridor, was a grate of steel bars with a slot for delivering meals. Double-deck bunks, stainless steel toilet-and-basin combos, and small desks left little space for the inmates to move. TVs flickered with daytime talk shows in a few cells, and radios crackled with rap music in others. The entertainment options were granted to inmate trustees—prisoners who performed assigned tasks for the administration—or shot callers with the cash to buy the equipment at the commissary.

Following Brady, Laura saw a guard walking toward her from the opposite direction. He smacked his baton against his palm and took steady, measured strides. Behind him, a line of inmates paraded in military fashion—in parallel lines, eyes straight ahead, silently. To Laura, the procession looked like a scene from a movie set in a nineteenth-century penitentiary. She stared straight ahead as the army of the living dead moved past her like ghosts.

Laura scanned the long row of caged residents. Most wore green shirts with name tags and matching green pants. Attica green.

Laura despised this barred world. The barbaric scene, combined with the dead air and rancid odors, kept heaving vomit into her throat. Decades after the historic riot, Attica had not fundamentally changed. Sure, more education and counseling programs were now offered to the prisoners to cover the brutality. The hospital wing actually had real doctors and nurses. Still, to this day, inhumane conditions, unchecked violence, and sadistic retribution ruled supreme. The guards issued punishment in darkened nooks out of range of the security cameras, their attacks ranging from belt whippings to sexual assaults.

For Christ's sake, she thought, these prisoners have it worse than the most mistreated zoo animals. Except, in *this* zoo, there were no moms pushing strollers, or kids hunting for the gorilla cage. Just broken men and unbroken bars, shining like guillotines in the shifting light.

The catcalls began falling like a putrid rain:

"Pussy on the block."

"Bend over, baby girl."

"Come get it, little mama."

Laura stared at Brady's back and kept moving as the jeers escalated in both number and crudity. She forced herself to maintain a blank expression, denying the cat-callers the pleasure of a response.

Now, what?

A guard approached. Devoid of any expression, the blue shirt had a prisoner cuffed to his left hand. The detainee had no shirt, wild eyes, and slash marks covering his bare chest. As the guard dragged him past Laura, the shackled inmate screamed in her direction, "I cut myself!" His terrified eyes locked onto hers. "I'm crazy! Get me out! I don't belong here!"

Brady took a sharp right into B-Block, and Laura followed. She cast her gaze down the long corridor, cringing at the rows of misery. Somewhere above the cells, pale light cut through wired windows. A few ancient, belt-driven ceiling fans circulated stale air.

Next, her guide led her onto the central catwalk—a raised walkway that connected the four cell blocks and oversaw the exercise yards. Men shooting hoops. Men tossing footballs. Men huddled in small groups. An old con hunting for half-smoked cigarettes like a starving chicken pecking at bare dirt. Laura looked up to see a guard peering down from a tower, an AK-15 slung over his shoulder. Just another afternoon recreation period for the boys.

She followed Brady down a darkened corridor to the main control room the inmates called "Grand Central"—the switching station the rebelling prisoners had seized to gain control of the facility back in '71. From there, they passed more sliding steel doors and grim-faced guards, then crossed over another leg of the catwalk to the Administration Building Annex.

The Tour had ended right where it had started.

"This is it." Brady pointed to a door. "Your client will be right down."

Laura took a deep breath as she stepped into the small room, then sighed with relief as she moved to the far side of the desk.

She'd made it. She'd survived the Tour. She'd gotten past the concrete walls, razor-wire fences, hostile guards, catcalling inmates, and putrid stench. After weeks of talking to Nash on state-monitored phone calls, she was finally going to look her client in the eyes.

5

Attica Correctional Facility
Security First
Thank Your Guard

LAURA SAT UNDER THE SIGN ON THE ATTORNEY'S SIDE OF THE SMALL white table. She shifted on the stool bolted to the floor and scanned the room. The walls were antiseptic white. The lights were harsh fluorescent. The floors were polished to a shine.

A grim-faced guard led Nash to the stool on the prisoner's side of the table. The massive CO—well over six-foot-six and three-hundred pounds— pushed the con into the seat opposite Laura. "One hour," the guard snarled. "I'll be watching you."

He took a position in the corner, standing ramrod straight, hands folded in front of him.

Laura smiled at her client. "Eddie Nash. At long last, we meet."

Eddie rested his cuffed hands on the tabletop. "Live and in-person."

An awkward moment passed before Eddie mused, "You look good in person. Better than your website photo."

"You look good yourself, my friend." Laura knew she was stretching it, but she had to set a positive tone. "Much better than your mugshot."

Eddie nodded. "Mugshots are so unflattering. It's something about the lighting in those police stations."

Laura smiled to hide her concern. She glanced at the deep ridges that cut across his forehead, and the fine lines that spiderwebbed across his face. His washed-out brown skin was starved for sunlight and as puffy as a blowfish. Deep purple veins ran down his neck and under the lapels of his green work shirt. His black hair was streaked with gray and thinning on top, and his dull, brown eyes were engulfed by dark circles. With his light brown complexion and even features, Eddie looked like an older version of Tiger Woods after a weeklong bender. On the other hand, Laura observed, the physique under his shirt appeared to be strong and fit, the frame of a man who worked out and cared about his body.

Eddie broke the silence. "Tell me again," he said. "How long have you—?"

"Been practicing law?" Laura interjected. "How long have I been a lawyer?"

"Interrupt me anytime," Eddie replied, shooting her a wry smile. "Cons love being interrupted mid-sentence."

Laura laughed. *Interrupted mid-sentence.* This con had a sense of humor. "To answer your question, I've spent four years as a staff attorney with the Council Against Wrongful Convictions. Four years working to get innocent people out of prison. A half-dozen of my clients are walking free today, dining on home-cooked meals, instead of prison swill. My whole hustle is freeing people who never should have been sent to prison in the first place."

Eddie nodded. "I get it. You specialize."

Laura nodded back. He was right. She'd been in the first generation of law school students at NYU who'd specialized in exonerating innocent men and women convicted of major crimes. Through the Council Against

Wrongful Convictions, she'd opened doors for innocent inmates and was a trailblazer in a movement that had exonerated two-thousand inmates, a number that just scratched the surface of those wrongfully convicted.

"Eddie, there are more than two-and-a-half million convicts serving time in the U.S. Two-and-a-half *million*. Five percent—a conservative estimate— were wrongfully convicted."

Eddie shook his head in disgust. "I see it all the time. The tagalong kid whose friends fingered him for *their* corner-store holdup. The scapegoat who went down, so the chief of police could be a hero."

Laura nodded. "Put all those people in one place, and you'd have the biggest prison on the planet. The biggest prison in the history of the planet. A vast pit of injustice. The tomb of the innocent."

Eddie gazed up at the ceiling, contemplating the statement. "You're telling me?" His chuckle carried a grim undertone. "I'm *in* the tomb of the innocent."

"That's why I'm here. We represent clients on the basis of actual innocence. Convicts who did not commit the crime that sent them to lock-up. We also expose police and prosecutorial misconduct and find new evidence that points to the actual culprit. We turn over every stone to find the truth and make sure real justice is served."

"Okay." Eddie nodded. "I'm your perfect client."

"I'm your best hope for ever walking out of this prison a free man. So, let's get down to business."

"Let's," Eddie replied. "Where are we?"

Laura doubled down on the lawyer-speak. "We've filed a writ with the federal court, stating that the police coerced your confession, fabricated evidence, and lied on the stand. The reckless prosecution violated your rights under the Fourth and Fourteenth Amendments. We also argued that your incompetent defense attorney denied your right to adequate legal representation under the Sixth Amendment.

"The federal appeal gives us a much better shot at overturning the original conviction. We'll give the federal judges plenty of grounds to vacate your conviction."

Eddie opened and closed the fingers on his shackled hands and shifted on his stool like an ADD kid who'd forgotten his meds. "Great. It all sounds wonderful. Just one question: Will anybody give a good goddamn?"

6

EDDIE STARED AT THE CONCRETE FLOOR. "I'VE BEEN SAYING ALL THAT stuff for years. My lawyers have been saying all that stuff for years. The courts have all heard it and said, 'Who cares?' It's been 'Guilty as charged,' 'life without parole,' "the appeals court affirms,' 'our law firm is unable to take your case'… those lines have haunted my nightmares for the past decade." Eddie winced like a man who lived with a butcher's knife stuck in the small of his back. "The system keeps throwing it back in my face."

It was true. Edward Thomas Nash had endured defeat after defeat for the past decade. Tried amid a circus atmosphere in the Erie District Courthouse outside Eden, *State of New York v. Edward Thomas Nash* had been a no-doubter. Wham, bam, you're off to prison, man. It ended with a guilty verdict, the maximum sentence, and a one-way van ride to Attica. A year later, the New York State Court of Appeals rejected his appeal, citing "a lack of reversible error." Now, Laura's challenge to the U.S. District Court of Appeals for the Second Circuit was his last hope. Only the federal court could reverse the original guilty finding and order a new trial.

Tears welled in Eddie's eyes. "No telling what I'll do if I lose again. I might just take a pine box parole."

Laura had heard that phrase before. In slammer world, it meant "leaving prison in a plain, wooden coffin."

"Look, Eddie. Let's keep our hopes up. Our goal is to get the federal court to order a new trial. I'll represent you in *State of New York v. Nash II: The Sequel.* I'll expose the prosecutor's outrageous lies, bogus evidence, and lying witnesses. I'll shine a light on the actual monster who hanged that poor girl. Shame on the cops for not doing it ten years ago."

A light returned to Eddie's eyes. "Okay. Okay. I'm down with it."

Laura decided to just roll on. "I'll introduce the jury to the real Eddie Nash. The small-town kid who overcame the odds to become a stand-up guy. The Army vet who served his country and came home to build a life. The victim of a terrible miscarriage of justice."

Eddie let the notion sink in before allowing a smile to cross his face. "Now, you're talking. I'll be exonerated. I'll walk out of the courtroom a free man. I'll announce it to the newspapers and TV. 'I'm innocent.' The whole world will know the truth. Eddie Nash is *not* a murderer. Eddie Nash is a good man."

"That's the plan." Laura shrugged. "No guarantees."

Eddie looked down to the polished tile floor before lifting his head and looking into her eyes. "I'm sorry, Laura. I never should have doubted you. I appreciate all you've done for me. You're a great lawyer. You're an amazing person. You've got a good brain, compassionate heart, and fire in your belly. I'm with you all the way. We'll fight the good fight."

7

LAURA STUDIED THE IRONMAN STANDING BEHIND EDDIE. THE GRIM-faced CO uncrossed his arms, checked his watch, and glanced in her direction.

She leaned in toward Eddie and whispered, "Look. We have to cover a lot of ground in short order. Give succinct answers to my questions. Just the facts. Be specific."

"Shoot."

"When did you meet Erin Lambert?"

"I met her in ninth grade. Homeroom. Mr. Lancing. Erin and me, we were cut from the same cloth. We skipped the same classes, flunked the same courses, crashed the same parties, and made friends with the same lowlifes."

"You were two of kind. Fellow rebels."

"Yeah. Go figure. This skinny black kid from the wrong side of town, and this pretty white girl from the right side. Her old man was one mean son of a bitch. He used to chase me away, cussing and calling me the N-word. 'Stay away from my daughter, you black bastard.'"

"But you stayed tight with Erin?"

"All through high school. Best friends. Allies. We drifted apart when I left for the military. When I came back eight years later, we reconnected. Or, I should say, she found me."

"How?"

"I was scarfing a burger at the Riverside Diner. Who walks in? Erin Lambert. She looked like the scum you scrape off the bottom of the shit can. Long, dirty hair. Black circles under bloodshot eyes. Turns out she was taking three-hundred milligrams of OxyContin a day and washing it down with cheap vodka from a gallon jug. Get this: She was working as a dancer at the Bottoms Up strip club. When I heard that, I wanted to puke."

"The Bottoms Up?"

"A windowless brick dive, full of losers, loudmouths, parolees, and per-verts—and most of the strippers did a lot more. But, that wasn't the worst of it. Erin told me she'd been dating the bouncer—this two-bit tough guy named Jimmy Dean Bernadi. I looked into her eyes and made her a promise. I said, 'Erin, I'm gonna walk you back from the goddamned cliff. I'm gonna help you get your life back.'"

"How did that go?"

"The girl was making a comeback—at first. Broke it off with Bernadi. Cut back on the dope and booze. She was building up the courage to quit the club; that was hard. The other dancers were her only friends. She called them her 'stripper sisterhood,' or some shit like that."

The big guard checked his watch again. Laura picked up her pace. "When did you learn of her death?"

"I was watching the local news on TV." Eddie lowered his voice. "I saw an old yearbook photo of her with white type spelling out, *'Erin Lambert.'* Then, the cops lowering a limp body on a rope tied to a bridge. I cringed at the words crawling across the bottom of the screen. Shit like, *'Stripper Hung from Footbridge'* and *'The Hangman of Eden on the Loose.'*"

Eddie lowered his head. "I can't talk about it. Let's just leave it there."

"No." Laura motioned with two hands in a keep-it-coming manner. "Every detail is crucial. Tell me about the arrest."

Eddie shook his head in disgust. "The cop, Detective Peter Demario, showed up at my apartment, pushed open my door, slammed me against the wall, patted me down, slapped on the cuffs, dragged me to the patrol car, and drove me to the county precinct."

Laura saw the CO shift his legs and stretch his arms. She turned back to Eddie. "What happened at the police station?"

"Demario dragged me into a small room with no windows, shoved me into a wooden chair, and cuffed my left arm to a water pipe that ran from wall to wall. Then, Demario goes, 'Confess, you black son of a bitch. Tell us how you killed that little piece of white ass.' Crap like that. I told him to go to hell."

"Then?"

"He pressed his gun barrel into my forehead and said, 'Confess. Tell me how you strung up the whore.' He pulled a phone book from the shelf, lifted it up high, and slammed it down onto my skull. I felt the room tilt, the floor spin, and everything faded into this kind of hazy, gray mist. My brain turned to scrambled eggs." A tear beaded in Eddie's eye at the memory. "Then, the bastard took out a plastic bag. He placed it over my head and pulled the drawstrings. When I came to, I told him whatever he wanted to hear. I figured no one would believe it. I was wrong."

"Your trial?" Laura asked. "What about that?"

Eddie leaned back. "Trial?" He said the word as though it tasted like shit. "I watched the cops pull fake evidence out of their asses. Tire tracks, clothing fibers, glass shards, beer bottles, piss with my DNA in it. The prosecutor produced this bullshit witness who put me at the crime scene. That bouncer from the Bottoms Up, Jimmy Dean Bernadi, lied like a fucking politician on Election Day. He testified that he'd heard me threaten to kill Erin the day before the murder. Lies. Lies. Lies. Nothing but lies."

"What about your lawyer?"

"My public defender sat on his hands from the opening gavel to the final verdict. Next thing I knew, I had my own place here at Attica. Rent-free. Meals included. Twenty-four-seven security. Everything a man could ask for. Except freedom and dignity."

The CO stepped forward and put a meaty paw on Eddie's shoulder. "That's it, Nash. Time's up."

As the guard led him away, Laura shouted, "Stay strong! I'll be back!"

Then, she watched him disappear back into hell.

* * *

As Eddie headed back to his cell, his mind circled with crude thoughts. Being locked up with virtually no female contact will do that to a man. He pictured his hot young lawyer stark naked, coming close to him and whispering in his ear. "Please Eddie. Let me take you away from all this." In Eddie's mind, the bitch had natural good looks and the physique of a long-distance runner. She was downright sexy for a woman who appeared to shun makeup and suggestive clothes. Her complexion was tanned and smooth. Her green eyes sparkled under thin, arching eyebrows. Her thin lips and button nose verged on being too cute for his taste. He couldn't get a good read on her contours under her drab clothes, but that could wait.

And once she got him out of here, the wide world of women could be his for the taking.

8

"HOME, SWEET HOME."

The hefty CO placed his right paw on the small of Eddie's back and pushed. The force sent him stumbling into the center of the cell. Eddie broke his fall with the palms of his hands. Standing back up, he flexed his arms and shook his head to reorient himself to the dark, dank space. Eddie stood still and remained silent, listening as the cell door locked, and the guard's footsteps faded on the catwalk. Certain that no one could see or hear him, Eddie balled his right hand into a fist and thrust it forward with a muted, "YES!", celebrating the performance of a lifetime, his version of a victory dance in the end zone following the winning touchdown.

Eddie was pleased—elated—with his role in the lawyer/client interview room. He had delivered his lines with conviction, never wavering from the script he'd etched into his gray matter like words etched into stone. As rehearsed, Eddie had started his tale of woe in the character of the demoralized lifer, the downcast convict with no hope of escaping prison alive. The whole bit about the pine box parole was brilliant. *Pine box parole.* What a line! Violin music should have been rising and falling in the background. A funeral dirge for a hopeless soul.

Later in the interview, he'd hit his second mark, shifting from the total loser to the proud survivor, clinging to hope. *"We'll fight the good fight."* Eddie was certain he'd expressed his confidence in her with heart-felt authenticity. Stroking her ego was fucking brilliant. Gushing about her being a "great lawyer" and "amazing person" was perfect. Who doesn't love praise? He'd cemented her trust, and he hadn't departed from his oft-told narrative of the case itself. The coerced confession, the planted evidence, the bogus witnesses, the guilty verdict, the ten years of torture at Attica. Now, Eddie's practice and patience were paying off. Now, Eddie Nash was boarding the Exoneration Express.

Yes, Eddie felt good. Real good. Nevertheless, there was something eating at him. What was it? Laura Tobias, the pretty white girl with the fancy law degree and impressive job with the Council Against Wrongful Convictions. Still, she was not his ideal attorney. She was so young. Her record was fairly thin. *Does she know what she's doing?*

Eddie had imagined his ideal attorney for years, in the darkness of his cell. For years, in the stillness of the night, he'd heard the voice of his perfect lawyer. Eloquent pleas resounded through the courtroom in his mind. Eddie's heaven-sent savior was a handsome, square-shouldered, African-American male who wore a three-piece Armani suit and spoke with a voice as deep and smooth as blended whiskey. A Morgan Freeman voice. This brilliant black attorney—a hybrid of Johnny Cochran and Thurgood Marshall—would thunder against this terrible miscarriage of justice. Articulate. Bold. Learned. Fearsome. The man's twenty-dollar words rolled through his imaginary courtroom like distant cannon fire:

> *"May it please this honorable forum. Edward Thomas Nash stands before you, the essence of innocence. Mr. Nash is a victim of venal allegations, overzealous prosecution, and unbounded prejudice. I beseech you, do not be distracted by the distortions and deceptions of his shameless tormentors. Look beyond their subterfuge to see the truth. Edward Thomas Nash is innocent. Return this man to his family."*

In the end, Eddie and his savior would emerge from the courtroom, arm-in-arm, basking in the cheers of the crowd, glowing in the bright lights of the TV cameras.

Laura Tobias had come out of nowhere. Two months ago, she'd sent him a letter under of the banner of the Council Against Wrongful Convictions: *We have an excellent opportunity to vacate your conviction.* Ms. Tobias had followed up with a few introductory phone calls. Just to feel each other out. Then, for the first time, in that cramped room, she'd looked into his eyes, and Laura Tobias had seen what he'd wanted her to see. Nothing more. Nothing less.

To Eddie, she'd looked like a pretty co-ed from a private girl's college. She'd sounded like a rookie lawyer who'd learned the law from a textbook. Under the surface, though, he'd sensed something more. What was it? What did she have? The woman came off as whip-smart, knowledgeable, and committed to righting the wrongs of a broken legal system. She had a few years of courtroom experience, and had gotten a half-dozen inmates out of lockup. At this point, Eddie figured that he was lucky to have her. Plus, Morgan Freeman, Johnny Cochran, and Thurgood Marshal were nowhere in sight.

Eddie walked to his bunk, sat down, and placed his head in his hands. In the dark world behind his eyelids, he saw home.

9

LAURA RETRIEVED HER KEYS AND CASH FROM THE INTAKE GUARD AND left the Administration Building. She stopped in front of the prison gate to peruse the stone monument bearing the names of the eleven guards killed in the '71 rebellion. Knowing that independent autopsies had showed all the dead guards, hostages, and inmates were killed by state police gunfire, she shook her head and whispered to herself, "A monument to a massacre." She continued into the parking lot and her car for the long drive home. She pulled her faded, blue 1998 Ford Mustang convertible out of the lot, top down, and started along a series of short, crisscrossing roads that led out of the twelve-hundred-acre prison compound. Laura passed through the first checkpoint, beaming as the brick-and-bulletproof-glass guard shack faded in her rearview mirror. She eased onto the two-lane street that would lead to Exchange Road and the highway. Her V-8, 460-horsepower engine had plenty of power to leave the place in the dust, but she kept a light foot on the accelerator, careful to stay within the 25-mph speed limit on the prison roads. A half-mile from the final prison exit road, Laura's mind drifted back to Eddie.

She recounted the reasons for believing in his innocence—or at least, believing he deserved a new trial.

One: The police forced him to confess, manufactured evidence, and lied on the stand.

Two: The prosecutor bought and paid for the one witness who put him anywhere close to the crime scene.

Three: His public defender failed to challenge any of the bogus evidence and lying witnesses. The PD even put Eddie on the stand without preparation to be eaten alive by the prosecutor.

Four: Eddie had answered all her questions without wavering from the testimony he'd laid out ten years before. He seemed to be telling the truth.

A quarter-mile from the final prison exit, she imagined a judge dismissing all the charges with one great crack of the gavel: "Mr. Nash, I also want to apologize on behalf of the State of New York. You are free to go." How she longed to hear those five magic words: *"You are free to go."* A not-guilty verdict in a second trial would be tantamount to exoneration. The state would be responsible for restitution, or they would face a massive lawsuit for wrongful imprisonment. True, the final settlement wouldn't make up for all those lost years, but on the other hand, the windfall would make for one hell of a fresh start. Eddie's family, friends, and neighbors would celebrate his return and help him make the adjustment back to the free world.

Then, Laura recalled a troubling part of the conversation: He'd played the victim card. What was that line? "I just might take a pine box parole."

A cliche, she thought, from a prison flick.

At times, Eddie had seemed to be playing the part of the shit-for-brains black kid from the racist town. This, she felt, seemed out of character for a man who had proclaimed his innocence for over a decade and seemed hell-bent on clearing his name. Contrived. Eddie Nash was not stupid. Eddie Nash was not weak. Eddie Nash was not a victim. Eddie Nash was a very smart man who acted only in his own best interest. Eddie Nash was out for freedom. Period.

She figured he'd been playing her. In fact, she knew it, to an extent. But, what the hell? That was okay. After all, the guy had his life on the line. Eddie had to get her to believe him. To believe *in* him. To fight for him. He *had* to play her. Manipulate her. It didn't mean he was guilty; he was just working to get the most out of her. At the same time, though, she'd been playing him, too.

She had her own reasons for wanting to win this case. The first trial had been a media sensation, and a second trial—if there was to be one—would sizzle with sensationalism, too. The media would devour it and regurgitate it, over and over, then over again. The rope. The noose. The broken neck. The Hangman of Eden. The names of the lawyers would be printed in newspapers, broadcast on TV, and spread through social media. When the jury announced, *"Not guilty,"* her notoriety would turn to fame. Her career would be jet-fueled, setting her up for even bigger cases. The name Laura Tobias would be known to every member of the New York State Bar. Reporters would turn to her as an expert source for high-profile cases. The incarcerated innocent would beg her to represent them. Every prosecutor in the state would cringe when she challenged one of their convictions.

Laura had to congratulate herself on her performance. Through the entire sit-down with the convicted man, she'd kept her ambition hidden behind a façade of righteous indignation. She hadn't let him see the gleam of hunger for fame in her eyes. She'd checked her selfish craving to bask in the limelight. Hell, Eddie had seen her as an idealistic kid out to save a poor black boy from becoming another statistic. Eddie had seen her as one more liberal do-gooder, fighting the big, bad, evil system—the Machine.

He had no clue. *New York v. Nash* was her ticket to the bigtime.

Laura was an eighth of a mile from the prison exit. Cruising at 20 mph, she glanced back in her rearview mirror. The reflection made her flinch. What the hell? An Attica patrol car had pulled off the service road and pushed to within a foot or two of her rear bumper. Squinting, she made out a uniformed CO behind the wheel.

Shit.

As Laura gazed back, the patrol car inched closer. She crawled down the hedge-lined drive with the blue-and-white vehicle on her tail. She vowed to keep going. Once she pulled onto the public road, this patrolman would have no jurisdiction. When she looked back again, the cop car was almost kissing her chrome. She exhaled long and slow, seeing the sign:

LEAVING ATTICA STATE CORRECTIONAL FACILITY.

How many people have thanked God at that sight?

The Mustang was maybe fifty yards out from the borderline when lights swirled behind it. The blast of a siren made her jump.

No fucking way.

Laura pulled off the prison road and came to a stop on the gravel break-down lane.

Stay cool. Don't explode.

Looking once more in her rearview mirror, she saw a tall, thin CO, swaggering toward her. He wore dark sunglasses and a scowl. He leaned into the open driver-side window, resting a hand on his service revolver.

"Laura Tobias?"

"Yeah."

"Come with me."

10

Attica Superintendent Leon Wilkes smiled from behind the double pedestal desk in his oak-paneled office.

"Thank you for stopping by, Counselor." Wilkes raked the long fingers of his right hand through his thick mane of white hair. "It's a pleasure to meet you."

Laura was seated in a comfortable leather armchair in front of his uncluttered desk. "How could I turn down the request from the nice officer who pulled me over with his siren blaring and lights flashing?" Her voice dripped with a toxic mix of anger and sarcasm. "The pleasure's all mine, Superintendent Wilkes. Now, what the hell is going on?"

Wilkes stared back through black-rimmed glasses, his bushy white brows arched over his penetrating steel-blue eyes. "Yes. Well. I apologize for summoning you in such a crude manner. I'd instructed my top lieutenant to escort you from your client visit to my office. However, he couldn't find you."

"I'm not surprised. I got there a little late. Your guards gave me the Tour. Led me on a forced march through the cell blocks."

"How unfortunate. I'm sorry for the inconvenience."

"Right."

"In the end, I had to send the patrol officer out to invite you to my office. I didn't want you to get away without making your acquaintance. Again, my apologies."

"Apology accepted." Laura leaned back in the chair. She gripped the walnut arms like she was choking throats. "Besides, this is a first for me. I can cross this one off my bucket list."

"Being pulled over? On prison grounds?"

"No." Laura shot him a "gotcha" smile. "Hearing the superintendent of a maximum security prison say, *'I didn't want you to get away.'*"

Wilkes laughed out loud and slapped his desktop. "Now, that's a good one. All right, then. I'm glad we have this chance to chat. I'm a fan."

"A fan?" Laura stalled for time to decipher his bullshit. "I'm flattered. I don't really have fans. This makes you the first member of the Laura Tobias Fan Club."

Wilkes adjusted his red power tie. It set off his gray suit coat. "I'm also aware of the Council Against Wrongful Convictions. I admire its work, and for the most part, I support its mission. Ms. Tobias, let me assure you, I shudder at the thought of a single innocent person being housed in this facility. Every one of our inmates should have been convicted in a fair and impartial trial, with all the protections of the New York State Constitution and the U.S. Constitution. There should be no doubt of their guilt."

"Superintendent Wilkes." Laura looked down and studied the hardwood before reengaging his sharp gaze. "Let's get down to it. What can I do for you? What do you want from me? You didn't summon me here to discuss the Constitution."

Laura was tempted to call him "Warden" Wilkes. She hated the way the prison establishment had whitewashed the language of incarceration, cleansing the DOCSS, when it was formed back in the '80s. Prisons became "correctional facilities," wardens became "superintendents," guards became "corrections officers." Attica now had a hierarchy of one superintendent, two deputy superintendents, four captains, eight lieutenants, and dozens of corrections officers.

"Counselor, let me assure you, I have no agenda. I simply want to exchange information in anticipation of a very interesting and important appeal." The superintendent leaned back in his cushioned swivel chair and clasped his hands behind his head. "As part of the discovery process, the New York State Prosecutor's Office forwarded your request for a copy of Mr. Nash's prison file. The entire file is being compiled as we speak. It will be forwarded to your offices in a few days. I think you'll find it very interesting—enlightening, even."

"Enlightening?" Laura narrowed her eyes, straightened her back, and ratcheted up her B.S.-detector, which was already soaring into the red. "Well, I look forward to examining the entire file. Now, if that's all, I'll be on my way. I have a long drive in front of me."

Wilkes leaned forward, planting his elbows onto his desktop. "Counselor. Again. We would never want an innocent man to be imprisoned at Attica. That would be a travesty. On the other hand, we would never want a guilty man to be released from this institution before his rehabilitation was complete. We would never want to send a deranged murderer back into the community to take more innocent lives. I'm sure you can understand our dilemma."

"*Your* dilemma?" Laura resisted the urge to slug him. She felt her blood pressure rise like the tide in the run-up to a hurricane. "What are you talking about, 'dilemma?' How did this come to be about you?"

"Counselor, may I share an important fact?"

"What?"

"Edward Thomas Nash is not the man you think he is. Edward Thomas Nash is not a poor, uneducated man from a struggling mill town in upstate New York. Edward Thomas Nash is not the victim of a broken legal system that feeds on black men."

"Is that so?" Laura glared. "What is he?"

"Edward Thomas Nash is a monster capable of unspeakable acts. A one-of-a-kind miscreant who can kill in cold blood and persuade the world of his total innocence. No. Nash is not innocent. Nash is an unrepentant murderer. Nash is a master manipulator. I urge you to reconsider your defense of this man. Don't make the mistake of putting a diabolical killer back into the world. Read the file. Study his pathology. You will see the truth."

Laura stared back in disbelief. *You arrogant bastard.* She buried the expletives running through her mind before finding her voice. "Superintendent Wilkes. Your actions are outrageous. First, you have your guards march me through cell blocks that reek of human waste. A rank attempt at intimidation. Then, you have me pulled over for no reason and escorted to your office. More intimidation. Then, you make outrageous claims against my client, none of which are supported by fact. Then, you ask me to step back from the case. A case that a federal appeals court has found worthy of review. I have a bit of advice for you, sir. Back off. *Way* off. Now."

Wilkes lost his grin as Laura piled on.

"Look. I can have a civil rights complaint on your desk by 10 AM Monday. You can explain your psychobabble theories to a federal judge, and the U.S. Department of Justice. You can spend the next three months with federal prison examiners burrowing up your ass—and if you know me by reputation, Superintendent Wilkes, you know I'll do it. I'll bring the whole power of the law down on you like a landslide. I'll make your life such hell that you'll want to exchange this fancy office for one of those cells. Do you hear me, sir?"

Wilkes straightened his back and cleared his throat. "Now, now, now, take it easy, Counselor." He extended his arms wide and turned his palms up toward the ceiling. He looked like a faith healer praying for heavenly intervention. "I meant no offense. I just wanted to make a simple suggestion. To give you a heads-up. For your own good."

"A threat?" she snapped.

"A warning," he answered.

Laura glared. "I'll show myself out."

"Before you go, Counselor, answer this one little question."

"What?"

"What do you get when you cross a psychopath with a sociopath?"

She glared back in silence.

"Let me tell you." Wilkes let a wicked smile cross his face. "You get a two-headed monster. Edward Thomas Nash."

11

"CHEERS!"

"Cheers!"

Laura clinked glasses with her father on the outdoor patio of the Blue Canoe Café on Lake Cayuga. It was a crisp Saturday afternoon, and three days had passed since her Attica adventure. They were sharing a bottle of 1982 Sauvignon Blanc Reserve from the Blooming Creek Winery on the slopes of Seneca Lake and looking forward to a nice lunch at the lakeside restaurant.

"This New York State white is absolute perfection." Laura lowered her glass onto the white tablecloth, gazing out at the slanting rays of afternoon sun on the shimmering water. "Hints of lime and peach with a perfectly clean finish. Love it."

"I'll drink to that." John Tobias took another sip and savored the flavor. "Here's to food, wine, and conversation. Then, you can update me on the case."

Laura's father was her number-one lunch companion and favorite off-the-books legal adviser. A retired prosecutor with the New York City District Attorney's Office in Manhattan, he was now all about his golf game, bass fishing, and his daughter's cases. He brought the perspective of a seasoned prosecutor to her work—and, naturally, never charged for the advice.

Steering clear of the case for now, John moved on to an even riskier subject. "How's what's-his-name?"

Laura shook her head in a "you've-got-to-be-kidding" way. "You know his name. Nick. Nick Drake."

"Of course. *The* Nick Drake." John shot his daughter a playful smile. "God's gift to stage, screen, and the unemployment line."

Laura shrugged off his jab. *Game on.* "The truth is I have no idea how he is. You'll be pleased to know that Nick and I are taking a break. We both need a little more space."

"You broke up with the guy?"

"We're on hold. We hit the pause button."

"It doesn't make me happy to hear that. That's up to the two of you. I just think you could do better than a thirty-year-old unemployed actor with a fixation on himself."

"Dad. Please."

"Nick could pick up a diamond and throw it away because he'd figure it was just a rock."

Laura groaned. "Please."

An image of Nick burrowed into her brain. He was handsome. Classic good looks. Strong features. Jet black hair. He was smart. A graduate of Columbia and the New York Academy of the Arts. Sure, he was a struggling actor in New York City. Sure, he just missed out on minor roles in off-Broadway plays, TV cop dramas, and underwear commercials. Sure, he was career-obsessed. Nick was a late bloomer who felt the clock ticking.

Be that as it may, Laura wasn't missing him. In fact, she was glad her on-again, off-again boyfriend was off-again. She'd stopped taking his calls after he'd begged off their last date to hang out with an old frat buddy who was in town for the night. It was a common theme—plus, she needed space to concentrate on the case.

Their lunch conversation paused as an attractive young woman in a white blouse and black slacks arrived with their meals. The tall, graceful woman served Laura her Cayuga Lake trout, and John his Cornell chicken. Farm-to-table veggies and fingerling potatoes complemented the dishes. They remained silent as they dug in.

Despite the mini-drama with Nick, her relationship with her father was rock-solid. All those back-to-school nights, father/daughter dances, and class projects had forged a bond that just seemed to grow stronger over the years. From bass-fishing trips on the Finger Lakes to Mets games under the moonlight. It was an essential relationship—especially with Laura's mother gone.

Today, John made a point of having her back. "I'm proud of you, punk," he said. "Have I told you how much I support what you do on behalf of innocent inmates? You inspire me. You are such a believer and a fighter. Mom would be proud, too."

Laura studied her empty plate like it held the answers to life's most confounding questions.

John downed his last bite of chicken and took a sip of water before clearing his throat and addressing the other elephant in the room. "Attica?" he asked. "How was it?"

"Glad to be out. Nice place to visit, but…"

"Nash?"

"Quite a character."

"But, is he innocent?"

12

"My gut tells me he is."

"How can you be so sure?"

"I didn't say I *was* sure."

"Why do you *believe* he's innocent?"

"The case against him doesn't add up. The police and prosecutors had it out for him from the get-go. The cops manufactured evidence and made up testimony. The prosecutor paid witnesses to lie on the stand. Nash's public defender just sat there like a bored spectator at a lopsided ballgame. No one followed leads on other suspects. Better suspects. I mean, talk about a frame-up. This was the mother of all frame-ups. All to make sure that this no-account, upstate black kid paid the price for a horrendous crime."

"How does Nash come across? I mean, what's he like?"

"Overall, he's rational for a guy who's doing life in prison with no chance of parole—and for a crime he insists he did not commit. He's really smart for a guy who slept through high school and never set foot on a college campus. Eddie Nash served eight years in the U.S. Army and left with an honorable discharge and a skill. He worked as a military vehicle mechanic and never saw combat. Nash has natural intelligence, good instincts, and his own best interest at heart. The man even has a sense of humor—even after serving ten years at Attica."

John rested his elbow on the table, lowering his chin onto his palm. "Go on."

"Nash understands his situation, proclaims his innocence, and never wavers from his original storyline. Coerced confession aside, he's been consistent for more than a decade."

"And on the other hand? There's *got* to be an on-the-other-hand."

Laura recalled the line about the pine box parole. "He seems to be playing me. Playing the victim card. Like he wants my pity. I mean, that doesn't make sense."

"Why?"

"Eddie's a naturally confident person. He's been proudly declaring his innocence for ten years. He's been working to get his conviction overturned from Day One. So, why does he play the woe-is-me card? Presenting himself as a dumb black kid from a shit-kicking, racist town made no sense. Suggesting that he might just end it all if the appeal failed did not ring true. It was an act."

"Oh." John looked out at the geese rising from the lake. "Not good."

"Let me explain it this way: It *is* true. This man is a victim of the Machine. He's been set up and smacked down. However, Edward Thomas Nash does not see himself as a loser. I've talked to him a half-dozen times by phone and sat down with him at Attica. This guy is confident, smart, savvy, cool, collected, and determined to clear his name. Maybe *too* smart. Maybe *too* cool. Maybe he's capable of fooling everybody. Maybe he is a master manipulator."

Master manipulator. Where did I hear that phrase? Oh, yeah. Attica superintendent Leon Wilkes had used it to describe Nash. Laura pushed aside her plate and the memory of her clash with Wilkes. Her father didn't need to know about her bizarre encounter with the Lord of the Lock Up. Or the

VIP Tour, or the prison patrol car. He would just worry—and try to take over her life.

John Tobias looked her in the eye. "So, what do you want?"

"I want the opportunity to prove his innocence in a brand-new trial, in a brand-new venue, with a brand-new judge, and a brand-new jury. I'll win. Even if I have to put the cops and prosecutors on trial for all their shenanigans during the first trial."

"Let me ask you this: If Nash didn't commit the murder, who did?"

"Good question."

"What's your plan?"

"To propose multiple theories of third-party guilt." Laura made the pledge with a straight face before laughing out loud. "I just have to figure out who to point the finger at. Or maybe I'll just go out and catch the real killer myself. That would solve everything."

"Well, if your guy is innocent, the real killer is out there."

"Chances are," she agreed. "Maybe he's killed again. Maybe he'll keep on killing." Laura decided to change the subject. She turned the conversation back on her dad. "Hey, how's that committee you were asked to join? You know the one. The old boys' club up in the state capital."

"The old boys' club?" He feigned outrage. "The proper name is the New York State Special Commission on Police Corruption. We'll be looking into bad cops and issuing a full report to the governor. Should be wrapped up by the end of the year."

"No kidding? How did you score that gig?"

John shrugged. "My stellar reputation."

"Your what?"

"My rep for prosecuting the scum of the Earth."

"What scum of the Earth?"

"Bad cops."

"What bad cops?"

"The corrupt few who shake down perps, steal drugs, extort money, plant evidence, and lie on the stand. The ones who lord over the drug dealers, gangbangers, and con artists until they're just as bad as they are. Worse. I loved putting 'em away. I hate corrupt cops. Make all of us look bad."

"I had no idea," Laura said. "You were a real crusader."

John's face took on a somber tone. "Just doing my job."

Laura shifted her gaze to the back corner of the restaurant, where a good-looking man was sitting at the bar, checking her out.

"Hey, Dad. Don't turn around. The fellow at the bar keeps looking this way."

"What? Who?"

"Don't look back. Just a guy. Mid-thirties. Short, blond hair. Killer blue eyes. Blue blazer. White golf shirt. He's keeps glancing over here."

"Just ignore him. Mind your own business."

"He looks familiar. Very familiar. I've seen him before. I know it. Where…?"

John decided to ignore her advice, glancing over his shoulder at the man in the blue blazer. After checking him out, John turned back to Laura, who was rolling her eyes at his obvious move. "I have no idea who he is. He looks like trouble to me."

"He looks so familiar. I know him. I know! Yeah, yeah, yeah, he was filling up at the gas station in the lane next to mine. Small world. He was cute then, and he's even cuter now."

"Just ignore him," John repeated. "Finish your lunch. Drink your wine."

Laura leaned toward her dad. Why not torture the old man a bit more? "Maybe I should stroll over and introduce myself. I'll tell him he looks very familiar and ask if we've ever met. There's no telling where an opening like that might lead. He is rather cute—and a sharp dresser, too."

"Young lady, forget it. You will do no such thing. Good Lord. I didn't raise you to approach strange men in bars. Do you know how dangerous that is? You're right about one thing: No telling where it might lead."

"Oh, come on." Laura pushed out her hands in a give-me-a-break motion. "You are so sexist. Men do it all the time."

"It is not sexist," John shot back. "It's common sense. You have no idea who this guy is. For all we know, he could be a serial killer. He could be savoring a drink before abducting his next victim. Do you really want to end up in his trunk?"

Laura suppressed a laugh. "Oh, please. Come on, old man. Get with the times. Hey. Maybe that's it. Maybe I saw his face on Tinder."

"Tinder?"

Laura groaned. "The dating app."

John looked over his shoulder again—clearly not caring if the stranger saw him.

The man in the blue blazer was gone.

13

Laura jumped into the bucket seat behind the Mustang's wheel, cranked the engine, slammed the gear shift, and lurched forward. She had one more stop to make—and it wasn't going to be an easy one.

Laura cruised down Saratoga Way and eased onto Evergreen Drive. She banked onto a narrow road and through an open gate under a black, iron sign for Longview Cemetery. She rolled down a winding interior road to a tree-lined lot. She parked in the back row next to a stand of spruce and climbed out of the Mustang. Strolling up a lush, grassy hill, she passed under a canopy of towering oaks, their interlocking limbs forming a cover for the rows of headstones and monuments. Above them, thick, gray clouds blotted out the setting sun.

She stopped at a plain granite marker at the top of the hill and read the inscription:

Janet Tobias
Loving Wife and Mother
Born
March 6, 1962
Died
January 16, 1996

Laura's eyes welled with tears, her mind conjuring up distant memories. Her mom. Beautiful. Vivacious. Loving. The most important person in her young life. A person—along with her dad—she couldn't live without. Laura remembered how her mom always seemed to have a smile and a kind word at the ready. Her touch and sage advice made the most insurmountable problems become no big deal.

Until the cancer came. Janet Tobias' battle against the disease turned out to be long and painful ordeal for everyone. The surgery. The chemo. The hospice nurse. Even an eight-year-old girl knew what it meant. Even an eight-year-old girl felt the pain.

A light rain started to fall on the cemetery grounds. It spattered the gravestones and the little flags left for the veterans. Wind swirled in the oaks. A flock of crows rose from the branches and vanished into the fog. Laura clasped her hands and closed her eyes. "I'm sorry, Mom. I should have been there for you."

Laura still had a secret locked in her heart all these years later. She knew she should move on, but she couldn't. The day before her mom's death, Laura had marched up to her mom's deathbed and screamed at the dying woman, excoriating her for abandoning her only child: *"I hate you! I hate you! I hate you!"*

Janet lacked the strength to respond and just drifted off to sleep. She passed away before Laura could take back the words.

After her mom's death, Laura retreated to her own room, feeling like the sun had been blotted out. The grieving girl tried to bury the pain, but it lingered like a dark force. How could she live without her mom? The woman who took her to school, held her hand when she was afraid, held her close all night when she was sick, and took her side when kids bullied her? Her champion?

Laura choked back tears as the rain droplets glistened on the cemetery lawn.

"I'm doing better now, Mom. I think you'd be proud of me."

Laura closed her eyes at the gravesite and conjured up an image of a girl's bedroom:

> *Pink walls. A puppy poster. The lights are dim. The door is locked. A teenage girl sits cross-legged on her bed. She wears cut-off jeans, a t-shirt, headphones, and a somber expression. A grim rock ballad blares through the speakers. The girl holds a razor in her hand. She rests the blade against her bare thigh. She presses the serrated edge to her flesh. As she slides it forward, glorious pain emerges from the crimson flow.*

Thunder boomed.

Laura snapped back into the here and now. It was raining harder, and the wind was picking up. Time to go. Before she got drenched. She stepped up to the gravesite and placed a hand on the tombstone. Then, she turned and headed back down the hill—careful not to slip, encircled as she was by the dead.

She stopped short when the parking lot came into view. A man stood at the trunk of her Mustang. Was he messing with her car? As she continued down the hillside, the man spotted her and slipped away into the nearby woods. From a distance, he looked a lot like the man in the blue blazer.

14

Laura cruised down the darkened country road, passing black pine forests, tree-shrouded lakes, and sprawling cornfields. She was anxious to get back to the city and resume the case.

The radio was set to an oldies station, and she sang along to "Bridge Over Troubled Water." At the chorus, she felt the car tilt hard to the left and heard a familiar thud, thud, thud, then the telltale sound of a rubber tire grinding on a steel wheel hub.

She slowed the car to a crawl and pulled the Mustang onto the gravel breakdown lane in the shadows of a stand of massive river oaks, their bare limbs reaching out and interlocking like skeletal fingers. Still in the car, Laura grabbed her phone and called the emergency road service. The words "no service" on the data screen said it all.

She was alone on a desolate road with no connection to the civilized world. Cicadas screeched. Tree frogs chirped. A dog howled in the distance.

What now?

She knew the answer to her own question—and how to jack up a car, remove a damaged tire, and mount the spare. The year before, one of her rear tires had picked up a nail on the way home from the beach. She'd begun to panic, when a Good Samaritan came to her rescue and showed her, step-by-step, how to change it out. Laura vowed to never be caught short like that again and followed up with a visit to the auto-parts store. Casting cost concerns to the wind, she'd spent $179 on a supercharged Emergency Roadside Survival Kit, a package approved by the New York State Police, complete with fluorescent orange vest, reflective triangles, and six powerful roadside flares.

Laura leaned out of the driver's-side window and looked up and down the long, straight ribbon of road. Seeing no one, she turned off the ignition, unfastened her seatbelt, and climbed out onto the gravel. She took long, purposeful strides to the back of the car, popped the trunk, pulled out the jack, grabbed the tire iron, and removed a couple of safety flares from the kit. With an eight-inch flare in each hand, Laura marched off ten paces from her rear bumper and knelt on the hard, roadside surface. She was positioning the first flare when she heard the whine of an engine behind her.

Looking back, she saw headlights. White eyes in the blackness. Coming on fast. The twin beams grew brighter as the car got closer. It passed, and Laura watched the Chevy Impala crawl to a stop on the shoulder, about fifty yards in front of her disabled Mustang. Her eyes narrowed. Her body tensed. Her heart raced. Her breaths came faster. She did not light the first flare.

The Impala idled for a long moment, engine purring like a beast resting in the bush. Its headlights remained on, illuminating the gravel roadside and the black woods. A darkened figure emerged from the driver's-side door, visible in the mix of headlights and moonlight. The man was clad in a black windbreaker, black pants, and black shoes. He stepped in front of the car, menacing in his own headlights.

Was this the man who'd been wearing the blue blazer?

Had he cut her tire to form a slow air leak back in the cemetery parking lot?

Had he followed her to this isolated spot, knowing her tire would go flat?

For what purpose?

Maybe this was just her overactive imagination, conjuring up a doomsday scenario. Maybe he was just another Good Samaritan out to do a good deed for a stranded motorist.

"Do you need help, Miss? Let me lend you a hand."

15

"No, thank you," Laura called to the man in black, still walking toward her on the dark country road. "Just a flat. I'll have it fixed in no time."

She rose from her kneeling position and stood erect, holding her head high, focusing her eyes forward.

He kept coming. "No, no, no. Let me help you."

The man took five or six strides forward, cutting the distance between them to within thirty yards. Then, he came even closer.

At twenty yards out, Laura could see his eyes, two gleaming orbs reflecting the mix of moonlight, starlight, headlights and taillights. A cocktail of fear and anger ran through her. Her father's words raced through her head: *"If your guy is innocent, the real killer is still out there."*

At fifteen yards out, there was just enough light to make out his appearance. His short-cropped blond hair moved in the wind. His intense blue eyes cut the night. His square shoulders hunched like a wolf on the hunt. This had to be him. The man who'd been shadowing her—in a black outfit this time, instead of a blue blazer. Then, she saw it. In his left hand, the guy twirled a tire iron.

As the guy got closer, twigs snapped under his black shoes. She studied his smile. There was no doubt. It was the same man from the gas station, the restaurant, the cemetery, and who-knew-where-else?

"Stop right there! I called the police!" Laura shouted the lie at full volume. "They're on their way! A state trooper will be here any minute! Take off before the cops get here! Before you regret this!"

"You called the police?" The interloper dropped his voice an octave, halting his forward progress to consider her words. He spread his arms into a wingspan, palms up, tire iron dangling from his left hand. "Now, that is strange. You see, there's no cell coverage out here in God's country. There's no way to dial 911. You called no one. No one's coming to your rescue. No one but me."

"You're wrong! I have a police radio!" Laura yelled that lie even louder. "They're on their way! When they get here, you're fucked!"

"Liar." The man spat the word and took a step forward. "What're you afraid of? I'm not going to hurt you. I just want to help. I just want to mount that spare for you. Maybe talk a little. Get to know you."

"No! Get away from me!"

"Too late for that."

She realized there was no more need to shout. The man had stopped just ten or so yards away. This was no Good Samaritan. This was a Bad Samaritan.

The man glared. "I know who you are. You're a lawyer. You represent a murderer. He killed little Erin Lambert. He nee—"

"Yeah." She took a step back. "I'm impressed. You did your homework."

"I'm going to ask you in a nice way," the man said. "Please, drop the case."

Laura shook her head. "No. Forget it."

"Drop it. I can make you. One way or another."

"Not happening. Who the hell are you?"

The stranger released a long, slow, guttural laugh, a contorted smile crossing his twisted face. He passed the tire iron to his right hand and raised it high. "I guess you'll have to learn the hard way."

Laura straightened her back and narrowed her eyes. She curled her upper lip and snarled like a dog. Her mind raced. Should she make a run for the woods? No. She couldn't show fear or panic. Plus, he'd hunt her down, anyway. The guy looked fit, strong, serious, and determined.

Laura dug the soles of her flats into the loose gravel, bracing her legs for possible impact. She kept her hands behind her back, not allowing the would-be attacker to see the safety flare in her right palm. With her left hand, she squeezed the ignition cord that would ignite its strontium nitrate core. She had to force the confrontation. She had to provoke him.

"Fuck you, asshole. Go to hell."

In the moonlight, Laura watched the man's face turn red as blood flooded his brain. He lifted the tire iron even higher, the cold, steel shaft reflecting the stars. Its reflection gave her a focal point as she calculated probabilities and plotted her next moves.

A tire iron. Not a gun. He wasn't carrying. Must be back in his car. "Eddie Nash is innocent. I won't drop his case, not until the day he walks out of that prison a free man. Not until the day you move into his cell."

The stranger narrowed his eyes, curled his upper lip, and lowered his head. She pictured him as a raging bull, snorting fire, feet pawing the ground, preparing to charge the matador As the man rushed forward, Laura felt like an unprotected quarterback being blitzed by an undefended lineman. She let the charging man get close before stepping to one side, then she squeezed the flare behind her back and yanked the ignition cord. She thrust her hand forward as a burst of sizzling, multi-colored light lit up the night. The dazzling fireball—a circle of red, orange, yellow, and blue—sent toxic smoke swirling in the crisp air. It looked like a blast from a military-grade phosphorus grenade, or the final fireworks on the Fourth of July.

Laura cracked open her eyes and stared through the circle of flames. Seeing the sizzling core of light starting to wane, she whipped the second flare from her back pocket and pulled the cord, creating another blinding flash, and thrust it into her attacker's face.

The man held an arm over his eyes, drawing back from the sizzling flames and backpedaling like a sand crab headed back to sea. His body tipped and tilted with each frantic, backward stride. Stumbling and gagging on the toxic, blue smoke, the intruder dropped the tire iron, rubbed his eyes, and blinked into the blinding, phosphorescent haze. The light in his panicked eyes was almost as intense as the streamers encircling him.

Sensing an advantage, Laura took another step toward the retreating thug, slashing both flares back and forth, whipping embers from side to side, ignoring the molten residue dripping onto her hands, spitting out smoke from her inflamed lungs.

Moving into a full retreat, the attacker held his hands out in a defensive position, before turning and running back to his Impala.

The car was still idling on the shoulder. The headlights were still on, and the driver's-side door was ajar.

"Hey!" Laura screamed like a mad woman, rushing after him. "Where you going, asshole?!" She lifted one of the flares over her shoulder as the man reached his car and crawled onto the front seat. "You know what one of these will do to your fuel tank?! Wait for the BOOM!"

Rushing within feet of his front bumper, she slid a sizzling flare under the chassis. She stepped back and yelled, "Hold on! Hold on! Here it comes!"

Laura looked through his windshield and into the stranger's wide, terrified eyes as he slammed the gearshift into drive. She had no idea whether a flare would ignite his fuel tank, but then again, neither did he. She raced down the embankment and dove behind a thick tree stump as his car lurched forward, the tires creating a shower of gravel. There was no BOOM.

Laura dropped the dying flare and watched as his taillights vanished into the darkness.

She managed to mount the spare and drive six miles to Hamilton Memorial Hospital. She told the emergency room doctor about the flat, improvising that a malfunctioning road flare had exploded in her hand. The physician washed out her eyes, applied ointment to the burns, and checked her lungs.

"Your lungs are good," he assured her. "You'll be fine. Just don't play with road flares for a while."

Later, a young nurse stood at her bedside with a pair of scissors, clipping away hanks of singed hair.

Finally alone in the recovery room, Laura relived the encounter. The man in the blue coat at the restaurant and cemetery. The flat tire on the isolated country road. The tire-iron-wielding intruder dressed in black. Was the real killer out to stop her from reopening the investigation and clearing Nash's name? Were the police out to stop her from exposing their frame-up and who-knew-what-else?

Reluctantly, Laura took out her phone, called her father, and told him what happened. "Yes," she agreed; he could come to the hospital to take her home.

"No." She would not drop the case.

16

GLASS OFFICE TOWERS GLISTENED IN THE MORNING SUN.

Wide sidewalks bustled with pedestrians, newsstands, food carts, bus stops, and taxi stands.

Laura strolled down the broad sidewalk on the east side of Atlantic Avenue in Brooklyn. She was relieved that the epicenter of the case was moving from the remote enclaves of western New York State to the metropolis of New York City. The next acts would unfold at the Council Against Wrongful Convictions offices in Brooklyn, and the United States courthouse just over the bridge in Lower Manhattan.

Laura kept scanning her surroundings for any sign of her attacker. She figured her roadside pyrotechnics had not scared him off for good. He would be back—whoever he was—to finish what he'd started. Was he the real Hangman?

The stranger was nowhere in sight, and that was good news for the time being. Laura swung the chestnut-colored leather briefcase her father had given her as a college graduation gift in her left hand and clutched a bagel with lox and cream cheese wrapped in a sheet of waxed paper in her right. Walking at a good clip, she lifted the briefcase to check her watch—9:37 AM. She took a bite of the bagel and picked up the pace, in a hurry to get to the office and update her colleagues on the case. She needed their backing to secure the resources that would supercharge her appeal.

She also had to begin preparing for oral arguments before the U.S. Court of Appeals for the Second Circuit, which would be held at the Thurgood Marshall Justice Center in Manhattan. This would determine whether a new trial would be granted.

Moving in the stream of pedestrians, Laura passed a classic New York City newsstand, where the balding proprietor made change for hurried customers. Garish headlines screamed from the tabloid racks. Political scandals. Subway shootings. Financial rip-offs. The sensational banners made her think of the media frenzy that loomed in her future. Challenging the conviction of a man the press had dubbed "The Hangman of Eden" in the first trial was certain to reignite the imagination of the headline crafters. Those creative news poets who worked in high-rise offices and sixty-four-point type had been in rare form in the aftermath of the murder ten years ago. STRIPPER SWINGS FROM HANGMAN'S NOOSE. EDEN WOMAN HUNG OUT TO DIE. What would they come up with this time?

Laura took long, hurried strides down the sidewalk, outpacing the parade of pedestrians. She was running late for a meeting, so she hustled into a modified trot. Feeling her phone vibrate in the back pocket of her black, cotton slacks, she stopped short, downed the last of the bagel, retrieved the device, and checked the data screen: Delilah Cole, the young paralegal assisting her with the Nash case.

"Delilah." Laura summoned a chipper voice to sync up with her perky assistant. "What's up?"

"Just checking on you. Where are you? What's your ETA?"

"Three blocks out. Be there in ten."

"Good."

"How's the prep work going?"

"Going great. I've got all the content ready to go for the three o'clock meeting. I've drafted the cover memo, compiled the agenda, and copied the trial transcripts, appellate drafts, discovery responses, and media clips. I've laid out the facts of the case in PowerPoint and placed hard copies in all the folders. Eight sets of papers in eight individual folders, one for each of the attendees."

"Ahead of the game, as usual," Laura replied. "You are the Get-it-Done Girl. I am glad you're on my side."

Delilah Cole *was* a stand-out paralegal. Mid-twenties, whip-smart, and task-oriented. Her goth attire, diamond nose stud, and arm tattoos also separated her from her colleagues.

"How's our client?" Delilah asked. "What's his mood? Is he hanging with us? Oh. Sorry. Bad choice of words."

"Nash is good. He's behind our strategy one-hundred-percent. The federal appeals court is reviewing our petition. The law journal coverage is favorable. The prosecutors are starting to sweat. We've got this. The three o'clock meeting should be a rubber stamp."

Delilah's deep inhale and slow exhale were audible over the phone. "Oh, shit."

"What is it?"

"I'm reading an email."

"What?"

"The three o'clock meeting is blowing up. Find me as soon as you get here. I want to go over everything with you."

"'Blowing up?' What does that mean?"

"It's not a meeting. It's an ambush."

Arriving at the Council Against Wrongful Convictions offices—based in an eight-story building that had once been a furniture warehouse—Laura stepped through the revolving glass door, plowed through the lobby, and hustled into a waiting elevator. She hit the button for the fifth-floor offices of the state's premier legal nonprofit, dedicated to exonerating the imprisoned innocent.

Time to go to war with her own colleagues.

17

EDDIE NASH PUSHED OUT OF HIS BUNK AND TOOK THREE STEPS TO THE desk on the far side of his cell. He sat in the plastic chair, opened the drawer, and took out a notebook and pen. He held the prison-issue pen up in the dim light and laughed out loud. Prison. How fucking stupid. The pen was made of flexible rubber, so it couldn't be weaponized.

Eddie opened the notebook and stared at the blank page. He wanted to unload his thoughts onto those pages—to express his excitement at the prospect of being cleared, to put the notion of being free into his own words.

But, words wouldn't come. Instead, he just had questions. What was happening with his case? When was his cute lawyer coming back to fill him in? What did those federal judges think of the appeal? Eddie looked to the ceiling, invoked the spirit of his literary hero, Etheridge Knight, and asked himself, *What would Etheridge write?*

Not that he knew much about books, authors, or literature. He didn't. How would a rebellious black kid from a shit-kicking upstate town know anything about literature? How would a kid who'd slept through high school know about prose and poetry? But, unschooled as he was, he understood the power of words, and he liked Etheridge Knight, a black man who'd begun writing poetry as an inmate at Indiana State Prison back in the '60s, and one of whose books had even been nominated for the National Book Award and the Pulitzer Prize.

Eddie liked to lose himself in the cold, hard words and cutting references in Knight's poems and stories. The writer's comparison of modern prisons to slave plantations made him think. Eddie had read Knight's meandering tale, *A Fable,* over and over, contemplating its meaning through his own plight:

Eddie puzzled for hours over the fictional conversation of seven wrongfully convicted black inmates.

> *Prisoner # 1 insists that the only viable route to freedom is through education. Learning to emulate the non-colored people, he tells the others, will persuade their jailers to set them free.*
>
> *Prisoner # 2 responds to that idea with a definite, "Hell no." He claims that only God can grant them freedom. If all seven adopt and adhere to Christianity, he proclaims, the Lord will lead them to the promised land.*
>
> *Prisoner # 3 replies to the God-will-set-us-free argument with one word: "Bullshit." Prisoner # 3 has been digging an escape tunnel. He urges the others to pick up shovels and join in the task. By working together, he asserts, they can all escape.*
>
> *No. No. No. Prisoner # 4 warns that escaping through a tunnel is "too risky." He suggests following the rules to please the white jailers. This will gain their trust and forgiveness. "So c'mon brothers and sisters and unite behind me."*
>
> *Prisoner # 5 responds to that with two words: "Fuck you!." Prisoner # 5 has a different escape plan. He wants the inmates to secure guns and shoot their way out.*
>
> *"No," interjects Prisoner #6. All of the plans, he declares, are flawed. Doomed to failure. Dead on arrival. Prisoner 6 explains the political dynamics behind their incarceration as well*

as the historical inevitably that justice will prevail. In time, he tells his comrades, "the bars will bend from their own inner rot."

Prisoner #7 dismisses all of the previous notions and turns against the other inmates. You see, Prisoner # 7 has his own plan. He will save himself by "ratting" out his fellow inmates to the non-colored jailers. "That is the one way!"

The inmates argue. Trust in God. Dig a tunnel. Take up arms. They continue to argue to this day, squabbling amongst themselves while caged like vicious animals.

After reading Knight, Eddie thought more and more about race. He began to doubt his belief that race—black, brown, white—didn't matter. As a kid, he'd tried to be colorblind. "Growing up," he often recalled, "I stopped seeing color and just saw people." Eddie used to believe that. He used to live by it. Back when he was running with the wild kids in Eden. Now, he saw that race and racism explained so much. It was no mistake that the vast majority of cons were black and brown. Knight's words were all about blackness. The beauty. The history. The pride. The challenge. The exploitation. The pain. Plus, Knight's damned stories made sense, and his poems rhymed.

Eddie knew he was no Etheridge Knight. He was just a con with a pen and paper and time to kill. He loved to write, anyway. Writing was an excellent time killer and he plenty of it to kill. Like the old man in A-Block had told him. "You kill time or time kills you." Eddie had taken two creative writing classes in the prison education wing, and the instructor had read out his stuff in class. Plus, the inmate-run *Attica Grapevine* had published one of his poems, as well as an essay he'd penned about the banning of the death penalty.

"The new death penalty is life without parole," he'd written. *"It is a long, slow form of lethal torture. Cruel and unusual punishment administered by cruel and unusual people."*

Now, in his darkened cell, Eddie Nash tried to find words to sum up his feelings:

American justice.
A work of fiction
Bad arrest.
False conviction.

Eddie knew his poetry sucked. What the hell? Maybe his words would make better song lyrics. Maybe the brother with the guitar in B Block could put one of his poems to a blues tune. Maybe one of the young guys in A Block could turn one into a rap. Maybe. Eddie closed the notebook and shut his eyes. He bowed his head and prayed. "Please, God. Let this be real. Let me go home."

Home. His current home was located in the heart of D-Block, with the prestigious address D-3-26. Cell Block D. Section 3. Cell 26. The dim space was lit by a cheap lamp he'd purchased in the prison commissary. A gray sweatshirt from one of his mother's care packages hung on a hook at the head of the bunk. Family pictures were taped to the wall. Home, sweet home.

Eddie had no cellmate and savored the solitude; although, at times, the loneliness got to him. In the darkest of times, it seemed like loneliness was his one companion, and despair was his sole confidante.

Eddie held his homemade mirror, fashioned from a flattened Campbell's soup can, beyond the bars of his cell door. He peered into the mirror and caught the reflection of men in the long row of cells. Murders, rapists, armed robbers, drug dealers, and a few innocent men. Sprawling on their bunks, pacing back and forth, or anticipating the next guard check.

Of course, Eddie hated prison, like all sane inmates. To him, prison was relentless boredom, interrupted by sudden terror. Prison was iron regimentation, exploding into total mayhem. Hope had left the building.

Eddie hated Attica. He called the grim citadel of New York's most dangerous inmates "an efficient hate factory."

Sitting at his desk, Eddie turned his notebook to a new page and picked up his rubber pen. He began to write in his journal, words flowing in a subconscious rant:

I want freedom from: The bars, buzzers, shanks, shivs, scars, skins, tats, Tasers, lifers, losers, posers, and perverts. The gangsters, gumps, dealers, dopers, Mexican Mafia, and Aryan Nation. Good riddance to choke sandwiches in the mess, chin checks in the yard, and shit shanks in the TV room.

I want freedom to: Hug my mom and hang with my friends. Chase hot women and down cold beer. Eat steak fresh off the grill and drink bourbon on the rocks. Getting it all back after losing it will make it all the sweeter. Taking it back after having it stolen will be my revenge.

Eddie had survived ten-and-a-half years of hell. Now, here he was, looking forward to the possibility of exoneration. His every move had to be calculated to keep himself alive—at least, until justice could be served. He had avoided the dry snitches, bad bugs, and shot callers who could fuck him up. He'd started each day doing two-hundred-and-fifty push-ups and four-hundred sit-ups on the concrete floor between his bunk and toilet. The workouts gave him the strength to fight off the bad jackets in the yard and the muscle-bound freaks in the weightlifting gym. The workouts gave his body the hard edge he needed to gain the respect of his fellow cons and hold his own in a fight. At the same time, his self-styled exercise regimen didn't bulk him up into a strong man—the attention-seeking bulk would have made him a target for the *real* muscle, the prowlers seeking to add to their rep or just experience the thrill of inflicting pain on another human being.

Eddie took extra care in D-Yard, ever since a Latino gangster stabbed him with an "ice pick," a long, metal rod sharpened to a point. His attacker— out to make a name for himself by murdering a murderer—had shoved the pick into his gut and angled it up toward his heart. It had taken Eddie two months in the infirmary to recover from that one. These days, Eddie spewed just the right amount of trash talk in the yard, aka "Central Park." His shit shanks were sharp enough to let the other cons know he wasn't afraid, and measured enough to never piss off the wrong shot caller. When working the slime line in the mess, he'd dole out larger servings of the decent food to keep certain inmates on his good side. It never hurt to have a little good karma coming back his way.

Eddie put the notebook back in the drawer and threw himself onto his bunk. He turned onto his side to face the cell door and scanned the grim confines. A cockroach crawled out from under the bed. *Well, look at that.* He resisted the urge to get up and stomp it into the concrete. He just watched. Truth be told, he envied its freedom. He craved that freedom. He smiled as it crawled across the floor and out of the cell.

18

LAURA STOOD IN FRONT OF A HALF-DOZEN ATTORNEYS, SEATED AROUND the oval, racetrack conference table.

"*State of New York v. Edward Thomas Nash*," Laura announced. "Let's start by running through the facts." She established eye contact with each colleague before continuing. "In July 2008, Edward Thomas Nash, twenty-eight, of Eden, New York, was arrested and charged with first-degree murder for the hanging death of Erin Lambert, twenty-eight, a longtime friend, and a dancer at the Bottoms Up Gentleman's Club."

Laura had just started, when Josh Linder—the charismatic founder and chairman of the Council Against Wrongful Convictions—interrupted. "Laura, remind me again, why is this case for us?"

"Nash was set up by the police, railroaded by the prosecutor, and sentenced to life without parole without due process," she replied, just as she'd rehearsed it. Linder started all these case updates with his favorite question. "This is a classic miscarriage of justice. The confession was coerced, the evidence was tainted, and the testimony was bought and paid for. I mean, the cops even photoshopped his mugshot for a photo ID. It is the most outrageous frame-up I've ever seen. The most important thing is this: He's innocent."

"Got it." Linder leaned back in his swivel chair. "Go ahead." His rumpled, navy-blue sport coat hung on the back of his chair, his wrinkled, blue shirt was rolled up at the cuffs, and his shaggy, salt-and-pepper hair framed his handsome face. "You have our attention, Ms. Tobias."

"Nash was grilled for fourteen hours at the police station. He broke down, signed a confession, and read it into a video camera. By the next morning, he'd been condemned by the sheriff, demonized by the mayor, and crucified by the media."

Ken Leveson—a hotshot appellate attorney with chiseled features, chestnut-colored hair, and a bright future—cleared his throat. "Just one moment, please, Laura." Ken's tone fell somewhere between confidence and arrogance. "I have a point to make."

Ken had been chilly to Laura ever since she'd turned down his third invite for after-work drinks. She hoped this was not payback.

"A fourteen-hour interrogation does not—repeat, *not*—equal a coerced confession." Ken lowered his voice to underline the seriousness of his statement. "At least, it doesn't show the level of coercion needed to prevail in a federal appellate court. You might want to consider leading with a better argument. I mean, police coercion is a non-starter. The courts are tired of hearing it. Everybody knows that."

Laura glared in his direction. How she hated that smug smile.

Fuck you, Ken Doll.

She buried those words and chose better ones.

"It's more than just the marathon interrogation and psychological pressure." Now, she fought back the waver in her voice, unwilling to give Ken the pleasure of watching her squirm. "I mean, Nash was cuffed to a water pipe and beaten over the head with a phone book. The perfect implement; it doesn't leave a mark. Then, the arresting officer slipped a plastic bag over his head."

"You have proof of that?" Ken placed two hands on the table and glared back at her. "Do you have anything beyond your guy's claim that he was tortured by the authorities? Believe me, in a federal appeal, the word of a convicted murderer against the word of a police officer is nothing. Your guy loses."

"Give me time." Laura felt like a boxer, ducking a series of jabs while knowing that the uppercut was coming. "I'm still laying out the facts here, Ken. The misconduct of the police and the prosecutor provides ample grounds for an appeal at the highest level. The trial was a farce."

"How so?"

In her appellate brief to the federal court, Laura had argued that the Erie County Police Department had coerced the confession, presented false evidence, and lied on the stand. She'd also argued that the Erie County prosecutor had made false and prejudicial statements to the jury and failed to disclose to the court that a key prosecution witness had been paid to testify. Concerned that those arguments were not unusual enough to persuade the three-judge federal panel to revisit the case, Laura had dedicated much of the brief to a stun belt that Nash had been forced to wear in the courtroom. She'd argued that the jury's knowledge of the belt—capable of delivering an eight-second, 50,000-volt electric shock that could send the wearer into convulsions—robbed Nash of the presumption of innocence.

"Okay, Ken," she said with a fake smile. "Picture the defendant wearing an electronic belt, capable of delivering enough voltage to cause a seizure. Consider the pressure this places on the accused, and the prejudicial signal it sends to the jury. I believe federal courts are itching to strike down the use of these devices."

Ken smirked in disbelief. "Stun belts are used as a precaution against sudden outbursts by defendants. To be honest, stun belts provide a more humane alternative to shackles. They're less prejudicial, too. The device is placed under the defendant's clothing, so the jury doesn't see it."

Linder shook his head, held up his hands, and raised his voice. "Time out. Let's keep this moving. At this rate, our client will die of old age in prison while we're still bickering over the facts." The room hushed. Linder spoke again. "Did the prosecution have an eyewitness to put Nash at the scene? How credible were the eyewitnesses?"

"One witness came close." Laura looked down at her court papers and scanned for the name. "Danny Boggs was a long-haul trucker from Eden. Boggs was returning home from a run to North Carolina in the early morning hours of July 2nd."

"Around the time of the murder," Linder interjected.

"Yes. Boggs testified that he saw Nash turn his red Silverado onto an isolated road off State Road 8. That service road led to one place: The pedestrian bridge where Erin Lambert was killed."

"Hanged," Ken interjected. "Hanged by the neck until dead."

"Yes, hanged," Laura replied. "It was a brutal murder. No denying that. It doesn't mean Nash did it."

Linder ignored the interruption from Ken. "Great eyesight for a long-distance trucker finishing a fourteen-hour run in the wee hours of the morning," he commented. "Great memory, too. This eyewitness account is tenuous at best. I can't believe that Nash was convicted on the basis of flimsy testimony like that."

"Yep. Boggs claimed that Nash's truck swerved in front of his eighteen-wheeler. Boggs claimed that he leaned on his horn, and Nash responded by giving him the finger. In court, Boggs identified Nash as the driver with one-hundred-percent certainty. He even described a red baseball cap that Nash was supposedly wearing that night. Prosecutors produced Nash's hat, and photos of his pickup truck. The prosecutor also linked tire imprints from the scene to the tires of Nash's Silverado."

"We all know that tire tracks are inconclusive." Linder ran a hand through his hair. "There are lots of pickups, and lots of tires. The imprints mean nothing. Where does Nash say he was?"

"Asleep at home," Laura replied. "Alone. There's more." Laura picked up the pace. "The prosecutor never revealed that he paid Boggs—his star witness—twenty-five-hundred dollars to testify. On top of that, he dropped a pending DUI charge against Boggs two weeks before the murder trial. Danny Boggs could not afford to take a DUI hit. He would have lost his trucking license. Danny Boggs had all the reason in the world to lie about Eddie Nash on the stand."

"Now, this is getting interesting," Linder said. "Dropping charges in one case to get a witness to perjure himself in another is unethical, if not illegal. This prosecutor was treading on very thin ice. I agree with you, Laura. Reeks of a frame-up."

19

As the meeting continued, Laura explained how the judge had paved the way for conviction with biased bench rulings and slanted jury instructions, and how the panel of twelve had conferred for an hour and fifteen minutes before passing judgement. How hair fibers, empty beer bottles, shards of glass, and DNA found at the scene were tested at a second-rate lab, known for inaccurate—if not outright falsified—results.

Laura sensed Linder's growing interest. She wanted him on her side. No, she *had* to have him on her side. Linder could make or break her case and career. Linder's admirers called him "The Vindicator," pointing to the scores of incarcerated men and women he'd freed from wrongful imprisonment, and to his best-selling book, *The Innocents*. His detractors mocked him as the "Loophole Lawyer," claiming he exploited legal technicalities to put guilty criminals back on the streets.

"What about the defense?" Linder asked the question in the deep, authoritative voice that had served him so well in the courtroom and on TV news shows. "Did our guy get a decent defense?"

"Paul Cox was the public defender," Laura answered. "Cox was unprepared, disinterested, and one-hundred-percent incompetent. Cox failed to challenge bogus evidence, debunk phony forensics, cross-examine lying witnesses, and object to biased bench rulings. He also put Nash on the stand with no preparation. Nash got creamed.”

“You can’t blame the defense counsel because his client choked on the stand.” This time, the challenge came from Leon James Melton, a former prosecutor in his fifties with a rotund build, oversized head, and an even larger ego. Melton wore the scars of twenty years of courtroom warfare like worn-out Boy Scout badges. He loved to brag about his big wins back in the day to anyone who would listen. He’d spent the past two years working to exonerate innocent inmates for the Counsel Against Wrongful Convictions without a single victory to show for his efforts. These days, Melton spent most of his time rehashing war stories for female interns and junior attorneys.

“There’s more.” Laura skewered Melton with her eyes. “*Much* more.” She explained how the cops had strung together a weak line of circumstantial evidence that came nowhere close to meeting the standards for a trial. She described how the prosecutor had unleashed a torrid, scorched-earth assault on the defense, demonizing the accused, his counsel, and his character witnesses.

“The prosecutor painted Nash’s character witnesses as ignorant black folk, whose faculties for truth-telling were compromised by generations of inbreeding.” She felt a sickening ooze in her stomach. “It was prejudicial, outrageous, and racist. You wouldn’t believe how the so-called ‘good people’ in these small towns treat their black neighbors. Hell, they still call them ‘colored.’”

“Let’s stick to the facts,” Linder advised. “What about the judge?”

“Superior Court Judge James P. Lorraine let those kind of characterizations stand. Lorraine sided with the prosecution on almost every objection. The judge might as well have been on the prosecution team. We’re talking small-town, good-old-boy justice. As we all know, certain places upstate can make the Deep South look downright progressive.”

Laura checked her watch. Time to change tactics. She picked up one of the folders Delilah had distributed before the meeting. "Take a look at Page Four of the prosecutor's final argument."

Silence fell over the room, as all eyes scanned the highlighted excerpt:

> "Again, ladies and gentleman, I ask you to look into the eyes of the defendant. Look deep into the eyes of Edward Thomas Nash. Deep enough to see the lies, distortions, and guilt that consumes him. This monster stalked a lost and troubled girl and beat her with a steel pipe. He placed a noose around her neck and threw her off a bridge—to her death. Ladies and gentlemen of the jury, I told you how he climbed onto that concrete safety wall and guzzled a beer while gazing down at her swinging corpse. Do you know what he did after that? Ladies and gentlemen, I struggle to even utter it, but the facts are the facts. He urinated on her dead body. From the top of the bridge, he urinated on her. He defiled her corpse."

Ken Leveson was the first to finish. "Jesus Christ!" He gasped. "Is this true? This creep pissed on the girl's dead body? What a—"

"No." Laura slammed the tabletop. "No, no, no. That's not the point." Laura looked from one face to the next before pushing on. "There's no real evidence to support that outrageous and prejudicial claim. Just a hack genetic test I can destroy in court. It never happened. I repeat, it did not occur. Do you hear me? Never. It was made up. By the prosecutor. For shock value. This was the Big Lie." Laura took a moment to compose herself before continuing. "You want to call my client a sick monster, Ken? Go ahead. The fact is that the *prosecutor* is the sick monster in this case."

"Calm down, Laura. Take a breath." Martha Barrack—the Council's Chief of Staff—turned to Linder. "Josh. We have to rethink our approach here. This is a complex case that calls for an experienced appellate attorney. I can't believe you're just letting Laura run with this on her own. She doesn't have the experience. She's always taken second chair and her cases have not been major felonies. Laura is just not ready to take first chair on a first-degree murder appeal in a federal court."

Laura almost snorted. So spoke the former corporate liability attorney, who'd made millions representing Fortune 500 companies in lawsuits over their faulty products. After the bank accounts, estate homes, and Ferraris lost their thrill, Martha had made the shift to nonprofit exoneration law. Now, she had it all—the good life, *and* a clear conscience.

"I'll say it again," she repeated. "This case requires a seasoned attorney at the lead."

Classic Martha. A mix of unchecked ego and highbrow condescension. Harsh words delivered in soft tones. A wicked sneer tilting upward into a fake smile. Direct threats delivered with flashing eyes. Martha Barrack, Smiley Face from Hell. Then again, Martha approached all her battles with a holier-than-thou attitude, camouflaged hostility, and a perfect hairdo. The woman was always perfectly coiffed, attired, and made-up, making a point to look better than everyone else in the room. Today, she wore a cashmere sweater set, suede boots, and a self-satisfied demeanor that had been honed at Harvard.

Martha rose from her seat, scanned the table, locked eyes with her peers, and commanded their attention, before letting her blue lasers rest on Laura. "I admire your ambition. I applaud your hard work. I love your determination. You're going to make a great appeals attorney. But, you're just not quite ready for a case of this magnitude. I'll take first chair; you take second. Think of it as a learning opportunity."

20

Martha's words hit like sugarcoated shrapnel. Each pierced Laura's skin, bore deep inside, and lodged itself into her psyche. Laura absorbed the pain and braced for battle. She took deep breaths to calm her nerves. She balled her fists to stall the shakes. Her face heating up, she ignored the impulse to either leap across the table at her colleague's throat or run away and never come back.

Keep cool. Let it pass. You can't afford to melt down in front of the entire team.

Laura stared back at Martha, rising to her level. "I've got this, Martha. One-hundred-percent. I appreciate your offer, but this is my case. I know it inside out. I have a relationship with the client. My name is on the appellate brief, because I wrote it. This is my case."

Bitch.

"Hold on one minute. Can I get a word in?" A deep male voice rolled through the room as if from on high. It blended the smoothness of a late-night radio DJ with the low rumble of a jazz crooner. Those pipes belonged to Charles Steel, the team's self-styled private investigator.

Lacking a law degree but abundant with arrogance, Steel was an unusual character to be sitting with the executive committee. However, his proven ability to investigate wrongful conviction cases, and his track record for freeing the imprisoned innocent, gave him considerable clout within the organization.

"Let me just say this: Laura, you've got yourself a helluva case here." Steel flexed the loose sleeves of his red-and-gold designer dashiki and flipped the dreadlocks off his shoulder. Steel was a smooth talker, and a sharp dresser. His dashikis, sweatshirts, cardigans, and jackets all bore colorful, African tribal patterns and motifs. "This is a classic miscarriage of justice, a tragic wrong to be righted. A complete breakdown of the legal system. We can't turn away from this; we have to intervene—it goes to the core of our mission. We either save this man, or he dies in prison. Plain and simple."

Martha sank back into her seat, and Laura returned to hers. It was clear that Steel was just getting started.

"Now, you all know I've investigated twenty-six felony appeals, and those turned into reversals or new trials for twenty-six defendants. Based on that experience, I can tell you something obvious about *State of New York v. Edward Thomas Nash:* We can win this. We *have* to win this. I can see it now. The classic photo we all love? You know the one: The innocent inmate, walking out of prison, surrounded by his legal team—smiles all around. Eddie Nash deserves to go free. We just have to do our jobs, find the facts, connect the dots, make the arguments, and win the case."

"Wait a minute, Charles." Ken's posture stiffened, as Martha fumed on the other side of the table. "Is this Eddie Nash our ideal client? Is this case the most winnable option we have in front of us? Is this middle-aged male the most deserving person to benefit from our precious time, talent, and treasure?"

Charles adopted a stern look, but Laura was sure he was beaming inside. *Step into the trap, Kenny Boy.*

"Look at it this way, Charles," Ken continued. "It seems to me that this man got a fair trial. A judge and jury heard the facts and found him guilty. The state appeals court reviewed his case and affirmed the verdict. Why would a federal court go against all that? Even if the federal court ordered a new trial, Nash would just be found guilty all over again."

"Who *does* deserve our precious time and treasure?" Steel asked. "One of *your* potential clients?"

"As a matter of fact, yes." Ken planted his elbows on the table and stared at Charles. "I have a thirty-two-year-old insurance executive who was convicted of fraud, embezzlement, and money laundering. He was sent up on the flimsiest evidence and convicted in a bogus show trial because the prosecutor wanted to make an example out of him. The guy was sentenced to a thirty-year stretch in a federal supermax. These kinds of complex, white-collar crimes are far easier to appeal than violent murder convictions. The guy is a sympathetic character. He didn't hang a poor, mixed-up girl."

Charles glared at Ken. "And he's white."

21

CHARLES MADE AN EXCEPTION TO HIS "NO RACE CARD" RULE FOR HIS friend, Ken. He lifted his gaze and cleared his throat, before his deep vibrato rolled through the room like a gathering storm.

"Kenny. I hate to explain the obvious, but it appears I must. Eddie Nash is the perfect client. His case is strong. His appeal is pending. His chances are good. And yes, his skin is black. Kenny, I'm sure you're well aware of the scourge of mass incarceration. The racial injustice that plagues our pitiful excuse for a legal system. I'm sure you understand how institutional racism has turned our prisons into warehouses for black and brown men and women. Hundreds of thousands of African-American and Latino inmates are serving time for crimes that never should have come to trial in the first place. There are more black men locked in prison today than there were enslaved black men in 1850. And you question this man's right to be represented by the Council Against Wrongful Convictions? What are we doing here, Ken? Why does this organization exist? What game are we playing? Are we here to challenge the system? Or are we just part of it?"

"No. You're wrong. You know me, Charles." Ken puffed out like a man who'd been falsely accused of molesting children. "I'm as dedicated to fighting racial bias in the legal system as anyone. I'm appalled by the number of minorities imprisoned in the United States. It's one reason I became a lawyer in the first place: To end racial injustice. I just want this organization to pursue cases it can win. My client is young. My client is intelligent. He has his whole life in front of him. He can come back from his ordeal. Okay, he's white. So what?"

"Kenny. Don't play the back side of the race card with me, bro. Or the age card. So, what's Eddie Nash? Thirty-eight years old? Are you saying that a thirty-eight-year-old black man isn't worth saving? We all know the stats, cat. As an African-American man without a law degree, that's why I work here."

Motherfucker.

"No, let me explain what…" Ken stammered, looking to Martha for help. Her gaze was focused on the floor. "I just, well, meant…"

"Ken, let me ask a question: Have you ever spent any quality time in those redneck enclaves up north?"

Ken's face was flushed. His eyes were blank.

"No," Charles concluded. "I didn't think so. Let me enlighten you, my brother. The black population in those parts is very small. Maybe five percent in the cities, and fewer in the country. The racism is ingrained. It's ever-present. Black kids have to walk the line between the redneck racists and backyard barbecue bigots. Blacks kids are happy to just survive in those parts. Let's give this one guy a chance to rebalance the scales of justice."

Ken stammered. "Um… well… now…"

Linder straightened his back and cleared his throat. "Charles, as always, thank you very much for your insight. Martha, I have to disagree with you; Laura is more than ready to take first chair on this case. However, you do have a point, so here's my compromise. Martha, I want you to take second chair. Laura calls the shots. You back her up. Got it?"

Laura and Martha nodded.

Linder went on. "Ken, I have to disagree with you; the Nash case is perfect for us. The pros and cons of representing your white-collar client are a separate matter; we'll take that up at a future meeting. Plus, we need your undivided attention on your own caseload. The Wyatt case is scheduled for retrial next month. It's winnable. You have to win that case, so stay focused. Give that man back his freedom. Keep your eyes on the prize."

Linder looked from one face to the next. "Let me remind all of you of a very important fact: More than fifteen-hundred men and women have been exonerated by organizations like ours over the past quarter-century. With each new exoneration, the world sees the flaws in the criminal justice system and supports our efforts to ensure equal justice for all. Let's stay focused on our mission. Let's work as a unified team, instead of a bunch of rivals. Let's use all our talents and resources to make this movement stronger than ever."

Linder leaned back in his chair, clasped his hands behind his head, and arched his right eyebrow. Looking to Steel, he said, "Charles, you're lead investigator. Get to the bottom of this." He turned to Delilah. "Delilah, you're paralegal support."

He paused one more time before stating, "Let's win this case."

22

THE INNOCENCE ALLIANCE
THE EXONERATION BLOG

The Innocence Alliance is a nationwide affiliation of organizations dedicated to providing legal and investigative services to men and women seeking to prove themselves innocent of the crimes that sent them to prison. The Alliance also works to correct flaws in the legal system that lead to wrongful convictions and supports the exonerated as they transition to life after incarceration.

NEWS ALERT:

The U.S. District Court of Appeals for the Second District has set oral arguments for September 15 in the appeal of the first-degree murder conviction in State of New York v. Edward Thomas Nash. The well-respected Council Against Wrongful Convictions will argue that the appellant was denied a fair trial, due to police and prosecutorial misconduct, and inadequate defense counsel. While appeals courts have been slow to embrace those arguments of late, this creative court challenge has an added twist. It also argues that the appeallee's right to participate in his own defense was compromised because the trial judge required him to be out-fitted with a stun belt, an electronic belt worn under the clothing, capable of delivering a 50,000-volt shock to an unruly defendant. Appeals courts have been growing more and more concerned with the rising use of these devices.

EVENT REMINDER:

Don't forget. National Exoneration Day will be observed on Tuesday, Oct 3.

23

LAURA SAT IN HER SECLUDED NOOK IN THE COUNCIL AGAINST Wrongful Convictions offices. A stack of court transcripts, legal briefs, hand-scrawled notes, and discovery exhibits cluttered her desk. She was combing through the fine details of the case, certain the answers to her questions were in there somewhere.

The spacious, open-plan office was non-profit chic. Laura's desk was made of an old, wooden door, painted red and set between metal sawhorses. The ceilings were low, the I-beams were exposed, and the red bricks on the walls were fake. On the wall behind her hung a block-letter poster that read:

"BETTER THAT TEN GUILTY PERSONS ESCAPE, THAN
THAT ONE INNOCENT SUFFER."
—William Blackstone

In the heart of the office, junior attorneys, administrative assistants, and interns stared into computers, jabbered on phones, and pulled paper from printers. Along the far north wall, more experienced lawyers toiled in small, glass-enclosed offices. CEO Josh Linder and Chief of Staff Martha Barrack worked in opposite corner offices with antique desks, comfortable sofas, and competing egos.

As for Laura, her quiet space in the back of the office was a good spot to prepare the federal court appeal. She'd spent countless hours researching points of law and legal precedents for the written brief to the U.S. Court of Appeals. She'd begun to prepare for oral arguments before the three-judge panel, plotting responses to the questions that were sure to be hurled at her.

Picking up a new document, Laura cringed at the sound of designer boots on pressure-treated hardwood.

Shit. Here it comes.

Martha walked up to her cube and planted her heels in the hardwood, sipping a lavender-infused latte. "Listen… Laura… I came to… I came to, well, to apologize. I didn't mean to shoot you down in the meeting last week. Believe it or not, I was trying to help. I just went about it the wrong way. You may have noticed that I can be a bull in a china shop. Sorry."

Laura had seen Martha's olive branch coming. The nonprofit was plagued with a passive-aggressive work culture that fueled personal rivalries, often undercutting the collaboration needed to win cases. After a blatant power grab, the aggressor—in this case, Martha—had to gloss over the conflict with the veneer of a professional whitewash. Just one more step in the competitive dance.

"We're good, Martha," Laura lied. "We're more than good. Trust is built on honest exchange. We had an honest exchange. That's how teams work. It's all about teamwork."

Martha nestled her cup between two palms. "I'm happy to take second chair. I will have your back."

"Thanks."

"You present oral arguments, launch the investigation, and build our case. I'll remain in the background, helping you with an overall legal strategy. I want you to win this case."

"I *will* win." Laura flattened her smile, locking in eye contact. "I have a strong case."

Martha tossed back her scarf. "Great. I like the confidence. Just don't get *too* confident. Don't be afraid to ask for help. Please know this, Laura: I'm here for you."

"Okay."

Martha glanced over her shoulder at an intern, making copies at a nearby machine. The senior attorney took two steps forward and leaned in closer to Laura, lowering her voice to a whisper. "If you need any advice with any aspect of this case at any time, come talk to me. Let's put that teamwork to good use."

"I will." Laura leaned back to regain her personal space. "I promise."

"Great." Martha looked up to the ceiling, studying the sand-swirl pattern. "We're good, then. Let's grab lunch next week. We've got to work up a solid strategy."

Martha spun a one-eighty and marched back toward her office.

Laura savored the dying scent of lavender, and the slow fade of spiked heels on hardwood. She pushed out of her cube and strolled to the long, rectangular window on the street-side wall. She looked out at fire escapes and air-conditioning ducts, climbing up red-brick apartment buildings. In the distance, slanting rays of afternoon sunlight poured through the skyline of Lower Manhattan. Down below, young men and women clad in colorful jogging garb trotted along the Brooklyn Heights Promenade. Couples leaned close on park benches, gazing out at the river, where working barges, crowded ferries, and slow-moving pleasure craft traversed on choppy waves. On the busy street, hipsters paraded in and out of artisanal coffee shops, expensive wine-and-cheese stores, and high-end clothing boutiques.

"Don't jump." The deep, rich, mellow voice rolled in from behind her. "It ain't that bad."

Laura turned to see Charles Steel.

24

PI CHARLES STEEL. OR AS *TIME* CALLED HIM, *"THE SHERLOCK HOLMES of the Innocence Movement."* Effortlessly hip, from his streaming dreads to his jet-black shirt with subtle tribal patterns embroidered over the pocket.

Steel tucked his hands into the pockets of his designer jeans and asked, "How goes the case? Or have you solved it?"

Laura shook her head. *No way.* "I was going to ask *you.* Where the hell are we?"

"Screw Martha." Charles did his best impression of a snarl. "Forget about her. Don't let her get into your head. She'll mess up your thinking and do a number on your self-confidence. It's what she does, and she's so good at it. You should see her in a courtroom."

"I can handle Martha," Laura replied. "I'll make her an asset."

"Good. From an asshole to an asset."

Laura swallowed a laugh. "I'm glad to have you on my side, Charles. You're going to make such a difference. I need a partner on this."

"Let's get going, then. No time to waste. I want to go over everything you have on the case. Timelines, witnesses, alibis, theories, alternative theories, *conspiracy* theories, the works. I'm putting on a second investigator to help with the legwork. We'll get to the bottom of this mess."

"You've read my mind. We have to scrutinize every word of testimony and shred of evidence from the original trial. We have to prove that certain testimony was false, and certain evidence was fabricated. I mean, half of the prosecution's case didn't prove anything about Nash's guilt *or* innocence. It was just fear-mongering, intended to shock the jury into voting guilty."

Charles nodded. "We may be able to find new witnesses who didn't come forward the first time around. We may be able to find new evidence that slipped through the cracks in the original police investigation. Who knows what the cops ignored, lost, buried, or burned? We'll turn over all the rocks, take down all the prosecution's bricks. I'm planning a complete rein-vestigation. Top to bottom." He spoke like a man who had done this before. "Who else had a motive to kill the victim? Who else had access to the crime scene? Why did the cops target Nash to the exclusion of all other suspects? It's all on the table."

"Thank you, Charles. You're right. But, there's something I have to tell you." She lowered her voice to a whisper and pointed to the corner window. "Come on over here for a minute. No one can hear this."

Laura led him to the far corner of the office, out of earshot of every-one else, and told him about the CO in the prison patrol car, and the prison superintendent who'd demanded that she drop the case. She described the stalker who'd attacked her on the isolated country road, and the gleam of his tire iron. She shared the eerie feeling of being followed, and the fear of being attacked again, immensely relieved that she could entrust those secrets to her colleague.

"Thank you for listening. It's been an ordeal."

"What's your cell number? We have to be in twenty-four-seven contact."

They exchanged numbers.

"Okay." Charles spoke at a deliberate pace. "If anything else happens— if anything unusual occurs, anything at all—contact me. I'll come running. I know how to deal with this."

25

Laura lay on her queen-sized bed in her cluttered bedroom of her three-room apartment. The second-floor walk-up was in a classic brownstone in Red Hook, a gritty urban neighborhood on the banks of the East River in Brooklyn, home to street gangs, drug markets, and industrial squalor; although, a slow influx of young, professional, urban pioneers was changing the social makeup. Laura had chosen to live there because the hardcore hipsters had not discovered it yet, and the rent was affordable.

Laura leaned on pillows piled against her headboard. She clutched a folder of court papers the way a new preacher clutches his Bible his first time in the pulpit. She began sifting through documents as she fought back sleep, stopping at the brief she'd filed with the federal appeals court:

> *The Council Against Wrongful Convictions petitions the Court to vacate the conviction laid down in* State of New York v. Edward Thomas Nash. *We contest the finding of guilt on multiple constitutional grounds. By the standards of the Sixth, Ninth, and Fourteenth Amendments to the U.S. Constitution, the defendant was denied even the semblance of a fair and impartial trial.*

She turned the page. The critique of the stun belt followed.

The defendant was forced to wear a stun belt, capable of sending 50,000 volts of electricity into his body with the flip of switch. Mr. Nash assured the judge that he posed no risk of a violent outburst and complained that the fear of being shocked— either by accident or on purpose—made it hard to concentrate on the case against him.

The judge responded that stun belts were standard equipment in murder trials in his courtroom. "The belt is just a precaution," the judge stated in open court, with the jury present. "You should be grateful. We could put you in hand restraints and leg irons."

We implore the federal court to send a clear message to the trial courts of New York: There is no place for these dangerous devices in our modern courtrooms.

She flipped pages, until she heard a noise coming from the kitchen. She was not alone. Out of nowhere, a small, lively dog ran into the bedroom and jumped onto the bed.

"Tripod." Laura laughed. "Come here, boy."

The pooch launched a furious onslaught of licks and nips, as Laura pulled a pillow over her head.

"Down, boy. Settle down. I know, I know. I know. I'm sorry for ignoring you. I'm home now. It's just you and me, buddy. Now, lie down and go to sleep. We have a big day tomorrow."

Tripod was a Border collie—a three-legged one, at that. Laura had adopted him after a car accident had damaged his left front leg. A benevolent rescue service took the dog in, paid for his life-saving amputation, and put him up for adoption. At the time, Laura was mending a broken heart from a break-up and figured a dog would be more loyal than any man. Perusing potential adoptees online, she'd spotted the three-legged collie, filled out the forms, and took him home. She'd nursed him back to health, retraining him to maneuver on three legs. Three years later, Tripod now scooted as quickly as most dogs ran. He was thirty pounds of nimble, perpetual motion, hopping faster than the squirrels he chased, angling his one front leg in the center of his body and bouncing off it like a pogo stick, bounding circles around his peers at the dog park and sniffing out rodents with the best of them.

"Did you have a good time today?"

Tripod took three or four short walks a day with Laura's downstairs neighbor, Mrs. Sanchez, and her miniature schnauzer, Mike, making it possible for Laura to work and keep the dog.

Tripod circled on the bed, lay down in a soft spot, rested his head on her leg, and closed his eyes.

Laura gazed down at the sleeping dog, wondering if he had four legs in his dreams.

Laura propped herself against the pillows and started to make a mental list of the next steps for the Nash case. She had to ramp up her preparations for the oral arguments. She had to begin working out a legal strategy with Martha. She had to launch the investigation with Charles and his number-two investigator. She planned to split Delilah's time between administrative tasks and actual casework; the young paralegal was ready to take on more responsibility. Laura needed to request a position for a forensic computer specialist to lead the online work. In the end, the entire team would be smart, talented, and driven, as well as up to speed on the latest high-tech methods of conducting legal research and investigating complex cases. They would have access to the latest computer technologies, applications, and databases used for these kinds of cases.

The Council Against Wrongful Convictions might be a pennywise nonprofit with doors for desks, but it knew the importance of modern technology and techniques. It used the same sophisticated equipment as big law firms and law enforcement agencies. Still, there was no way around the need for good, old-fashioned legwork, too, and their work would have to go beyond re-examining old witnesses and finding new ones, reviewing old evidence, and uncovering new evidence. They would also have to confront the police and prosecutors about their apparent frame-up.

Laura looked up to the ceiling and asked herself the same nagging question. Who killed Erin Lambert? Who, who, who?

Her concentration was shattered by the buzz of her cell phone. Laura grabbed the phone and checked the data screen.

26

"Nick Drake" flashed on the screen like a neon emergency sign. Her on-again, off-again boyfriend was calling for the third time that day. This time, she answered, though she wasn't sure why.

"Nick," she deadpanned. "What gives?"

"Just checking in. How are you?"

"Busy."

"The case?"

"Yes."

"How's it going?"

"It's going great."

He told her his acting career was not going well. "It's only a matter of time. Talent will win out."

"Listen, Nick. It's late. I've got to go."

"You're working, right?"

"Right. Besides, we're supposed to be taking a break."

"The break's over," Nick stated. "How about I come over? We'll take a break from the break."

Laura's mind sped back to where they'd left off. The time he bagged their date in favor of an old frat buddy. Laura had given Nick a choice: His buddy or his girlfriend. Nick had chosen his buddy.

"No," Laura said. "Got to go. Bye, Nick."

"Well, okay. Goodnight, Laura. Sleep tight."

Laura flipped onto her side. "I am *not* calling him back. At least, not until the case is over."

Her mind replayed the highs and lows of her six-month fling with Nick. The instant attraction at that party in SoHo; the romantic dinners at those trendy restaurants; the unleashed passion and great sex. After the first flush of a connection, Nick's obsession with himself had taken center stage. Then, there were the restaurant bills and bar tabs he'd left for Laura to pick up, as well as the former frat buddies and old flames who'd seemed to take precedence over their own plans. *No,* Laura told herself. She would not call him. She would not take his calls. She would steer clear.

Laura plunked her papers on the bedside table and turned off the lamp. She looked at the glowing numbers on her digital clock—1:59 AM. Laura rolled onto her right side and closed her eyes. Lingering in the netherworld between awake and asleep, she felt a frightening sensation. The presence of a man emerged in the shifting shadows of her room. She opened and closed her eyes to make sure he wasn't real. Just her imagination. Except, he *seemed* so real. Was he actually there? Clad in black, he stood over her bed, breathing over her, dangling a rope.

In the deep recesses of her nightmare, she knew it was the Hangman of Eden.

27

LAURA WOKE THE NEXT MORNING TO A WET NOSE ON HER FACE. SHE pushed Tripod aside and sat up in bed.

"All right, I get it; it's Dog Park Day."

She put the collie on the floor, crawled out of bed, grabbed a bathrobe from a door hook, and sleepwalked into the weekend routine. As the coffee brewed, she moved, zombie-like, into the shower and let the cold water snap her awake. From there, she wrapped herself in a towel, scooted back to the bedroom, and rifled through her dresser.

She pulled on a sweatshirt, embossed with a photo of Tripod and emblazoned with the words, *"Who Rescued Whom?"* Then, came well-worn blue jeans, black ankle socks, and her chartreuse Brooks running shoes. After tying the orange laces in double knots, she hustled to the bureau and found a rubber band to hold her hair in a ponytail.

A few minutes later, she was sitting at the counter, sipping black coffee from a mug that read, *"I Dig Dogs."* With Tripod's eyes fixed on her every move, she emptied the cup and placed it in the sink. "Come, boy," she called to him, leading him to the door, where she attached his six-foot leather leash to the ring in his imitation-diamond-studded collar.

"Let's do this. Let's get you to that dog park."

Just as she reached the door, her phone buzzed with a text. Laura looked at the screen and dropped the leash.

She stared at the message.

DROP THIS CASE.

What? She reread it.

DROP THIS CASE.

Her brain flashed red. Her blood chilled. *Who the hell?* She looked at it again:

DROP THIS CASE.

Tripod looked up. His head tilted as he began to whine at the door.

Laura stared at the screen one more time. There was no name or incoming number. She clicked the data screen, in search of some clue. The message must have come from an unregistered cell phone.

Who? The question ricocheted through her mind like a gunshot in an empty barrel. Her skin crawled. *The real killer?*

Like she'd told her father, she was eighty-percent certain that Eddie Nash had not killed Erin Lambert. That meant there was a good chance the real killer was still out there. The real killer would want Nash's conviction to stay on the books. The real killer would not want the original murder investigation to be reopened. The real killer would want Eddie Nash to remain behind bars for committing the horrendous crime of hanging a human being.

The next thought to enter her mind was just as chilling. *The police?*

Were the corrupt cops working to keep her from exposing the coerced confession, courtroom lies, tainted evidence, and bogus witnesses? Was the prosecutor in cahoots with the cops to keep her from exposing his lies, distortions, and paid testimony? Did the corruption run so deep that the authorities had to resort to scare tactics to hide their own crimes?

She forwarded the message to Charles Steel and added:

JUST RECEIVED. UNKNOWN SOURCE. KEEP PRIVATE.

Laura pocketed her phone and looked down at Tripod. "Let's go."

28

Laura led the collie down the narrow stairs and into the bright sunshine on Clifford Street, trying to put the text message out of her mind.

She continued to the crosswalk and looked in both directions. To her left was a long, littered street populated by open-air drug peddlers, and suburban users cruising for a fix. To her right was a tree-lined street with brick row houses, shrubs, and the occasional statue of the Virgin Mary. She turned right and headed to Carol Gardens—a safe, secure neighborhood a few blocks away.

This old Italian neighborhood seemed a million miles from the hard-scrabble Red Hook and the gentrified cityscape of Brooklyn Heights. Gone were the tatted-up gang-bangers, dolled-up hookers, and destitute down-and-outers. Gone were the too-cool hipsters, trendy art galleries, and boutiques. In their place were older women in cotton dresses, aged men in baggy pants, and teenage couples, walking hand-in-hand. Sweet aromas wafted from the Napoli Restaurant with its classic biscotti, Napoleons, and ricotta cheesecakes gleaming in the glass display window.

The scent made her feel better. She promised herself to put the threatening message aside for now; she wanted to enjoy the beautiful fall day with her dog.

Leading Tripod farther up the street, she forced herself to pass by Napolitano Pizza. Leaving the scent of simmering tomato sauce behind her, she stopped in her tracks at the window display of Giovani's Wedding Supply. She gazed through the glass at a flowing, hand-beaded bridal gown that looked like a piece of art. The exquisite fabric was tailored and stitched to perfection. The cut was low and styled to hug feminine curves. The dress exploded at the waist in a shimmering, white cyclone of graceful movement. She admired it for a long moment. *How would I look in that?*

Her phone buzzed. Nick fucking Drake. She let it go to voicemail.

Then, the real question forced itself back into her brain. *Who sent that text?*

Their route took Laura and Tripod to the riverfront promenade back in Brooklyn Heights. The morning sun backlit the towers of Manhattan, and roller-skaters rocketed down the walkway along the East River. "Come on, Tripod," she called, tugging his leash. "Let's get you to the dog park."

Tripod hopped into the lead and pulled on the leash, dragging Laura forward. He needed that romp and wasn't going to stop pulling until he got it. The dog was frantic by the time the Brooklyn Heights Dog Park came into sniffing range.

29

THE PUPPY PARADISE WAS SET ON A LOT AT THE TOP OF A RISE IN THE far northwest corner of the bustling Mario Vance neighborhood park. Dog owners let their pets run wild in the fenced-in enclosure, while kids swung from monkey bars and soared in swings in the adjacent playground.

She led Tripod toward the park. A half-dozen cars were parked in the lot of a nearby minimart, where a large, green dumpster stood in the rear. It cast a pungent scent that drifted in the wind, distracting the cavorting canines beyond the fence.

Laura led the collie through the parking lot, past the dumpster, and through the entrance gate, then released him into the park. A shepherd, poodle, pointer, and Lab all congregated at the gates, forming an enthusiastic welcoming committee. A scattering of purebreds and mixed-breeds frolicked in the grass across the two-acre spread. A Jack Russell raced to the top of the mound of artificial turf, challenging the others to a game of King of the Hill. Laura smiled as Tripod bounded into the fray. The sound of dogs barking and children laughing on the nearby swings fused into a joyful concatenation that took her mind off everything else.

Maybe I'll just come back as a dog in my next life. A turf war over soggy tennis balls seems much easier than a courtroom.

Laura strolled to an aluminum picnic table set under a pavilion near the top of the rise. She watched Tripod pounce at an Irish Wolfhound at the bottom of the rise, luring the larger dog into a chase. The hound was unconcerned that a smaller dog with three legs was out-pacing him. Two middle-aged women standing nearby cooed at the sight.

As Tripod scampered from dog to dog, Laura thought about the text. Who the hell would send such a threatening message? This was real life. Not a Netflix series. So, who had sent it? The real killer? The police? By now, both knew Nash's new lawyers had filed an appeal. The media was picking up the story.

Laura was lost in her thoughts. Time passed without her even noticing. The wind picked up and died down, then picked up again. Dog owners led their pets out the exit gate, while new ones led theirs through the entrance. The sun was back out from the clouds when her phone buzzed with a text.

Again, no name, no number:

WHERE'S TRIPOD?

Laura's brain went red with rage, panic coursing through her. *What the fuck?*

She scanned the dog park. There was no sign of Tripod. She leapt to her feet and climbed atop the picnic table. From that vantage point, she could look out over the entire space. No Tripod. She jumped down from the table and raced down the rise, looking right and left. She didn't see her dog. She approached a middle-aged man in a flannel shirt who was tossing a ball to a young Lab.

"Hey!" She was breathless, her chest heaving. "Have you seen a three-legged Border collie?"

"Nope." The man shrugged, turned, and tossed the ball. "Go get it, Chester!"

Laura hurried toward the gates. A small cluster of trees shrouded the area just south of the entrance. Maybe Tripod had followed a dog under the canopy; maybe he was wrestling with a terrier, digging up an old bone, or resting in the shade. She scanned the area. Nothing. Goddammit.

Laura started following the chain-link fence around the perimeter of the park. Hustling, she traced it for thirty or forty feet, then stopped to look around. No sign of him. She raced another forty feet and put on the brakes again. Still no sign of him. She reached the far side of the park, but he wasn't there, either. She approached a tall, young woman standing near the fence, her eyes glued on her setter.

"Have you seen a three-legged Border collie?"

"Yeah," the woman replied. "What a cutie. What's his name?"

"Where? Where?"

"Well, it was like a half-hour ago. I'm not sure where he went. Let me think. Oh, yeah, it looked like he was heading for the trees over by the gate."

Laura retreated back to the grove, but no Tripod. Her brain shifted into overdrive. *Where are you? Who the hell would do this? What the hell do they want with you? I'll find you, I promise.*

Her phone buzzed with another anonymous text.

She stared at the screen, and her eyes glazed over. Her skin burned, and her brain felt like a dagger had been jammed into it, then twisted to maximize the pain.

THE DUMPSTER.

30

Laura dodged rollicking canines and confused owners as she exited the dog park. She ran back toward the minimart parking lot, stopping forty feet from the filthy, green dumpster. She squatted down like a baseball catcher and took a deep breath.

Is he in there? Is he...?

She looked in every direction. No one to her right; no one to her left. She snapped her head back over her shoulder to confirm that there was no one behind her. She stood up straight, sucked in a lungful of air, and began stepping forward. Putting one foot in front of the other, she made painstaking progress toward the receptacle. She pushed through an invisible barrier of dread with each step. Images of her dog ran through her mind. Tripod at the beach, Tripod in the woods, Tripod taking a walk. Laura could not bear the thought of losing him. She could feel her fear turning to white-hot, searing anger. Who would steal her dog?

Laura was maybe twenty feet from the trash bin. She smelled rust and rotting waste. She was ten feet away when she stopped and listened. A faint scratching sound came from inside the bin. She was five feet away when she called out, "Tripod...?"

She listened for any response. More scratching. Two feet away. She reached out to touch the filmy, metallic surface. She was so intent on finding her dog that the stench of decay did not matter. Rising to her feet and reaching for the lid, she heard a scream.

"Stop!"

She spun toward the voice.

"Come back here!"

Shit. It was just a kid on the sidewalk, calling to his runaway dog.

Laura turned back to the dumpster. She gripped the grimy handle, lifting the metal plate.

Please, God. Let him be okay.

She winced and looked inside.

A small gray creature scurried in the refuge and leapt up. The rat screeched, bared its yellow teeth, and swiped its claws at her.

Damn it.

She slammed the lid shut. After a long moment, she opened it a crack and peered in. The rat was curled up in the corner, hiding in the mounds of rotting meat and banana peels. The smell of sour milk mingled with the aroma of rancid mayonnaise. Pools of vomit would have been less disgusting. She leaned over the edge, sweeping her hand through discarded paper plates, cardboard boxes, and cabbage stalks, choking back the vile she vowed not to puke and avoiding the rat.

No Tripod.

He's not here. Laura exhaled. *What gives?*

She closed the lid as her phone buzzed with a new text message:

FINAL WARNING. DROP THE CASE.

She looked in all directions. Nothing. No one.

She took out her phone and composed a text to Charles Steel:

DOG STOLEN. MORE THREATS.

Laura was fighting back a growing sense of panic when she heard the bark. She would know that yap anywhere. "Tripod!" She snapped her head back toward the dog park. There he was, standing at the fence, wagging his tail, and calling out to her.

She raced back to the park, scrambled up the rise to Tripod. She bent to one knee and snatched him up, hugging him for a long moment. She never wanted to let go of him again.

"Who took you? Thank God, you're okay. Let's get out of here."

Laura put him down, snapped on the leash, and ran him out of the park.

There it was again. The taste of bile in the back of her throat. The bands of invisible steel constricting her ribcage. The panic always started this way.

I can't melt down. Let the fear pass.

Speed-walking down the sidewalk, she forced herself to take deep, even breaths, one shaking hand lingering over her solar plexus. She had to find her center and calm down. What should she do? It might not be safe back at her apartment. Whoever sent the texts and snatched her dog was smart enough to know where she lived. Laura had no desire to go home just to come face-to-face with her stalker—whoever it was.

She paused on the sidewalk to send another text to Charles:

Meet me at the Red Lion Café.

31

Laura sat at an iron mesh patio table at the outdoor bistro. Tripod stood by her side, drinking from a metal water bowl.

A tall, skinny waiter with dishwater hair and a challenged complexion hovered next to her with a notepad in hand, staring down at the dog. "How did the little guy lose his leg? Poor thing. Can he walk?"

"Just a latte, please," Laura said. "A small latte."

Asshole.

The kid cocked his head at her brusque tone and retreated back into the kitchen.

Laura looked up and down Essex Street. A diverse parade of pedestrian traffic navigated the wide boulevard. A Latino man in blue coveralls emerged from a work van and hustled into A-1 Custom Auto Parts. A middle-aged woman in stretch pants exited Pronto Dry Cleaning, hangers with shirts, pants, and dresses flopping over her shoulder. A woman in a flowery smock gazed into the window of the Sweet Smoke Vape Parlor at the corner of Essex and Carroll.

Laura looked farther up Essex. She was on the lookout for anything or anyone out of the ordinary. A teenage boy ascended the broad, brick steps of Saint Patrick's Church. He could have been an altar boy, arriving to set up for evening Mass. A city worker pushed a plastic barrel on rollers at the corner of Essex and Grand. The whiff of rotten vegetables from Key Nam Thai Soup mingled with car fumes and street dust.

The vibe on the street was reassuring. These mom-and-pop businesses and second-floor apartments were the real Brooklyn—no trendy bars serving eighteen-dollar cocktails, prepared by mixologists using "artisanal ice."

An abrupt realization snapped her back to reality.

Laura realized that her mysterious starker knew a lot about her. Her name. Her cell number. Even her dog's name. Just what she needed. A psycho who does his homework.

Laura looked up and down the street one more time. Still nothing unusual. Then, she fixed her gaze on a short, bulky man, walking—no, limping—in her direction.

Who the hell is this?

The middle-aged guy had a head like a bucket, a body like a granite block, and legs like redwood stumps. He wore an Army surplus jacket, oversized blue corduroys, scuffed combat boots, and a vintage Dodgers baseball cap. This was not a unified look.

Laura peered at the oncoming man. The closer he got, the more menacing he seemed. At fifty feet out, Laura made out a scar slashing across his forehead, and tattoos on his neck. Forty feet out, she noticed his crooked sneer and flattened nose. At twenty-five feet out, she looked into his cold, empty eyes, the color of thick, white haze in a sun-bleached sky. Despite their hazy gleam, those eyes were focused dead ahead, right at her.

He could have been a homeless meth-head—or a thug hired to kill her.

32

LAURA CLUTCHED TRIPOD'S LEASH AS THE GRIZZLED MAN STEPPED OFF the sidewalk and onto the patio.

Run. Run. Run. She ignored the impulse and froze in place.

The man limped toward her, shoulders squared, arms braced, and his white eyes narrowed to sinister slashes. Five feet from the table, he held out two meaty paws in a stop sign.

"Don't run," he grunted. "I'm a friend. I'm your new bodyguard."

The strange newcomer pulled a steel-framed patio chair up to the table and lowered his massive body onto it. He scanned the space, moving his glazed eyes over a half-dozen patrons. Turning back to Laura, he held up an iPhone, hit a button, and handed it to her.

"This is Charles. Laura, say hello to Lou. He's one of us."

Laura gave the phone back to the stranger. "Hello, Mister…?"

"Hello." His croak suggested one too many billy club whacks to the larynx. "Just call me Lou. No last name."

"Okay." Laura leaned back, easing her grip on the leash. "Thanks for coming."

"You're safe now. Your dog's safe." Lou's voice was sandpaper-rough and foghorn-low. "You're now under surveillance, one-hundred-percent-coverage, one-hundred-percent of the time. Whoever's harassing you will show themselves, and we'll be there to take care of them when they do."

"'We?'"

"You won't even see us. Until you need us."

"'Us?'"

Lou grunted. "Yep. Us. No need to say more. We have you covered."

"You work for Charles Steel?"

"Yes."

Jesus, no wonder he's a legend.

Tripod stood at attention under the table, sniffing the stranger's boots. No growl, no bark.

"Look." Lou studied her with those hazy eyes. "I'm here to get this situation under control. I specialize in these kinds of cases. I know you didn't expect a mash-up of Quasimodo and the Incredible Hulk, but you got one."

"Okay, it's—it's just that—"

"I get it, you're traumatized. You've had a bad morning. Fill me in, and we'll go from there."

Laura leaned back in her chair. There was something she liked about this brutish, likely bare-knuckle brawler who'd just stomped into her life. Maybe it was his bulldozer personality. A hint of brilliance hid behind the brawn, scars, and tats. Undoubtedly, a colorful past had educated him on handling danger. If he worked for Charles Steel, she was sure he shared a knowledge of the law and investigations.

"Yeah, I guess I am traumatized. The stalker's methods worked."

"Sending a threatening text was meant to get your attention. Snatching your dog was meant to shock you into compliance. Now, their tactics will escalate. Next time, they'll threaten to shit can you. These people are not nice."

"I'm getting over it." She smiled. "I'm dealing."

"Good."

Laura and Lou looked up at the reappearance of the kid waiter.

"Miss." He looked at Laura, while ignoring Lou. "Is this man bothering you?"

"Bothering me?" Laura was stunned by the kid's brashness. "Hmmm, no."

"Is he with you?" the waiter demanded. "Or is he from the street?"

"What?"

Lou curled his right hand and coughed into it.

"We've been having problems with—" The kid stopped short of completing his sentence. Undoubtedly, he'd meant to say homeless men, filthy vagrants, vile street people, dirty beggars, or bums. "We've had trouble with them bothering our customers."

"No problem," Laura assured him. "We're cool. He's with me."

"Just bring the check, sonny." Lou issued the order in a low, serious tone, with one glazed eye targeting a spot in the middle of the waiter's forehead.

The waiter turned red and marched off.

The next voice came from nowhere. "I see you two started without me." Laura and Lou looked up to see Charles, well-dressed in a black sweater with muted African designs and slim-cut jeans. He laid his hands on the back of Laura's chair. "And I see you've met Lou. He's gonna look out for you. He's gonna protect you from these bastards."

Lou sprang from his chair, and Charles moved to take his place. The transition was as efficient as a military maneuver or a scene choreographed on Broadway.

"Who exactly is that man?" Laura asked Charles, as Lou began his peculiar walk away.

"Lou is my number-two man. The guy is a master of personal security, and a hell of an investigator. He can keep you safe while assisting with the investigation. From now on, Lou is engaged one-hundred-percent."

"Where did you ever find him?"

Charles shrugged. "Lou was riding with a bikers' club in Queens. The Night Riders. He got rung up on a breaking-and-entering beef. The cops locked him up in the Tombs. I heard about it, checked it out, and figured out he had nothing to do with the B&E. I pointed out the holes in the case to the DA and got the charges dropped. Lou paid me back by working with my investigative team. The rest is history."

"You have an eye for talent."

"Always on the lookout for fresh blood. I'm looking for a new under-cover guy as we speak. A smooth operator who can fit into any situation. Lou kind of… stands out."

"I'll keep my eyes open."

Charles continued urgently, "Now, tell me what happened. What the hell is going on?"

Laura didn't answer immediately, watching Lou limp away into the distance. She smiled with appreciation as he vanished into the parade of humanity.

33

THE OLD MAN HAD A FRINGE OF HAIR, A WIZENED FACE, AND BLUE EYES that hid in purple flesh. His shoulders were rounded, his back was hunched, and his hands quivered most of the time. He had the resigned look of one who knows that at his age, life has stopped giving and only takes away. His memories both warmed and haunted him, sometimes drawing a smile, but most times, a tear. He had long since forgotten what it felt like to have joints that moved freely without pain. He had almost forgotten what it was like to live freely, to walk on a beach, to feel the rain, or watch the stars. The old man knew one thing for sure. Time was the thief he'd always suspected it to be, picking off his loved ones and friends, one by one. *Everybody seems to want to have a long life*, he told himself, *but what good is it if you're not free? What good is it if your retirement home is a cell block? What good is it if your destiny is to die in shackles?* He would describe old age as bobbing on an ocean in a boat, not knowing when death will finally come to sever the rope that anchors you to the ocean floor and binds you to this earthly coil.

* * *

Eddie Nash wanted to retch, as usual, as the slime slinger piled his plastic plate with what the sign said was "Turkey a la King". The putrid pile of off-white mush looked more like reheated puke, poured on regurgitated potato chunks. It had the smell of rancid poultry, and the consistency of runny shit. God, how he hated "Quick Chill," the state's new, cost-effective prison cuisine program. The scarf was cooked up at a minimum security facility three hours away and shipped to Attica, where it was reheated and served up as "gourmet fare." Eddie carried his tray to the end of the line, stopping to fill his metal cup with coffee the color of sewer water.

"More swill," he muttered, navigating the rows of rectangular wooden tables to the back of the mess hall, scanning the security cameras and tear gas dispensers mounted on the walls. Eddie strode past the Plexiglas-enclosed control room, careful not to eyeball the screw who stood ready to push a button that would—at the first sign of trouble—trigger a shower of tear gas on them all.

Eddie passed the tall columns and archways that gave the mess the false atmosphere of a cathedral. He reached a table near the back wall and nodded to an old man sitting at the end by himself.

"Hey, Doc," Eddie greeted him, as if he were an old friend. "Doc Gleason."

In contrast, the elderly con lifted his head in slow motion and managed a half-hearted nod. "Nash... sit."

Eddie placed his tray on the pinewood and lowered himself onto a chair opposite the old lifer.

"The famous Doc Gleason." Eddie let his mouth drag out a smile. "The MD of A-Block."

Doc coughed into a curled hand and said, "In the flesh."

"What the hell you doin' dining with the big dawgs of D-Block, Doc?"

"Got my blood pressure checked today. Made me late for A-Block swill call."

"How was it? Your BP?"

"Two-hundred over one-hundred."

"Stroke territory. You get meds?"

"Maybe next week."

"Oh."

Eddie had shot the shit with the old man in the past whenever their paths crossed. Eddie liked listening to his stories but hated how the encounters left him thinking about dying in prison. He'd heard the story of Doc's murder rap on the grapevine and never forgot it. How Doc had overdosed his wife with painkillers, signed the death certificate, and shipped her body off for cremation. How the cops had caught up with him at the airport with a ticket to Panama, and a suitcase full of cash.

Crack. Crack. Crack.

Eddie looked up to see a C.O. slam his baton against a table of Latino inmates. Their Spanglish chatter went silent.

Eddie turned back to the old man. "How old are you now, Doc?"

"Eighty-three, and the oldest con in stir." Doc ran a hand through a balding, mottled cap of hair. He ignored the trails of white drool seeping from the sides of his mouth. "The last fifty-two right here in this death factory."

"Fifty-two years." Eddie shook his head and forced back a wince as he pressed a plastic fork into the turkey. "Parole?"

"Yep. Up next month. Compassionate release."

"What's your pitch?"

"Let myself get sick enough for 'em to feel sorry for me, but not sick enough to die before they let me out."

"Maybe that'll be the charm. No sense keeping you locked up at the taxpayers' expense."

Doc dipped his spoon into his remaining gruel. "My daughter's gonna speak up for me."

"Good luck, Doc. You deserve your freedom. Nobody should have to die in this place."

"Amen."

Eddie closed his eyes and plunged a chunk of white-coated potato into his mouth, allowing that grim thought to hang in the air.

"YOU'RE A FUCKING DEAD MAN."

Eddie swung his head toward the source of the threat. It came from a con at the far end of the table. The white con had blonde dreadlocks—a strange sight in itself—and tattoo sleeves on both arms. Skulls. Dragons. Spiderwebs. The man was leaning over the table and glaring at the inmate opposite him.

"You're dead, you fucking diaper-snipper."

Eddie froze in his seat. "Don't move, Doc."

Three guards pounced on the troublemaker in seconds, battering him with batons, then dragging him out of the mess.

Once the hoots and hollers subsided, Eddie muttered, "Fucking drama queen."

"Could have gotten us all gassed," Doc added. "At least we're getting dinner and a show."

Unsure where their talk had left off, Eddie decided to change the subject. "You know, we've never talked about the '71 riot. I got a lawyer now; she's all into that; made me think of you."

"It wasn't a riot." Doc raised his hunched back and leaned in closer. "It was a revolution."

"Revolution?"

Doc put his spoon onto his plate and lowered his tone to an audible whisper. "The Black Panthers and Black Muslims ran the show. Seized the yard. Took the hostages. Set the rules. As the hours ticked off, though, a strange thing happened: The usual prison factions broke down. The whites joined in. The Puerto Ricans followed. Black. Brown. White. Clenched-fist salutes and cries of 'Attica! Attica!' We all believed the uprising would spread to prisons all over the country. The idea was to overturn the whole miserable system."

"Didn't work. The system survived."

"Right. Four days of negotiations ended with five-hundred state cops blasting their way back into control. The troopers fired wildly. Smashed heads with gun butts. Stuck gun barrels in the mouths of downed prisoners. Yelled, *'White power!'* while gunning down black prisoners. When the smoke cleared, the yard was lined with dead inmates and hostages."

"You mean the troopers did all the killing?"

"The cons had no guns. The troopers had all the firepower. Even guards were mowed down by so-called 'friendly fire.'"

"What did you do when it was going down?"

"I was an MD. I had value. After the inmates took Time Square and D-Block, I was drafted to tend to the injured hostages and prisoners. Finally, a medical corps from the outside was let in to tend to the wounded. I stood down. I found myself an abandoned cell out of harm's way."

"You hunkered down and survived the siege."

"Except, it didn't end there. The worst part was the days and weeks after the siege. Retribution ran wild. The guards beat and tortured the surviving ringleaders and sympathizers. I put my head down and avoided the beat-down crews. Maybe the hacks gave me a pass because I was white."

"Fucked-up," Eddie muttered. "One-hundred-percent fucked-up."

Doc nodded. "Yeah. Behind us now. So, what's up with you? What do you got going on?"

Splat!

Eddie heard the mound of Turkey a la King land next to his plate and felt drabs of white mush splatter his shirt. He looked back in the direction of the projectile, but the culprit must have put his head down. Eddie wiped his shirt and returned to his conversation.

"What do I have going on? My girl lawyer and her hotshot PI are getting me a new trial. I'm looking forward to proving my innocence and walking out of here a free man."

Doc nodded. "A free man. Just like Corkscrew."

"I ain't Corkscrew." Eddie's smile snapped straight, his posture stiffening. "Fuck Corkscrew."

Corkscrew was the handle of a gangbanger named Manuel Sandoval. An enforcer for the Latin Kings, Sandoval earned his nickname by the way he disemboweled his victims. He'd been convicted of double murder for executing two bangers who'd crossed the Kings, and he had been sentenced to life-plus-sixty.

"'Member how them innocence lawyers got him a new trial?" Doc asked. "Claimed his rights were violated."

"I remember. Everybody does."

"'Member how Corkscrew walked outta here? Strutting like a goddamned peacock on parade."

Eddie glared in silence.

Doc laughed. He swallowed a spoonful of swill. "Innocence. Exoneration. What a load of shit."

34

"LULLABY AND GOODNIGHT..."

The CO's soothing baritone echoed through the cavernous cell block, soothing the murderers, rapists, drug dealers, and gangsters. The fall of his steel-toed boots on the iron mesh catwalk formed a rhythmic backbeat to the song. As he approached Eddie's cell, the short, compact CO stopped singing and called out in a loud whisper, "Brother Nash."

Eddie stepped into the circle of light cast by the guard's flashlight, gripping his cell door bars. "Hey, Fridge."

The nickname underscored the guard's ice-box physique, but it was his personality that made him stand out to the cons. One of the few African-American COs at Attica, his storytelling, advice, and willingness to lend an ear had opened up even the most withdrawn men in D-Block. The cons never referred to him by the names they'd applied to the other guards. Fridge was never a bull, a hack, or a screw. Fridge was just Fridge.

Fridge stopped at Eddie's cell during lights-out five nights a week. The two jawed about the food in the mess, the fights in the yard, and the bad jackets in keep-lock—an order confining misbehaving inmates to their cells for twenty-four hours a day.

"Brother Nash," Fridge repeated. "What's the good word?"

"Freedom," Eddie replied. "Sweet freedom."

"Freedom from?" Fridge asked. "Freedom from what?"

"The bars and razor wire," Eddie shot back. "The shot callers and shower stalkers."

"Freedom to… what?"

"Eat steak, drink beer, drive fast, and make long, slow love to a beautiful woman."

"Got it." Fridge nodded. "No bars, razor wire, or surprises in the shower. Just sirloin, suds, and Halle Berry."

"You got it. The good life."

"How are you going to come about this freedom?" Fridge asked, his black skin glistening.

"My lawyer is gonna get it for me," Eddie whispered. "She's ready to tell the appeals court how my rights got violated. She's expecting the court to rule by the fall."

"Got it; new trial."

"I'll be proven innocent. Then, I'll be home free."

Fridge held up a flat palm, arm clad in his standard blue shirt, and whispered, "Shush." The sound of laughter rolled from down the catwalk. Signaling to Eddie to hold his thoughts, Fridge looked over his shoulder and hollered, "Lights-out, gentleman! Don't make me come back there!" Pausing a moment to make sure the laughter had been silenced, Fridge turned to Eddie again, resettled his black DOCSS cap, and asked, "What's so great about this girl lawyer of yours? How's she gonna pull off this miracle?"

"She's from the Innocence Project. She's one of those special lawyers who get cons out from under all this hurt, who exonerate inmates who got a bad deal in the courts."

Fridge stepped back from the cell, his smile melting into a sneer. "Corkscrew all over again."

Not that again, Eddie thought. "No. No. No," Eddie pleaded. "It ain't like Corkscrew."

Fridge moved closer to the bars, standing face-to-face with him. "Corkscrew. Manuel Sandoval. Vengeance for the bloodiest crew in the 718. Goes down for double murder and becomes the most feared shot caller in Attica. Then, the Innocence Project comes in and starts whining, *'His rights were violated.'* Corkscrew gets a new trial."

"That wasn't my lawyer," Eddie pleaded. "My lawyer ain't like that."

"This time, Corkscrew plays it smart. He gets his home dawgs on the outside to threaten a couple of weak spines on the jury. In the end, the weak spines hang the jury—out of fear for their lives and their families. Corkscrew walks."

"I'm different," Eddie insisted. "I am innocent."

Fridge stepped back from the bars, pausing before adding a final thought. "Look, Brother Nash. I've been a guard here for seven years. I've walked every catwalk in this place. I've met cons of every kind: Serial killers, repeat rapists, kidnappers, gang leaders, you name it. How many times have I heard those lines? 'I'm innocent; I was framed; I was set up. I don't belong here.' On and on, over and over."

"I'm sure you heard it plenty."

"I can't count the times. But, there's one thing I know with absolute certainty from my years working in this pen."

"Just one?"

"Yep. There's one fact that I know without a doubt." Fridge held up one stubby finger. "One, and only one."

"What's that?" Eddie asked.

"The most important fucking thing of all."

"Yeah, okay. What?"

"Every con to ever enter this prison was guilty of something."

35

THE MASSIVE GRANITE STEPS. THE WHITE MARBLE COLUMNS. THE DAZ-
zling gold dome. The chiseled busts of ancient lawgivers: Plato, Aristotle,
Demosthenes, and Moses. Laura felt just the right degree of intimidation as
she entered the Thurgood Marshall United States Courthouse at 40 Foley
Square in Lower Manhattan. Her briefcase swung like a pendulum as she
marched on the marble floors of the main hallway under the glimmering
chandeliers that hung from the ceiling thirty feet above. The courthouse
served as home to the U.S. Court of Appeals for the Second Circuit, which
reviewed cases from New York State and Connecticut.

Laura stepped into the elevator and got out on the seventh floor. She
strode to Hearing Room #746—set aside for *New York v. Nash.*

Laura entered and marched down the aisle, taking a seat at a mahogany
desk with a sign bearing her name and affiliation. She turned to a matching
desk to her right, catching sight of a middle-aged man unpacking a briefcase.

Square-jawed and blue-suited, State's Attorney Robert McCall did not
acknowledge her nod. His stare was intense.

In the awkward, pre-hearing silence, the three judges—all clad in black
robes with gold sashes—took their places at the raised mahogany bench. Each
justice opened a folder and began scanning a document known as a "bench
memo."

The moment of truth was here. Oral arguments were about to commence. The fate of Edward Thomas Nash hung in the balance, even though Eddie was hundreds of miles away, locked in a cell, unaware that his fate was being debated at this moment in one of the highest courts in the land. Only lawyers attend oral arguments, period.

Laura ran through the facts, observations, insights, and anomalies she'd laid out in her written brief. The coerced confession. The paid-for testimony. The prosecutor's rants. She also reviewed her research on the three judges: Their judicial philosophies, previous rulings, and pet peeves.

I've got this. Laura felt no sign of her old anxiety. Maybe she'd conquered the beast.

In fact, she felt confident, optimistic. She had a strong case to present. At the same time, she had no illusions. She was not going to persuade these sophisticated jurists that her client was an innocent man who should be set free. She didn't have to. She just had to show that the trial court had reached its verdict—whether right or wrong—by an erroneous route.

At 2:06 PM, an attractive female judge of Japanese descent spoke from the elevated bar. Laura and McCall rose to their feet.

"Counsel. Let me start by commending each of you. Your written briefs are both thorough and illuminating. The legal issues are clearly delineated. I'm going to dispense with any repetitive opening statements and go straight to Q&A. Justices, questions, please."

Laura hid a flash of relief. Doing away with opening statements meant the justices wanted to cut to the chase. Justice Sandra Chen, the presiding judge, was an Obama appointee with a liberal record on police and prosecutor misconduct.

A male judge with close-cropped, gray hair and a poker face looked out over his designer tortoiseshell glasses. "Ms. Tobias." Justice Edward Manning was a George W. Bush appointee who tended to give prosecutors and police wide latitude. "Much of your argument hinges on alleged misconduct by the police and prosecutor," he stated. "Would you agree?"

"Yes, Your Honor."

"Now, you're aware that we hear these arguments quite often. In fact, allegations of police and prosecutorial misconduct are included in ninety-percent of all major felony appeals."

"I'm sure of it, sir."

"And I'm sure you'd agree that our police and prosecutors face serious challenges to enforcing the law."

"Yes, sir."

"And our state and local prosecutors face serious challenges to proving guilt beyond a reasonable doubt. Protecting society is not for the faint of heart."

"True, Your Honor."

"Can you cite one example of egregious misconduct that may have slanted the outcome of this trial against your client?"

"The false characterizations made by the County Prosecutor to the jurors," Laura fired back. She pointed to the grotesque—and baseless—claim that he'd urinated on the dead, suspended body. "The facts of this case did not support these outrageous accusations, Your Honor. The statements were outlandish, prejudicial, and wrong, and should have been stricken by the trial judge."

Judge Manning looked to the state's attorney. "What about it, Mr. McCall?"

"Your Honor, the state views my colleague's allegations against the police and prosecutors as overblown and irrelevant. The premeditated hanging of this poor young woman was a hideous crime, committed by a vicious and violent man. The prosecution had to describe the horror of the act, and the depravity of the actor. I urge you not to give this monster a second chance to kill."

"That presumes the guilt of my client, Your Honors. The state failed to meet the burden of reasonable doubt."

Laura beamed inside. McCall had just done her a big favor.

36

McCall had refused to engage with the factual and legal points that Laura had laid out in her statement. He had written her arguments off as unworthy of a response and—by extension—had advised the appeals court to overlook the flaws in the original trial. By refusing to recognize the relative strengths and weaknesses of her claims, the state's attorney had undercut the court's ability to weigh the defense claims against the prosecution's counterclaims. McCall was expecting the court to wish away the facts.

Judge Manning narrowed his gaze and cleared his throat. "Mr. McCall, what about this stun belt? Why force the defendant to wear it?"

"It was placed under his clothing, Your Honor. It was out of sight of the jury."

"Mr. State's Attorney," Manning said, annoyed, "that wasn't my question." He glared at McCall. "Again, why force the defendant to wear it?"

"The trial judge required it as a precaution against disruptions." McCall seemed uncertain on this point. "He'd determined that the accused could disrupt the proceedings with violent outbursts."

"Did Mr. Nash exhibit a previous proclivity to disruptive behavior?"

"Um." McCall looked down at an open binder on the desk. "I am not—"

"Ms. Tobias?" the appellate judge barked. "*You* must know."

"No, Your Honor, Mr. Nash had no prior criminal history and exhibited no violent reactions while in police custody. At the same time, Mr. Nash's preoccupation with being shocked made it hard for him to concentrate, undercutting his ability to take part in his own defense. Furthermore, the discussion of the belt in open court biased the jury against my client. Why was a man who was presumed to be innocent wrapped up in a dangerous electronic device that might electrocute him at any moment?"

"Thank you," Manning said. "Thank you for clearing that up."

Justice Chen followed up. "Mr. McCall, why was the presence of the belt discussed in the presence of the jury?"

"Your Honor, the trial judge told the jury that the defendant was being outfitted with the belt as a precaution. He instructed the jurors to make no inference of guilt or violent tendencies—to ignore it."

After several hard questions by Chen, and vague answers from McCall, the justices turned back to Laura.

"Ms. Tobias. How powerful are these belts?" Justice Manning leaned toward her to hear her answer.

"Your Honor, these belts are capable of delivering a fifty-thousand-volt shock to the wearer over an eight-second period. This causes the recipient to lose control of his limbs, fall to the floor, and flail about in severe convulsions. The promotional literature claims the belts provide *'total psychological supremacy over troublesome defendants.'*"

"How widespread is the use of these belts?" Justice Chen asked.

"The belts have been used for years. However, that is changing. Dozens of jurisdictions have banned their use after being sued by wearers who suffered severe convulsions that required hospitalization. Amnesty International has branded the belts 'cruel and unusual punishment' and demanded a nationwide ban. Your Honors, I ask this court to send a strong message to the trial courts of New York. I ask that you restrict—or outlaw—the use of the belts and grant my client a new trial."

37

EDDIE NASH BOUNCED ON THE BALLS OF HIS FEET IN THE HALL OUT-
side the main visitors' room. He'd been waiting in a line of restless cons for
more than an hour for a long-awaited visit with his mother. Cassandra Nash
had made the bus trip from Eden.

The other cons were busting with anticipation to see their loved ones.
Eddie was minding his own business when he felt a large hand on the small
of his back. A split-second later, he felt a push and sprawled forward, rico-
cheting off two men in line ahead of him. Regaining his balance, Eddie spun
a one-eighty to confront the creep who'd pushed him. Eddie glared at the
square-shouldered white man with the shaved head, cold eyes, and spiderweb forehead tat. Eddie had never seen the man before, but he knew he was
trouble.

"What the fuck?" Eddie snarled as the white con stepped forward, nar-
rowing the space between them to less than a foot.

The con who'd pushed him sneered, flexing a swastika tat on his thick
left arm. "Come on, mud man. Let's go."

Eddie stared into his cold eyes and contorted face. Racist bastard. He
felt the need to plant a fist into his forehead and an elbow to the side of his
head. To fuck him up bad. To send him to the hospital wing, then back to

his white-boy gang. Eddie's heart raced, his face flushed, and his hands balled into fists. His muscles coiled, preparing to strike.

The thug's eyes blazed, and his face was burning red. At the same time his arms still hung at his sides. The fool had not raised his defenses; the troublemaker must not have been a skilled fighter. Eddie envisioned his move: He would lower his stance and thrust a strong right uppercut into the creep's balls. As he folded over, Eddie would drive a knee into the motherfucker's face. Then, kick his wobbling legs out from under him. With any luck, the con would hit the concrete floor headfirst, and a sweet stream of crimson liquid would pool around him.

Then, Eddie heard the voice of reason in his head: *No, not now. Don't fuck this up. Keep your cool. You don't need a beef with the Aryan Nation men. You don't need to be written up. You don't need to be sent to the Box. Not now. A fight could ruin everything.*

Fighting back his instinct, Eddie faced forward, shrugging off the shit shank, as a guard tapped a night stick in his right palm and sauntered over.

Eddie smiled as the guard passed. He had to remain calm. Keep his cool. All he had to do was wait until the doors to the visiting room swung open, and the bulls began herding the inmates inside. He wanted to see his mother.

He'd learned the hard way, long ago, that any disturbance in the line would get the offender, or offenders, sent back to their cells without their scheduled visit. Their loved ones would be sent home with nothing to show for their trip to the isolated prison.

Patience was the key. Patient inmates were rewarded with the coveted one-hour contact visits. They could hug their parents, kiss their wives, hold their kids, or just catch up with friends from back home.

Don't fuck this up; you have to see her, he told himself. Eddie needed to hug her, hold her hand, hear her voice, and share his news.

This visit would be so different than his recent non-contact visit with Laura Tobias. That had been held in the sterile lawyer/client room, a locked-down holding tank reserved for inmates meeting with their attorneys.

"Come on, mud man," the con spat. "Let's do this. You and me."

* * *

Cassandra Nash waited with equal patience on the guest's side of the wall. She studied the faces of her fellow visitors. The wives. The kids. The parents. The friends. The clock on the wall told her the visit was an hour behind schedule.

Cassie—as her friends called her—was exhausted from the two-hour bus trip, followed by the forced march through the spired gates. But, she was there, and she'd wait as long as it took to hear more of the "big news" Eddie hinted at over the phone.

Finally, the door swung open, and the cons began filing in. Dour faces lit up. Tears. Hugs. The lure of coffee and donuts wafted from the service table.

"Ma!"

"Eddie."

The two embraced for a long moment.

Eddie led her to a vacant table, pulled out a plastic chair, lowered her into it, and settled down next to her.

"Thanks for coming, Ma. How're you doing? You're lookin'—"

"I'm fine for an old lady. How are you, baby?"

"Had a little issue with a con in line behind me. He pushed me, insulted me, wanted to fight."

Cassie closed her eyes. "What did you do?"

"I asked myself, 'What would Jesus do?' Then, I turned the other cheek."

"You did not."

"I ignored him and waited until the guards got between us. You know how it is, Ma. I mind my own business. I stay out of trouble. Just like you tell me to."

After the small talk, Cassie started in with her hometown update; all of their visits started this way. "Remember Chandra, your cousin?"

"The skinny one with braces?"

"She's twenty-one now, and beautiful. She's engaged to a boy from Franklin."

Eddie smiled. "Time flies."

Cassie nodded. "Too fast."

"Is he a good man?"

"We'll see."

Eddie rolled his eyes. "What else?"

"The Reverie Baptist Church is moving. The congregation is building a beautiful new church, high up on Heaven Hill in Grande Vista. One wall is gonna be all glass. It's gonna look down over the whole valley, over all of Eden."

Eddie looked at the floor and laughed. "I've been looking down on that town for years."

"Stop it, it's going to be beautiful."

"Heaven Hill?" Eddie raised his head, as if consulting the Divine. "Heaven Hill is just fine for a new church, Ma. The flock will be that much closer to God."

"Oh, Eddie." Cassie cringed at his sacrilege. "How many times have I told you? Don't poke fun at the Lord. You need Him more than ever now. Remember, John 5:1-9 tells us 'the angels of the Lord will see you through the troubled waters.'"

"Ma, how many times have I told you? God's big enough to take a joke."

Cassie scanned the room. The inmates and visitors huddled around the two-dozen rectangular tables, sipping coffee from Styrofoam cups and nibbling donuts from paper plates. Couples held hands and kids ran in circles, shouting, "Daddy, Daddy, Daddy!" The atmosphere was almost festive—a reunion in hell.

"Reverend Garret sends his best. You know, he still prays for you."

"Reverend Garret is a good man." Eddie conjured a picture of the rotund, black preacher.

Cassie studied his eyes. "My dear, beautiful son."

"Ma, this is too hard on you."

"You're such a good man, Eddie."

"Maybe you should just stop coming, Ma. Just make believe I'm back in the service."

"No, never." She wiped away the tears with a lace handkerchief. "Now, what's this big news of yours?"

Eddie cleared his throat. "I told you about my new lawyer. This one is the real deal. She's smart, knows her stuff, and is making great progress. She's getting me a new trial—a *fair* trial."

"That's wonderful!"

"This time, we're gonna win. This time, I'm coming home. We'll go to church together up on Heaven Hill."

"We will."

Eddie told her all about his appeal. He explained how Laura and the Council Against Wrongful Convictions fought for inmates who never should have been sent to prison in the first place.

"This hotshot investigator is finding new evidence and witnesses. It's gonna prove my innocence. Believe me, Ma. I'm gonna walk away from this place and never look back."

Cassie clutched his hand and forced a light squeeze. "You're gonna come home. You're gonna come home to me. My prayers will be answered."

"Keep praying, Ma. It can't hurt."

"Yes." She sighed. "I have my prayers. I have my pastor. I have my church. It's just not enough."

"What do you mean?"

"I want my son back."

38

LAURA AND CHARLES SAT AT A RED VINYL BOOTH AGAINST THE BACK wall of Brooklyn Heroes—a popular diner featuring pastrami on rye, cherry cheesecake, and fast service from surly waitresses.

"What's wrong?" Charles asked. "Distracted?"

"Yeah. Jennifer—my best friend—is coming next weekend. To get ready, I sent Tripod to my dad's place and set up my spare room. I still have to stock up on good wine. Jen and I are both wine snobs."

"First things first. Focus on the case."

Focusing was not in the cards. Laura scanned the wood-paneled walls, lined with actors, athletes, politicians, and pundits from New York City. Kirk Douglas. Sophia Loren. Tony Bennet. Even Rudy Giuliani.

"How ironic." Laura pointed to a studio shot hanging above their booth. It captured a scene from the 1975 movie, *Dog Day Afternoon*, in which a bank robber squares off with police outside the First National Bank of Brooklyn. "What a flick," Laura said. "Al Pacino. He was fantastic," she added, recalling the actor's portrayal of the hostage-taking bank robber named Sonny. "In this one scene, Sonny steps out of the bank, raises his fist and yells to the cops, *'Attica! Attica!'* Remember, Attica became the counterculture call of the times."

Charles seemed distracted now. He cast his eyes up and down the Wall of Fame.

"VIPs," Charles squinted as he scanned the images. "Very important people."

"Very, very important," Laura said. "New York icons."

Laura and Charles looked up to see a tall, slim waitress in a blue uniform, a notepad in her hand, her dark hair pinned into a bun. Laura ordered a grilled cheese, and Charles ordered the pastrami.

"So, who do you think is stalking you?" Charles whispered, as the waitress trudged off to place the order.

Laura took a deep breath. "Theory One?"

"Okay."

"The real killer. The actual Hangman of Eden. He can't allow Eddie Nash to be vindicated. An exoneration would beg the question: So, who really *did* kill Erin Lambert? That would force the police to reopen the investigation, and that would endanger him. Don't forget, the real killer beat his victim with a tire iron before hanging her. My stalker came at me with a tire iron."

"Makes sense. Theory Two?"

Laura scanned the diner before answering. No one within earshot. "The cops. Detective Peter Demario of the Eden Police Department. The police can't allow Nash to be retried, either. Their corruption gets exposed. So, they're going to great lengths to persuade me to drop the case."

"Chances are the police and the prosecutor worked together to frame Nash."

As they thought about that, they heard heavy footfalls and spotted Lou approaching the table, holding a folder under his right arm.

Squeezing his massive frame into the booth next to Laura, Lou said, "You ain't gonna believe this."

39

"The *POLICE* have been stalking Laura," Lou croaked softly. "They are out to get her to back down and keep her client a permanent guest at Hotel Attica." The grizzled investigator/bodyguard looked from Laura to Charles, then back again. "I've spent the past few weeks following up on the dog-snatching and text threats. Me and my guys have kept Laura under 'round-the-clock surveillance. The threats stopped. The stalker backed off. Kept his distance. Played it cool. Now, get this."

Lou opened the folder and withdrew a black-and-white surveillance photo. He slapped it onto the Formica. The image showed a handsome man, clean-cut, with sharp facial features and close-cropped, blond hair. Tailored, dark blazer and light golf shirt—both expensive.

Laura studied the photo. "It's him. The man in the blue blazer."

A self-satisfied grin crossed Lou's face. "Meet James Gorman: Caucasian, male, thirty-eight, six-foot-two, one-eighty, blond hair, blue eyes, and snazzy threads." Lou put a paw lightly on Laura's arm. "Gorman has been in the background of your life recently."

Laura's expression froze.

Lou pulled a second pic from the folder. This one showed Gorman sitting on the driver's side of a Chevy Impala, parked on a street in an urban neighborhood.

"Gorman has shopped for eggs in your local grocery store, he's eaten calzones at your neighborhood pizza joint, and he's spent countless hours parked on your street, looking up at your apartment. James Gorman has been your shadow."

Charles grabbed the photo. "Who is this guy?"

"He's a cop. Former." Lou shook his head in disgust. "We got a facial recognition match through the state police database."

"What kinda cop?" Charles asked.

Lou leaned back in the booth. "Officer James Michael Gorman started out in 2001 as a patrolman for the city of Eden. He got promoted to the detective squad in 2004 and worked his way up to lieutenant. He worked narcotics, robbery, and homicide. The guy became a legend. Hell. He had the words 'Final Justice' engraved into the handle of his service revolver. Earned him the nickname 'Final Justice Jim.'"

"Final Justice? Where is he now?" Laura asked.

"He left the force last year. Hung out his own PI shingle. He has a concealed-carry license and rolls with his own personal Glock. He duplicated his shield, which he keeps in his wallet. You never know when a counterfeit police badge is going to come in handy."

"What else?" Charles pressed. "Got to be more."

"Got an interesting tidbit from my source. A few years back, Gorman testified on behalf of a fellow officer at an Internal Affairs inquiry. Gorman stood up for a detective rumored to be shaking down mom-and-pop stores for protection money."

"Who might that have been?" Charles asked, with a smile that said the answer was obvious. "Let me guess."

"If you guessed Detective Peter Demario, you'd win the jackpot."

"What do we do about Final Justice?" Charles asked. "How do we shut him down?"

"We're going to invite Gorman out to Flanagan's for a drink this evening. We're going to show him a series of surveillance photos, showing him stalking the lead attorney in a federal criminal murder appeal. I'm going to suggest that he go back home and resume the lifestyle of a small-town PI."

Charles smiled. "Or?"

"Or those photos go to New York State Police Internal Affairs, the State Attorney General's Police Corruption Commission, and *The New York Times*. We'll also let him know we're aware of his connection to Detective Demario, and we're prepared to reveal it. My guess is this: Gorman will pack up and head home ASAP. We won't have to worry about him again. I'll put a couple of men on him, just to be sure."

"Good work, Lou," Charles said.

Laura nodded. "I knew I was being followed. I also knew you were following whoever was following me. Maybe now, we can focus our attention on the case."

Charles leaned back in the booth, looking up at the ceiling, before speaking. "Okay. We are now one-hundred-percent certain that the police have been the ones harassing Laura. Their thug cut her tire, followed her down that road, and came at her with a tire iron."

"Got to love those roadside flares," Laura quipped. "Never leave home without them."

Charles swept his eyes back over the V.I.P.'s on the Brooklyn Heroes Wall of Fame. "I guarantee you one thing. The police and prosecutor were not the only ones who engineered the frame-up of Eddie Nash. They had to be protected by very important people."

40

THE PRISON JACKET SENT BY ATTICA SUPERINTENDENT LEON WILKES hit Laura's desk with the explosive power of a mail bomb. Titled *"Edward Thomas Nash, #88417,"* the four-inch-thick file detailed Nash's life on the inside.

Laura started reading the section on his classification as a high-risk offender. It claimed that Nash's propensity for violence required imprisonment in a maximum security facility.

The classification was wrong. Nash had no record of violence prior to his conviction. She could make the jury see that he never should have been sent to Attica. That the cops and prosecutors had been out to bury him.

Laura read the disciplinary write-ups that got him a day or two in keep-locked, and the fighting beefs that landed him in the Box. *I can deal with those, too*, she thought. *The inevitable hardships of prison life. You fight, or you die.*

Then, she came to the bombshell that Wilkes had promised. Documentation of four years of psychiatric tests, conducted by consulting psychiatrist Edward J. Peters.

Dr. Peters painted Nash as a cross between a psychopath and sociopath, a rare breed of madman capable of cold, cruel, unspeakable acts. She cringed as she read:

Edward Thomas Nash exhibits a rare form of antisocial personality disorder that blends the attributes of a cunning psychopath with the qualities of a violent sociopath. The inmate combines the cold calculation and tactical thought patterns of the psychopath with the twisted fantasies and warped delusions of the sociopath. This volatile mix makes him capable of the worst forms of human violence. In my twenty-one years working as a prison psychiatrist, Mr. Nash is the most disturbed and frightening person I have ever examined.

The chilling report didn't end there.

This dual pathology enables him to present a different version of himself to different people within his social sphere. Nash presents one version of himself to his attorneys, another to his family members, another to his friends, and still another to his fellow inmates. His fellow inmates see the most authentic version of his distorted personality. This accounts for the three signed affidavits from inmates who swore that Nash admitted to them that he had killed Erin Lambert. These inmates knew details of the hanging that the killer—and no one else—could have conveyed. Edward Thomas Nash is a psychopath, a sociopath, and a danger to society.

Laura put down the report, totally dismayed.

41

Laura scanned the framed diplomas on the wall:

Bachelor's Degree with High Honors
from Harvard University

Doctor of Medicine with High Honors
from Boston University

Certificate of Excellence from
the American College of Psychiatry

Outstanding Achievement Award
from the National Alliance of Mental Health

She looked across the desk at Dr. Charlene Meyers, a renowned psychiatrist, and a sought-after courtroom expert. Laura hoped the forty-six-year-old leader in her field would take the stand and debunk the diagnosis from the prison shrink. She had messengered her a copy of Peters' report before paying her a visit at her Manhattan office.

"What do you think?" Laura looked past Dr. Meyers and out the window to the bustling street, eight floors below. "Is this report valid?"

"This is an excellent report." The elegant woman with long, brown hair and tortoiseshell glasses held the report in front of her. "Outstanding analysis. Splendid summary."

Laura blinked. "What? I thought…"

Dr. Meyers smiled. "Let me clarify. The report is first-rate. For a work of fiction. For a horror script. For a scary movie intended to scare the bejesus out of people. Are you sure this report was prepared by a certified psychiatrist? I would have guessed Stephen King. When is the film coming out? What's it called? *The Two-Headed Monster?*"

Laura laughed. "It scared the hell out of me. I mean, a psychopathic sociopath? Although, I guess most people use the words interchangeably. I mean, either way, a psychopath *or* a sociopath is bad news. "

"True. Hollywood has blurred the meanings. Pop psychiatry has perpetuated it." Dr. Meyers rolled her eyes at the ceiling. "The generic 'psycho' of the movies might be dubbed a 'psychopath' *or* a 'sociopath.' In professional psychiatric terms, however, these terms represent two separate types of anti-social personality disorder. Each of these terms was created by psychiatrists to explain two different mental states. Blending the terms together just distorts the science. To psychiatric professionals, the terms have distinct meanings."

"Oh?"

"Yes. Sociopaths and psychopaths also exhibit distinct traits."

"Such as?"

"Sociopaths challenge authority, show aggression, obsess over themselves, and are easily bored. Sociopaths are impulsive, prone to rage, and can be driven to violence. Their condition tends to result from environmental factors, such as childhood physical or emotional abuse. On the other hand, a sociopath does have a conscience and can blend into society. They have a moral compass —they just choose to override it. Sociopaths know that killing is wrong, and that's why they love doing it."

"Ted Bundy?"

"Yes. A pillar of society—and a mass murderer."

"And psychopaths?"

"Psychopaths have no conscience. Psychopaths feel no remorse. They inflict pain—even kill—for personal gratification. Psychopaths are cunning and manipulative. Even charming. Furthermore, psychopaths are made, not born—their conditions are genetic."

"Hannibal Lector?" Laura asked.

"Exactly. Brilliant. Calculating. Deadly. A true psychopath can torture a human being without feeling the slightest bit of guilt. Killing a person has the moral equivalence of eating a ham sandwich."

"So, what would you tell the prison shrink?"

"Pick one. Your subject can't be both."

"Then, you'll appear in court to refute Dr. Peter's findings? You'll take the stand for the defense?"

"I'll challenge every word in it. None of this is based on sound medical or psychiatric principles. This whole psychopath/sociopath combo is pure nonsense. For whatever reason, this prison shrink created a fantasy to make your client look like a monster."

"Thank you." Laura beamed. "Consider yourself hired."

The famous psychiatrist held up her right hand—palm up. "I'll have to examine the patient, Mr. Nash. I'll have to administer a number of tests, including a series of brain scans."

"Brain scans?"

"Brain scans typically show that dangerously deranged patients have a much smaller amygdala—the part of the brain responsible for emotion and judgement. Based on what you've told me, my guess is that your client will present a normal amygdala. Of course, I can't guarantee what I'll find in Mr. Nash, but I promise it won't be Doctor Jekyll *and* Mr. Hyde."

"No problem examining Nash," Laura promised. "I'll set it up."

"Well, don't celebrate yet." Dr. Meyers interlocked her long fingers and took a deep breath. "I'll have to take on the prison psychiatrist in open court. The battle of the shrinks may end in a draw. It usually does. The science often goes over the heads of the jurors. It might leave them confused. Dr. Peter's ridiculous narrative might stick in their minds, while my clinical analysis gets forgotten."

* * *

Laura's phone buzzed while she was waiting for the elevator outside the doctor's office. Delilah Cole.

"Delilah. What's up?"

"Do we have a psychiatric expert?"

"Yes, and she's fantastic. She assures me the prison psych report is shit. She's willing to testify to that in court."

"I may have more for you on that—the psychiatric report from the prison shrink, I mean."

"What?"

"Well, I spent the past three nights comparing Peters' records with prison employee and contractor records in the public domain. It turns out that Dr. Peters is not a full-time psychiatrist at Attica. He's part-time—not on staff."

"Okay."

"The records show that Peters only works in the Attica psychiatric ward two days a week—Tuesdays and Thursdays. The rest of the time, he works at a public health clinic in Buffalo."

"Interesting." Laura let the elevator door open and close. "Go on."

"Okay. So, Peters based his psychopath-sociopath theory on twenty-four one-hour sessions with Nash in the prison psych ward. The problem is this: Eight of those sessions were supposedly held on days when he was out of the prison. He was not there to conduct those sessions. The records are clear: Peters did not conduct those sessions. Those sessions never happened. Peters falsified his report."

42

LAURA LOOKED AT THE TRIAL TRANSCRIPTS, APPELLATE BRIEFS, POLICE reports, and crime scene photos piled on the long table.

"I have news," she told the team gathered in the case room. "Important news."

"You have our attention," Charles replied. "Enlighten us."

Delilah and Lou nodded in unison.

"I hold in my hand a letter from the United States Court of Appeals for the Second Circuit." Laura didn't let her face reveal her feelings about the content. "This letter will tell us whether the appeal will move forward. Or whether we start banging on the door of the U.S. Supreme Court."

"This is it," Charles said. "The moment of truth."

Lou beat a drumroll on the desktop.

Delilah sat still, eyes closed, hands folded.

Lifting the envelope, Laura let a slight smile cross her face. Holding the letter at eye-level, she began to read. "The United States Court of Appeals for the Second Circuit hereby rules in the case of *State of New York v. Edward Thomas Nash*." Enunciating every word drew out the tension. "The Court finds sufficient grounds to grant the petitioner's request for relief, and hereby orders a new trial."

Cheers filled the cramped space.

"Was it—?" Charles never finished his question.

"Yep," Laura interjected. "Unanimous. Three out of three. Chen wrote that the trial was *'rife with the aroma of prosecutorial misconduct,'* and all of them condemned the use of the stun belt. That's what put us over the top— the damn stun belt."

"Yes." Charles slapped the tabletop. "Bring it on!"

"Damn right." Lou thrust a clenched fist into the air. "Let's do this thing."

"Away we go," Delilah chimed in. "What next?"

"We prepare for trial," Laura said. "We prepare to prove that our client was convicted without cause. We build a case for his complete and total vindication."

43

IN THE NEW TRIAL, NASH WOULD BE CONSIDERED INNOCENT UNTIL proven guilty. The burden of proof would shift back to the prosecution. Laura felt good about her prospects of winning an acquittal. Discovery suggested that the Assistant District Attorney was essentially planning to rerun the original prosecution. Hair fibers matching Nash's on the victim's body. Empty beer bottles found at the scene, bearing Nash's DNA. Same shit. *"This murderer... this madman... this monster."*

True, the prison psychiatrist's report was new, but it could be torpedoed by the defense's highly respected shrink. The prosecution *did* plan to parade out one of the prison snitches, who would testify that Nash confessed the murder to him. *No worries,* Laura thought. *Prison snitches are chronic liars. Prison snitches make terrible witnesses. The jury can smell "slammer world" all over them. The jury can feel the brutality of their crimes and sense their willingness to say anything to get out.*

* * *

Martha Barrack tossed her floral-print, silk scarf over the left shoulder of her red, designer sweater.

"I read your interview in *The Columbia Law Review.*" She placed her elbows on her redwood desk and flashed a fake smile at Laura. "You are quite the prolific quote machine."

Laura gripped the arms of the leather chair and pretended to smile back at her rival, her mind circling around the words *"jealous bitch."*

"I was pleased with the interview." Laura held her head high and maintained eye contact. "It set up a strong case for police misconduct."

"It also alerted to the prosecution to our approach." Martha lost the smile, her wide eyes glaring under expensive mascara. "You gave away our strategy."

"Oh?" Laura shrugged her shoulders and looked away. "Really?"

"Yes." From the corner of her eye, Laura saw Martha running long, elegant fingertips over her auburn hair, making sure no strand had gone astray. "Look. Laura. Let me share a lesson that I had to learn the hard way. This case is not about *you,* or *your* career. This case is about your client. You remember him? The guy with the rest of his life on the line? The man who may spend the rest of his life in slammer world?"

Laura looked to the ceiling, as if considering. She had to admit, her more experienced colleague was probably right. Martha had a lot more experience than her—and had exonerated dozens of wrongfully convicted inmates. Conceding the point, Laura muttered, "Let's get back to forming that strategy."

Martha leaned back in her swivel chair and issued a list of carefully chosen words. "We let the prosecution dish out its weak evidence, sketchy witnesses, and out-of-date forensics. We let the prosecution feel confident of winning another conviction. We let them overplay their hand."

"Okay."

"Then, we launch a withering counterattack. We eviscerate their case. Witness by witness. Exhibit by exhibit. Expert by expert. We play rope-a-dope."

"Rope-a-what?"

"Rope-a-dope. You know. Muhammad Ali. The great heavyweight boxing champion. He'd let his opponent trap him on the ropes and tire himself out, throwing harmless punch after harmless punch. Then, Ali would lash out, destroying his depleted foe."

"We counterpunch." Laura narrowed her eyes. "We play defense."

"Yes. Until we launch our violent onslaught."

Laura had to give it to her. Martha knew her stuff. The strategy was sound. Even so, Laura had her doubts about the final outcome.

"No matter how effective we are, questions remain," she told Martha. "Can a new jury give the benefit of the doubt to a man once convicted of such a brutal homicide? Can a new jury see the defendant as anything other than The Hangman of Eden? Can the new judge apply the law without bias or prejudice?"

"Time will tell," Martha replied. "Time will tell."

* * *

Team Nash gathered in their new, high-tech case room that hummed with digital power. A FASTRA II desktop supercomputer sent images to a one hundred-eight-inch curved plasma monitor. The screen was suspended from ceiling cables in the back of the room. Six high-powered laptops shared software designed for researching legal precedents and storing electronic evidence files. The walls of the room were coated in a film that served as an electronic erase board, allowing the team to mark up the surface with schematics and plans. High technology would power the investigation: Criminal databases, electronic legal files, automated evidence searches. The same technology used by leading police labs and law firms. Those tools would be backed up with good, old-fashioned legwork. The probe should lead to new evidence, witnesses, precedents, and theories of the crime.

"We will reassess every word of testimony and shred of evidence from the first trial," Laura told the team. "New witnesses will be uncovered and new evidence unearthed. We'll use all that to undercut the prosecution at every turn. We'll have to shed light on the underlying question: If Eddie Nash did not kill Erin Lambert, who did?"

"A SODDI defense," Charles said.

"What?" Delilah asked.

"SODDI," Charles repeated. "Some Other Dude Did It."

Lou grinned, and Charles continued. "We'll also have to answer this question: What motivated the Erie County Police Department, and the Erie County Prosecutor's Office, to frame Nash in the first place? We'll have to find out just how deep the corruption went. Then, we'll have to share that knowledge with the new jury without having the jurors think we're trashing the authorities. Blaming the cops always backfires."

44

THE GLOW FROM THE CONCAVE COMPUTER MONITOR MOVED LIKE FOG through the darkened office. The time signature in the upper-righthand corner of the screen read 11:26 PM.

Rain pelted the long, rectangular windows like projectiles. Thunder crashed in the distance.

Laura studied each word and each phrase in the gruesome police report that flashed on the screen. Certain words and phrases bore into her brain like starving parasites. *"Blunt force trauma. Severe rope lacerations. Severed vertebra."* Her mind's eye pictured the killer—the Hangman—slipping the noose over the victim's head, yanking the knot tight around her throat, and hurling her body into the abyss.

The rain stopped. The thunder died.

A noise broke the eerie silence. Laura scanned the abandoned workstations. She looked into the empty offices. Were there telltale glimpses of a figure moving in the shadows? Or was it just the settling of an old building? She tried to ignore the distractions and gazed back at the screen.

The hunt was on. The police reports shimmering in front of her had secrets to share. She was certain of it. Clues hid in the rambling text and gruesome photos. She just had to find them.

She studied the next document on the screen. Under the letterhead of the Erie County Police Laboratory, the title read, *"Forensic Tire Imprint Analysis."* The findings were set in bold type:

> **The tire imprints taken from the crime scene indicate the heavy-duty pickup truck used in the commission of this crime was equipped with the Goodyear 1500 Series tires. The imprints at the scene were a direct match for the tire/ tires on the defendant's 1996 Chevrolet Silverado.**

Laura keyed on the words *tire/tires.*

Strange. Did they check all four tires, or just one? *Tire/tires.* What strange wording. She called up images of the tire tracks imprinted at the scene. Four distinct crime lab photos filled the four quadrants of the screen. Each photo showed a tread imprint from an individual Goodyear 1500 Series tire. Oh, of course; the tread on each imprint matched the other three tires. Goodyear 1500s. Standard for the make and model of Nash's truck.

Laura called up a new set of the images. This time, the crime lab photos detailed the actual tires on Nash's truck. Those photos were taken the day after his arrest. Four separate images of the tires on his Chevy Silverado, taken from distinct angles, each capturing the tread pattern of the individual tire. She zoomed in on each one.

Holy...! Now, that is amazing.

Nash's '96 Chevy Silverado had four different brands of tires mounted on the axles. One Goodyear 1500, one Michelin Defender, one Goodrich BF, and one Cooper Cobra 275. All those tires worked fine on that model of truck. They also all left very different tread patterns. The tread on each tire was worn, suggesting that each had been in use for some time.

The implications raced through her mind. *So, the imprints from the crime scene captured four matching track imprints from four matching Goodyear 1500s. Meaning, the truck at the scene was equipped with four standard tires. Meanwhile, Nash's Silverado had four different tire brands with four distinct tread patterns. His truck would have left four distinct tracks in its wake. The prosecution must have hid this fact from the jury. This was evidence that Eddie's Silverado did not leave those tracks at the crime scene.*

45

THE INNOCENCE ALLIANCE
EXONERATION BLOG

BREAKING NEWS:

The opening of the new trial in the case of State of New York v. Edward Thomas Nash *is set for Oct. 27 at the Erie County Courthouse in upstate New York. Since the defendant's request for a change of venue has been denied, the trial will be held in the same courtroom as the original high-profile, media-saturated proceeding. The first trial resulted in the original guilty finding more than ten years ago. However, a different defense attorney, lead prosecutor, and judge may quell the circus-like atmosphere that prevailed at the time. The order for the new trial was won by the Council Against Wrongful Convictions, which has formed an elite team of attorneys and investigators to advance this case, hoping to add it to its impressive record of exonerations.*

REMINDER:

The Future of Innocence Conference will be held at the Pritzer School of Law on the campus of Northeastern University on Nov. 2. Following the opening day luncheon, Professor Edwin

R. Sutton will deliver an address entitled, "The State of the Movement: Exonerating the Innocent or Excusing the Guilty?."

46

THE INNOCENCE ALLIANCE
EXONERATION BLOG

BREAKING NEWS:

Mass. Reverses Drug Convictions
Thousands of Inmates to Go Free

Massachusetts Attorney General Reginald Bartholomew announced today that the state will dismiss more than 21,000 drug convictions and charges in light of the revelation that a former state medical examiner falsified evidence against thousands of criminal defendants.

The tainted drug convictions were linked to a disgraced state chemist, who admitted to faking test results to incriminate defendants and forging coworkers' signatures on faked evidence reports.

It's the largest single dismissal of convictions in U.S. history, according to the American Civil Liberties Union.

Forensic chemist Jeanie Marie Stratford worked as a consulting medical examiner at the Hinton State Laboratory Institute outside Boston for nine years. Stratford tested drug evidence for state prosecutors to use in criminal trials. Stratford admitted to faking thousands of tests to prove that she was the most prolific chemist in the lab. She reported testing more than 500 samples a month, compared with 150 for a typical chemist. Her colleagues called her "Superwoman." She is now serving a five-year sentence for falsifying records.

As the scandal has unfolded, hundreds of people have been released from prison, and hundreds more will have their charges dismissed.

REMINDER:

The Exoneration Alliance workshop, "Combating Tainted Evidence in Criminal Court Proceedings," will be held Sept. 14 at NYU Law School. The workshop will show how doctored, mishandled, or inadequate test results lead to thousands of invalid guilty verdicts each year.

47

LAURA GAZED INTO THE PLASMA MONITOR. SHE ENTERED A SERIES OF commands, and the screen lit up with the words, *"National Incident-Based Crime Reporting System."* Then, the screen resolved into lurid crime scene photos of female attack victims with corresponding names and dates. Laura began combing the state and FBI criminal databases for murders involving female sex workers. She set her search for a seven-hundred-and-fifty-mile radius of the Eden crime scene in a three-year period after the imprisonment of her client. She was looking for attacks on women in the sex trade after Nash was locked up.

She ran through crimes of passion between husbands and wives, and boyfriends and girlfriends. She dismissed a justifiable homicide case in which a woman killed her abusive partner. In the end, Laura narrowed the results to three homicides in the western New York region.

One: Wayne, New York. A twenty-two-year-old prostitute was beaten with a blunt object and strangled to death in a hotel parking lot. She was found sprawled on the asphalt in a pool of her own blood, dumped outside her own car. Case still open.

Laura grimaced and waited for more.

Two: Lockport, New York. A twenty-year-old stripper was found dead with a plastic bag over her head on a secluded dirt road, four miles from the club where she worked. Case still open.

Three: Yates, New York. The thirty-six-year-old female proprietor of The Adam & Eve Gentleman's Club was beaten to death with a lead pipe. Her battered body was dumped in a swampy marsh adjacent to the club. Case open.

Laura studied the screen, focusing on the names of the victims and dates of the homicides. Someone was murdering female sex workers in upstate New York, while Nash was locked in a cage. The police had made their case against Nash and never bothered to pursue the possibility of a serial killer, a cold-blooded murderer with an eye for strippers and hookers. Pursuing a serial killer would have complicated their narrative, though, so the cops would argue that these were random, unconnected murders. None of these killings proved that the Hangman of Eden was still out there. But, then again, maybe he was.

"What am I missing?"

Exhausted, Laura opened an email and started typing:

From: **Laura Tobias**
To: **Delilah Cole**
Subject: **Incident Search**
Message: **Check Suicides.**

* * *

Delilah sat at her computer two days later. She focused on her search, while under her desk, she tapped her pink loafers with ornate lettering on them—one read, *Ciao,* and the other read, *Bella.* Delilah wore a gray, lace-up hoodie, and a black gothic skirt with a ruffled, steampunk-style hem.

"I widened the search to include suicides," Delilah told Laura, looking over her shoulder. "I spent last night scouring police files for reports of hanging suicides that might have been murder."

"And?" A chill ran down Laura's spine, settling in her bones.

"I found a case. Susan Carlson, aka Heather Night. Twenty-nine. High-end escort. Lived in a swanky apartment in downtown Rochester. Worked for an exclusive service that catered to corporate executives on business trips."

"Okay."

"Heather spent a lot time entertaining out-of-town guests at the Plaza Suites or the Grand Marquee… until the police found her in a black negligee, hanging from a rope looped over a reinforced steel shower curtain rod."

"When?"

"January 2010."

"After Nash went to prison."

"Yep."

"Ruled a suicide?"

"At first. At first glance, it looked like she'd hanged herself."

"What about at second glance?"

"The cause of death was changed to 'suspicious' after the police found a partial sneaker print on the toilet seat. The barefoot woman didn't hang herself. The killer wore sneakers, stood on the lid, and hoisted her up. He also used a three-quarter-inch climbing rope with thirteen loops."

Laura shook her head. *Oh, my God.* The ramifications raced through her mind like a horror flick on fast-forward.

Three-quarter-inch climbing rope. A call girl.

"This means that a homicidal hangman was stringing up female sex workers within a three-hundred-mile radius of the original crime scene after Eddie Nash went to prison. It also means the Hangman of Eden may have killed again."

48

Laura and Charles boarded the 6 AM United Airlines flight to Buffalo. By eight, the innocence attorney and exoneration investigator had rented a four-wheel-drive SUV and set out for their destination. By ten, the SUV was rolling down the gravel road that led to the bridge where Erin Lambert died.

"The West End Pedestrian Bridge," Charles said. "Right on the boarder of Eden and Genesee."

Laura and Charles lugged their gear three-quarters of the way down the concrete bridge walk and set up at the scene of the hanging that had terrified the community a decade before. Charles snapped open the lid of a large, metal trunk that would serve as a portable crime lab. Laura opened a folder and began flipping through police crime scene maps and diagrams obtained through discovery.

Charles pulled a long strand of rope from the case and turned to Laura. "This is the same kind of rope used in the murder. Three-quarter-inch climbing rope, meant to scale rock faces and traverse canyon walls. Same diameter. Same length. Same fiber core."

"It looks thin," Laura said. "Must be strong."

"Make no mistake." Charles flexed his arms in the loose sleeves of his dashiki. "This was the rope of an expert hangman. It had the ideal strength, resiliency, and flexibility for this particular job."

"Let me get this straight: The killer made a conscious and calculated choice to use that particular rope?"

"Yes, no doubt about it. To select it, the killer had to make a precise calculation. He had to factor in the density of the twisted core fiber, the torque resistance, the height and weight of the victim, the speed of the fall, and the length of the drop. This rope was the perfect selection."

"How so?"

"It was strong enough to support a five-foot-four, one hundred-and-five-pound body through a sixteen-foot fall at a ninety-degree drop. It was flexible, too. Easy to use. Plus, he could have purchased it at any outdoor store."

"You know your rope. You know your hangings."

"Hanging murders are few and far between, but I've worked one or two in my day."

Laura looked over the concrete barrier at the rushing water below. "Why hang her in the first place?"

Using his right index finger, Charles tracked the direction of the rope fiber. "What does the rope tell you about the killer?"

"You're the expert. You tell me."

"He had to know the fall would produce more than twelve-hundred foot-pounds of torque on the neck at the break of the fall. The mathematical precision suggests that our killer has a calculating mind. I've seen cases where would-be killers use the wrong rope, which then breaks, and the victim lives."

"Doesn't sound like Eddie Nash." Laura narrowed her focus on the rope. "I doubt if he ever took algebra." She stepped back from the barrier. "What about the knot?"

* * *

Charles looked out over the river, as a long-buried memory hit him like a clean kidney punch. A teenaged boy. An African-American kid. Hanging from a swing set. Other kids gathering around, shouting, *"No! No! No!"*

He shook off the image and regained his composure. "Where was I? Our killer tied the classic hangman's noose." Charles began looping the rope around itself. "The rope was coiled thirteen times above the knot. Thirteen coils for a very unlucky person. Thirteen coils made by the skilled executioner for the doomed prisoner. The traditional knot used in public executions two centuries ago used thirteen coils. The killer knew this."

"Jesus." Laura cringed. "This monster knew just what he was doing."

"Laura, this was ritualistic. The killer might be fixated on the fine points of execution and very adept with death by hanging. He went to great lengths—no pun intended—to do this deed. This was an execution."

Laura squinted in the morning sun. "No rope was found at Nash's apartment. No rope was found in his truck, and none at his mother's place. There weren't any residual rope burns on his hands. Plus, a calculating, mathematical mind? Ritualistic reenactment? That's not our client. That's not Eddie Nash."

"Check this out." Charles reached into his case and withdrew a crime scene photo. "I warn you—this one is rough."

Laura scanned the photo of Erin Lambert, suspended in mid-air. Her eyes were closed, her mouth agape, and her head crooked to the right. The rope ran from her neck in a straight line back up to the bridge.

"The length of the drop is critical in hanging deaths," Charles said. "Any drop lower than four feet is classified as a short drop. Any drop beyond four feet is classified as a long drop. This was a *very* long drop. Before the length of rope ran out, the body bounced, and the noose tightened. With such a long drop, death was immediate."

"Maybe that was a blessing."

"It was. The fall fractured her cervical vertebra—meaning, it snapped her neck. Had it been a short drop, the impact would not have broken her neck—it would have caused gradual asphyxiation. In other words, she would have strangled to death. It would have been long, slow, and painful. At least this way was quick." Charles bent down and pointed to a short length of steel pipe, protruding from the concrete. "The killer tied the end of the rope to this rebar to anchor it." Charles took two steps to his left. "The hangman stood at this spot when he pushed the body over the edge." He tapped the flat surface of the barrier. "He supposedly stood here when he drank his beer and urinated on the suspended body."

Laura shook her head in disbelief. "The police found urine on the victim's body that tested positive for Nash's DNA. But, who urinates on a body, knowing it will leave incriminating evidence? Who leaves two empty beer bottles with their DNA at the crime scene?"

"It doesn't fit this killer's MO. The person who took such careful steps to plan and carry out this crime would not leave evidence behind in plain sight. Unless he left it there to incriminate someone else."

Laura considered the point. Feeling the wind from the river, she could hear the words of the prosecutor in the original trial circling in her head like vultures: *This monster stood on that bridge and looked down at the corpse. He sipped a beer as the victim's dead body swung in the breeze. Once he finished his celebratory brew, this monster stood on that ledge and urinated down on the swinging corpse.*

She cringed with disgust. *The Big Lie. Works every time.*

"This is interesting." Laura stared at the enhanced photo that Charles had given her. "It's not a police photo." She pointed to a stamp on the white border of the picture. "Property of *The Eden Herald.*"

"The newspaper photographer beat the cops here and snapped a shot of the undisturbed crime scene," Charles explained. "It got added to the police file as evidence."

Laura studied the details in the image—the gravel walkway, concrete barrier, and dirt road at the far end of the bridge. She squinted narrowly, searching for that one inconsistency that would point to the lie in the prosecutor's case. "What's that?" Laura held up the photo and pointed to a white speck in the upper-left-hand corner. "That white mark on the dirt road. Where the killer would have parked. What do you think it is?"

Charles leaned toward the image. "Not sure. There's no mention of anything like that in the crime scene reports."

* * *

Charles pulled out his phone and called Delilah back in the case room. "Delilah. Bring up police crime scene photo #124."

A pause. "Done."

"Now, isolate the white mark in the area of the dirt road."

Fingers tapped a keyboard before Delilah replied, "Got it. I'm sending the concentrated images to your tablet. You should get a high-resolution copy."

The enhanced picture resolved on his screen. The white mark filled the tablet screen. Laura and Charles studied it with disbelief.

"Holy—" Laura gasped. "What in the world?"

"It looks like a white rag," Charles said. "Maybe a white towel."

"Are those...?" Laura asked, peering closer at the enhanced image. "Could those be...?"

"Looks like it," Charles said. "Bloodstains."

49

LAURA AND CHARLES WERE FINISHING UP THE WALKTHROUGH OF THE ten-year-old crime scene. The two stood on river stones under the bridge, close to the spot where the victim's body was retrieved.

"No white towel was ever logged into the police evidence locker." Laura recalled a detailed collection list she'd studied in the file. "No white towel was ever presented in court."

"What happened to that towel?" Charles wondered aloud. "The cops had to find it at the crime scene."

"The question is," Laura said, "what did they do with it? What does it mean?"

"It could be just an old, mud-stained rag that'd been lying around the site for days before the killing," Charles speculated. "Just a piece of litter that has nothing to do with our case."

"Unlikely," Laura replied. "Or?"

"It could be a towel the killer used to wipe blood from the victim. After all, he beat her with a tire iron before hanging her. Maybe he wiped her down before he strung her up."

"Makes no sense. Why clean her, just to kill her? Plus, no smeared blood or white fibers were found on the vic's body at autopsy. No. It's got to be something else."

"Okay," Charles conceded. "Try this: The killer was injured during the fray. He used the white towel to clean his own blood off himself."

Laura's mind raced back to the police report. "The detectives found shards of glass at the scene but never linked them to the crime."

"And? What's your point?"

"Eddie told me that Erin drank vodka by the jug. What if her vodka bottle broke during the attack? What if she used a broken shard to cut her attacker?"

Charles' eyes went wide as he picked up the story. "Then, the attacker pulls out a towel to wipe himself off. In all the chaos, he drops the towel and drives off without it."

"Makes sense," Laura said.

"Except the detectives must have found it at the scene and sent it out for testing. Then, it just vanishes? Never makes it into evidence? That doesn't happen."

Laura built on his thoughts. "Why does a bloodstained towel found at the murder scene never get logged as evidence? Why doesn't a bloodstained towel found at a murder scene become the centerpiece of the case?"

"By the time the results came back, the cops had Nash in their sights," Charles surmised. "Maybe the test results didn't match Nash's DNA. The cops must have buried the results to keep the focus on him. Bastards. Finding another person's DNA on that towel would have undercut their case against our guy."

"Yep. Distinct possibility. It would have forced them to drop the charges against Nash and start all over again—from scratch."

"So, Detective Demario and company lost the towel. How convenient. How corrupt."

"Poof," Laura said. "Gone."

"The cops may have destroyed the towel. Or at least, buried it in a deep hole." Charles' said. "We have to try to find it. We can still extract the bloodstains to get the DNA. The DNA of the real killer."

"That towel could exonerate him," Laura said.

"Or convict him once and for all," Charles added in a grim tone. "The DNA could be his."

"I don't think so," Laura insisted. "Nash had no visible wounds or scars when he was arrested. The blood evidence will point elsewhere."

"Could be."

"This could be Gary Dotson all over again."

Everyone in the Movement knew the name. Back in 1989, Dotson was convicted of first-degree rape, based on the eyewitness testimony of the teenage girl who had accused him. Even after the girl recanted her story, the judge and prosecutor refused to reopen the case against Dotson. *Was she lying then?* they asked. *Or is she lying now?* In the end, a DNA test on the semen in the rape kit proved that Dotson had not raped her. It turned out that the girl had been having consensual sex with her boyfriend and accused Dotson rather than confess her sin. Dotson was exonerated, and the Innocence Movement was born.

"This whole damned thing has to be dragged out of the shadows and held up in the light of day for the world to see," Charles said. The possibility that the cops conveniently lost the bloody towel wouldn't be the first time Charles had dealt with disappearing evidence. He turned to Laura. "This reminds me of a case."

"Do tell."

"Michael McNeal spent six years in prison for a crime he didn't commit. A crime he *couldn't* have committed."

"What happened?"

"A rape took place in McNeal's Brooklyn neighborhood, while he was at Disney World with his wife and kids. When he was arrested, the police confiscated a time-stamped receipt from the Magic Kingdom from his back pocket; it proved his alibi."

"So, he was cleared."

"Nope. The police and prosecutor never turned the receipt over to the defense. It just sat in the evidence room for six years. I got access to the file and found the receipt. McNeal was exonerated, and the real rapist was arrested and convicted."

"Damn. One more piece of 'misplaced' evidence."

Charles shook his head in an incredulous motion. "I went to court for the vacating hearing. I wanted to see the conviction get thrown out. In the end, the judge just looked down at McNeal and uttered a simple phrase. *'You are free to go.'* And with that, he walked out of that courtroom a free man."

50

LAURA CAUGHT THE 9 PM FLIGHT FROM BUFFALO TO JFK AND CABBED it back to Brooklyn. She trudged up the bare wooden stairs to her second-floor apartment, passed through the door, made a beeline to the kitchen, pulled open the freezer, and said, "Yes!"

There it was. A quart bottle of Vintner's vodka—a local blend made from organic grapes. Laura filled a glass tumbler, floated to the living room, and crashed on the couch.

Long, slow sips of the clean, white liquid did not erase the images that circled in her mind. Coiled rope. A sliding noose. A lifeless body, swaying in the breeze. In the silence, Laura could almost hear the death cry of a terrified woman, and the deep, evil laugh of a madman in the darkness.

She took another long, slow swallow of the white liquid. The grape vodka hit the spot. She sank into the couch like it was a pool of cool water on a hot day. The alcohol burned its way down her throat and numbed her mind but didn't stop the questions. *Does this confirm that the real killer is still out there? How many other women has he hung out to die? Is he stalking his next victim at this very moment?*

That's when she heard it. Faint, at first. A muted footstep? A hushed voice? The sound was coming from the west side of the apartment, down the hall from the living room. It wasn't Tripod; he was at her father's place for the weekend.

She sat up straight. She listened with full concentration. *Maybe I just imagined it.* She heard it again, and again. Light footfalls on old hardwood. The sound of the stalker? Did he have his tire iron? Or a gun this time?

She tiptoed to the hall closet, eased open the door, and withdrew a titanium bat, a Louisville Slugger from her fall softball league. Laura crept toward the source of the sound: The back bedroom. Standing in front of the door with eyes focused and bat cocked, Laura watched the knob turn. She inhaled as the door opened.

A figure emerged from the shadows. Laura double-clutched and swung. At the last instant, she stopped short. Her heart jumped. The bat barrel stopped a fraction of an inch from the head of a tall, thin woman wearing a white nightgown and looking terrified. The intruder was Laura's childhood friend, Jennifer Conner. Laura had forgotten all about Jen. She was spending the weekend and had a key to the apartment.

"What the—?" Jen stumbled backward, breathless. "What are you doing? Trying to kill me?"

"I thought you were—" Laura lowered the Slugger. "Never mind."

After realizing the situation, the best friends doubled over with laughter. They stumbled to the couch and plopped themselves down.

"Laura, you look like hell."

"Nice to see you, too, Jen."

"Seriously. What's going on?"

"Let's see. I spent the day at the scene of a hanging murder. I just downed a water glass full of vodka. I'm *supposed* to look like shit. *Shit* is a look I cultivate."

Jen moved closer and took her hand. "Are you okay? Tell me. What's going on? I worry about you."

"Well, let's see. I've been back and forth to Attica. My dog was stolen. I've been stalked by corrupt cops, and a vicious murderer may be planning to kill me. In other words, life is good."

"This case is getting to you? It *should* be getting to you. Murder. Prison. Courtrooms. You must be exhausted."

"No. I'm fine. Now that my best friend is with me."

"Laura. I know you too well. I've seen you crash and burn too many times. Is it back?"

"Is what back?"

"The anxiety?"

"Come on, Jen."

"Remember sophomore year? The chemistry final? You rushed into the girl's bathroom, scrambled to a stall, and puked your guts out."

"I aced the test," Laura countered.

"Remember junior prom? You kept that cute senior waiting while you threw up in the upstairs toilet."

"I made his night."

"Stress makes you crazy."

"I've got this, Jen. I promise. It's cool."

"You're not hurting yourself, are you?"

"Please."

"Are you?"

"Of course not." Laura lowered her head and studied the patterns in the carpet. The faded scars on her thighs began to throb.

"I won't let you go there again." Jen's voice was absolute. "I won't."

"Those days are over. I'm no longer a stressed-out adolescent with no one to talk to. Plus, if the anxiety gets too bad, I have Xanax."

"Okay." Jen put a hand under Laura's chin and drew her face up to meet hers. "If it's not the case, it's the boyfriend."

"Nick?" Laura drew back from her, looked at the ceiling, and laughed. "Nick is history. Out of the picture. Finished. Kaput."

"Good. I hate to say it, but I never liked him. He wasn't good enough for you."

"Why? You sound like my father."

"You and Nick have only one thing in common."

"What?"

"You're both in love with the same man."

"Shut up, Jen."

"Here's this thirty-year-old man who took an acting class and expects to be movie star. All he can talk about is how amazing he is."

"He's a late bloomer." Laura felt an irrational need to defend him. "He's working hard to make this acting thing work. You know, he can be a sweet guy. A *very, very* sweet guy."

"You're slurring your words."

"More vodka, then?" Laura asked. "One more."

Jen put a hand on her friend's shoulder. "Laura Tobias, do me one favor."

"Anything."

"Don't break under the pressure."

* * *

Laura and Jen relived old times until one in the morning. Old teachers. Old friends. Good times. Then, the air seemed to leave the room. The atmosphere changed, like a thunderstorm was brewing. Laura saw tears well up in Jen's eyes.

"What is it?" Laura took her hand and leaned in close.

"I wasn't going to tell you."

"Tell me what?"

Jen rubbed her eyes. "It's my mom."

"Your mom?"

Jen lowered her face into the palms of her hands and blurted, "She has cancer."

"What?"

"Lymphoma."

"Oh, my God, Jen. I am so sorry. Is it—?"

"It's bad. Very bad."

Laura wrapped an arm over her shoulder and felt her friend's body convulse with emotion.

"And I've been such a bitch to her," Jen sobbed. "I caused her so much stress. No wonder…"

For the next hour, Laura offered condolences that sounded like platitudes. "Life's not fair. You have to be strong. There's still hope. Make the most of this time." Then, she did the one thing that might help—she shared her own story.

"I was eight when my mom was diagnosed with cancer. Toward the end, I marched into her room and screamed. 'I hate you! How can you leave me?! Don't you even care about me?'"

"You were eight." Jen sniffled. "Just a kid."

"After my mom passed, the guilt stuck with me. Sure, I was an A-student through elementary school, middle school, and high school. Only because I put pleasing the teachers above making friends and having fun. You were a true friend, Jen, but you were it."

"I remember."

Laura looked at the ceiling and continued. "I got lost in my own thoughts. The same questions kept circling in my brain. *Why? Why is the world so unfair? Why did God take my mom? Is there even a God?* The answers never came. My mom wasn't there to explain any of it."

This time, Jen wrapped her arms around Laura's shoulders and pulled her close. "I tried to be there for you, Laura. But, I was just a kid, too. What did I know about grief and guilt?"

"You were my one real friend. I loved you. I *still* love you. I just didn't connect with any of the other kids. Intimacy made me twitch. To tell you the truth, it still does."

Jen choked back tears. "You and me. Me and you."

Laura smiled. "Yeah. The other kids thought I was weird and kept their distance. Most times, I didn't mind it. It gave me more time to study, which made for good grades, and a sense of self-worth. But, sometimes, the loneliness—the sense of being an outcast—hurt like hell. Sometimes, I just wanted to be a bubble-headed teenager who cared more about lip gloss than the rights of her fellow man."

Jen nodded. "I get it."

Laura placed a hand on Jen's arm. "You're suffering right now. Your mom is very sick. You're sad. You're mad—no, you're fucking *furious* at the world. It's okay. You have to go through it."

"Thanks."

"Just don't blame yourself. Don't torture yourself for feeling abandoned. It's natural."

Laura leaned back on the couch and rolled up the sleeve of her sweatshirt. She balled her fist and held it out.

"This is what guilt gets you."

The two best friends stared at the hairline scar on her wrist.

* * *

Laura was still tossing in her bed at 3 AM. Sleep seemed a million miles off. The news of Jen's mom curled in her head. Jen's take on Nick followed:

"I never liked him... you're both in love with the same man." Love? Was it love? Despite her friend's warning, Laura understood Nick. In fact, she missed him. Sure, he was self-centered. But, he could also be kind and caring. She trusted him and—at times—loved having him around.

It was close to three-thirty when her phone buzzed. Laura fetched it from the bedside table, checked the caller ID, and answered.

"Nick. What are you doing? It's three-thirty in the morning."

"I had to talk to you. I miss you."

"We're not getting back together."

"I know. I'm not calling to beg."

"What, then?"

"I'm sorry."

"For what?"

"For being an asshole. A self-centered jerk."

"True."

"Laura. I want to be there for you. I want to make it up to you."

"Come on, Nick."

"I read about your case in the paper. I figured you could use a friendly voice at the other end of the phone."

"Okay. Goodnight. Sleep tight. I'll see you sometime."

"I just want to say one thing: I admire you. I love your sense of purpose—your passion to do the right thing. Your drive to make a difference. Laura Tobias, you inspire me. Honest. There it is. I had to say it."

51

LAURA STARED AT THE LANDLINE PHONE ON HER CLUTTERED DESK IN the fifth-floor offices of the Council Against Wrongful Convictions. The phone was scheduled to ring in less than two minutes for her weekly client call. Given the recent swirl of discoveries, she took this rare moment of downtime to collect her thoughts.

The court's decision to grant a new trial changed the game. The debunking of the tire track evidence undercut the crime scene investigation. Dr. Meyers' refutation of the prison shrink's report promised to thwart the prosecution's campaign to paint Nash as a special breed of monster. The bloodstained towel in the crime scene photo could lead to the DNA of the real killer. Then, there was the hanging death of the sex worker a year after Nash was locked up.

In addition, her stalker was gone. Laura no longer cringed when she checked her phone messages. She no longer looked over her shoulder when she walked down the street, or out her apartment window for mysterious cars parked out front. It appeared that Lou's presence had scared off the thugs who had been trying to scare her into dropping the case. Even Tripod seemed to be resting easier, now that he was back from his vacation at her father's place. He was his old self back at the dog park. Their visits carried no surprises.

Laura even had a good phone conversation with her dad. It was about her mother. She'd shocked the old man with a new idea for celebrating the holidays. Laura suggested they drive out for a mountain hike that her mom had loved all those years ago. There was a long, winding trail that her mom had insisted on taking every Christmas break.

She was forgiving herself—or the eight-year-old kid who didn't want her mom to go away.

There was no doubt about it; all the breaks seemed to be falling her way. Still, Laura was nagged by one recurring emotion: Guilt. The fact was, she'd been fixated on herself since reading the appeals court letter granting the new trial. The letter promised to put her career on the fast track. Her moment in the limelight was as close as the new trial. She knew the sensational nature of the crime would trigger extensive media coverage. Reporters from most of the newspapers and TV outlets in New York would demand a piece of her. The blogs and websites would feed the twenty-four-hour news cycle. *"Ms. Tobias, why did you believe so much in your client's innocence? Ms. Tobias, how did you build such a strong case for his exoneration? Ms. Tobias, have the police asked you to help find the real killer?"*

The story might even go national. *The New York Times* might run a front-page news analysis, and an op-ed inside. CNN might gather its talking heads to pick the case apart. The ranting attorney host of the cable show, "The Guilty Party," might rave about the justice and injustice of it all. The pundits would have a field day with the perfect rope, the snapped neck, the beer bottles, the piss, and all the rest. She dreaded it—and she welcomed it.

The phone rang. Laura picked it up to hear the familiar, automated voice: *"This is New York State Department of Corrections and Community Supervision. You have a collect call from… inmate Edward Nash at the… Attica Correctional Facility in… Attica, New York. Do you accept the charges?"*

"Yes." Pause. "Eddie?"

"Yes."

"I have good news."

She filled him in on all the developments, including the image of the bloodstained towel. "It could have the real killer's DNA on it."

"Fan-fucking-tastic!" Eddie exclaimed. "Freedom's coming!"

"Eddie." Laura wanted more information about his background. She wanted more insight into his childhood influences. "Eddie," she said. "Tell me about Eden, New York."

52

Eddie's mind drifted back to his hometown. "Eden was no paradise," he told her from the small, glass-enclosed inmate phone room in D-Block.

The once prosperous mill town had been on the decline, ever since the closing of the ironworks and fish canneries on Lake Erie in the '80s. By the time Eddie came along, life was hard for most everyone in the remote village on the far edge of western New York. But, no one in the rural enclave had it worse than the three percent of the population that happened to be African-American. The black families had fled the big cities of Buffalo and Rochester for a simpler life in the country, only to run into a harsh backlash from many of their white neighbors. For Eddie, growing up poor and black in a white town had been one long endurance test as he navigated a maze of racial slurs, bigoted attitudes, and backward thinking.

"I was always being picked up by the cops and pressured to confess to some bullshit charge, or implicate a friend. It seemed that every little thing—a stolen bike or shoplifted toy—started with a visit to the Nash place."

"Go on."

"I got used to hearing racist shit from white kids—and their parents—until I had to turn off the noise. I learned to ignore the fools and misfits. I stopped seeing color and just saw people."

In fact, he'd made a conscious effort to survive in redneck Eden, New York. He avoided the haters and steered clear of trouble. In middle school, he hung with a band of free-spirited kids who had no time for skin color, race, ethnicity, or any of the categories that occupied the minds of most people. "To these kids, as long as you were cool, you were in. So, I became the coolest of the cool. The leader of the pack. We were all living on the edge in that hopeless town. Except, we didn't know it was hopeless. We thought *every* place was like Eden."

Eddie recalled his old haunt with a sense of nostalgia. "Our crew hung out at this abandoned mental asylum. I'll never forget it. The Angel's Gate Mental Asylum for the Permanently Insane. What a name, right? We made up this game called 'Doctor Lunatic.' We pretended to give each other lobotomies. Then, we walked around like brain-dead zombies, out for fresh blood. Just kids. Having fun."

"A mental asylum was your playground?"

"Yep. Picture this grand, three-story, stone estate home—this country mansion that housed mental patients back in the day. We used to go out to the abandoned house at night and make believe ghosts were floating around. One time, I picked through the old children's ward. I found this filthy, one-eyed, stuffed gorilla. I took it home and put it on my shelf. I swear, one night, the damn thing winked at me—with its one eye."

Laura cringed.

"What else do you want to know? Nash asked. "I got nothing to hide. How many different ways can I say it? Eden was a shithole."

"That's good for now," Laura said. "We'll pick it up on the next call."

"When are you coming back to Attica?"

"I'm not coming this time, Eddie." Her voice softened. "I'm sending you a friend."

* * *

Laura leaned back in her chair, closed her eyes, and relived the conversation. She knew what he was talking about. She'd spent plenty of time in those struggling towns, and the rural outback. Her time in college, screening applicants for pro bono legal appeals, had taken her to prisons and jails across the state. Her work as an innocence attorney had taken her to dozens of small cities and towns, plagued by joblessness and poverty, and a surge in opiate addiction. The nice homes and good schools had gone to ruin. The railcars had rusted in shut-down switchyards. Boarded-up shops cried out for the wrecking ball. The drunks wasted away in the bars; the meth heads gathered down by the tracks; the old-timers paraded down Main Street in their walkers; the pimple-faced kids took suicide prevention classes at the middle school.

And, although New Yorkers hated to admit it, racism flourished. In its own way, the bigotry was as bad as it was in any part of the Deep South.

She also knew about those mental hospitals. There were scores of those old, shut-down institutions throughout upstate New York. Back in the '40s and '50s, the high-priced shrinks in Manhattan sent the real crazies up-country for "the treatment," which meant lobotomies or electroshock therapy. After *The New York Times* exposed the abuse, the worst places were closed down but never demolished.

Someone was going to have to check this one out.

53

I_N THE CRAMPED PRISON CONFERENCE ROOM, THE BELEAGUERED CON-_
vict stared across the table at the stylish PI.

"Charles Steel." The PI smiled. "Private investigator."

"Eddie Nash," the con replied. "Convicted murderer."

Eddie wore his green work shirt over a white tee. Charles Steel, dread-locks flicking his shoulders, sported a black leather jacket with a colorful tribal pattern stitched above the front pocket.

"Welcome to Attica," Eddie joked. "Garden spot of the state."

"I'd say it's nice to be here, but…"

"Seriously." Eddie looked down at his shackled hands, before reestablishing eye contact. "Thanks for coming. I appreciate all your work."

"Save the gratitude. Thank me when you're home free."

Eddie smiled at the thought. "What's the latest? What are you finding out?"

Charles scanned the room before leaning in and whispering, "I've been running the financials on your friend, the amazing Detective Peter Demario. He owns a brick colonial in Eden, and a beach house on the river. Nice dock for his twenty-two-foot powerboat. Pays alimony to two exes and supports four kids. The guy is living high on a meager detective's salary."

"He's crooked," Eddie whispered back. "You guys can nail him in court."

Charles twisted his smile into a smirk. "Nope. His crooked dealings are not directly linked to your case. The trial judge will rule that it's irrelevant and prejudicial. We'll have to show how Demario coerced the confession and fucked with the evidence."

"We can do that. Easy."

"Yes, we can. No problem."

"What about the evidence?" Eddie asked. "What have you found?"

"The good detective was not the only one faking the goods. The police lab was just as much a part of the frame job. The tire track evidence is bogus. Your mix-and-match truck tires were different from the matching casts taken at the crime scene."

"Finally," Eddie exhaled. "I told my public defender that, and he said it didn't matter."

"The hair samples were bogus, too. The microscopic tests conducted by the police lab showed a 99.999% probability that the three hairs found on the victim came from you. We ran our own DNA tests on the same samples that proved the hairs belonged to Erin, the victim."

"Damn it." Eddie dropped his shackled hands on the desktop. "I knew it."

"We're still stumped on those urine samples taken from the victim's body."

Eddie shook his head in disgust. "The ones that supposedly prove I pissed on the corpse?"

"Yeah. Those. The lab tests showed the urine on her upper torso had traces of your DNA in it."

"How'd they pull that off?

"Not sure yet. Still working it."

"Okay."

"What about the towel?" Eddie asked. "The one with the bloodstains."

"We're still looking for it. Hopefully, the cops didn't burn it."

"The towel will tell the story." Eddie's voice grew stronger with a matter-of-fact tone. "No way my blood is on that towel."

Charles leaned back in his chair, shifting gears. "Tell me about Jimmy Dean Bernadi."

"Former bouncer at the Bottoms Up. Former boyfriend of Erin Lambert. Bad news dude. Mean son of a bitch. Haven't laid eyes on him since the trial. Not sure where he is."

"Jimmy Dean Bernadi," Charles mused. "Next on my hit list."

"Be careful," Eddie warned. *Very* careful."

Charles filled Eddie in on more details of the investigation. "More tests refuting the police account. Certain evidence that the cops were trying to intimidate the good guys. No progress in IDing the real killer." Then, he changed the subject altogether. He wanted to get to know Eddie a little better. "So, you're a writer?"

"Yeah."

"What do you write?"

"Poetry," Eddie replied. *"Bad* poetry."

"Can't be *that* bad."

"Just finished a lyric for a rapper over in B-Block."

"No shit?"

Eddie closed his eyes and recited:

"You're arrested and tried
Justice is denied
Prison is proscribed
Tears are cried
Gates opened wide
Your senses are deprived

Your brain got fried
And you go dead inside."

54

LAURA DROVE DOWN A LONG, STRAIGHT RIBBON OF HIGHWAY TOWARD the western frontier of New York State. The focal point of the case was moving back to the rural enclaves, east of Lake Erie. The proximity to the crime scene, witnesses, and trial venue made it ground zero for *State of New York v. Edward Thomas Nash II.*

Laura admired the view as the Mustang passed farmland and pine woods. She watched as the snowcapped mountains gave way to rolling hills, and the rolling hills gave way to barren fields. She saw deer in the woods, hawks on the wing, and dappled sunlight on the icy, roadside streams. She passed rivers, lakes, and towns with rich histories and Native American names. Chautauqua. Allegheny. Seneca. Mohawk. It wasn't easy, but she passed up many chances to stop for local delicacies at roadside eateries. Tomato pie— thick pizza with the cheese under the sauce—or grape pie made from native Concords.

Laura spotted a mud-smeared sign, rising from an icy drainage ditch: *"Welcome to Eden."* She continued past the old farmhouses and ramshackle barns on Burnt Mansion Road, before turning onto Commerce Boulevard, a four-lane stretch of fast food joints, used car lots, thrift stores, tattoo parlors, and bail bondsmen.

Welcome to paradise.

She pulled onto a dead-end road and stopped at a white, clapboard house—24 Lost River Road. The paint on the small house was peeling. The shutters hung loose. The shingles were shifting on the roof. The front porch needed new planks.

Laura stepped onto the uneven porch boards and knocked on the door, pushing back her hair as she waited. After a long moment, the screen door opened, revealing a thin, older, black woman in a floral-print smock.

"Hello, Mrs. Nash."

"Miss Tobias! I've been expecting you. And call me Cassie."

Laura smiled.

Cassandra Nash stepped outside and threw her arms around Laura. After the long embrace, Cassie took Laura's hands, pulling her through the threshold, then engulfing her on the other side with a second long embrace. "Thank you for coming. I've heard all about you. Thank you for all you've done for my son. Eddie sings your praises all the time."

"No, no, no," Laura protested. "Just doing my job. Eddie deserves it. What's happened to him is a shame. It's an honor to be representing him. We're doing everything in our power to get him out."

"You're pouring your heart and soul into this. God bless you."

"I believe in Eddie."

"Eddie believes in you."

"I'm doing my best." Laura looked into her warm, brown eyes. "It's looking good at the moment. We have a strong case, and it's getting stronger all the time. Still a long way to go, though."

Mrs. Nash led her through the old-fashioned kitchen to a worn sofa in the living room. Sitting together, they talked about the case, and the importance of hope. Cassie retrieved an old photo album from a nearby shelf and guided Laura through the pictures. Eddie as a baby. Eddie chasing his two sisters in the backyard. Eddie at the lake with a fishing pole. Eddie with his first car. Eddie on the front porch with his arms around his father. His dad had died several years ago from cancer, and Cassie had carried on alone. She'd remortgaged the house to pay for Eddie's appeal. She'd tapped her savings to send him cash for the commissary. She'd made dozens of trips to that Godforsaken prison. Now, she was fighting off death and waiting for the truth to emerge.

Laura looked up from the scrapbook and saw the pain in the woman's eyes. She also saw the intelligence and resilience.

A tear welled up, but Cassie ignored it. "I can't think about much of anything, except Eddie. I pray that God will put all this right."

"You've been there for Eddie," Laura said. "He needs you now more than ever. The jury needs to see that his family is standing behind him."

Cassie wiped another tear. "I'll be there."

Of course, Laura knew about the hardships facing the scattered African-American population in the remote reaches of western New York. It wasn't that she believed these rural backwaters were any more or less racist than anyplace else. But, she'd read news account after news account of dreadful incidents in these small towns. Police violence. Attacks. She'd read a study that singled out the region as the most hostile place in the entire country for blacks. On a percentage basis, the most racist Google searches—using the N-word—came from rural western New York. Then, there was the infamous YouTube video from Cheektowaga. It captured a white woman, hurling racial slurs at a black shopper in a Dollar Store parking lot. There was also the city councilman who sent out the mass email calling Michelle Obama a "chimpanzee in high heels."

There was something gurgling right below the surface around these parts.

55

Eddie saw his mother, reaching out to him. Her luminous form was bathed in the radiant light of countless stars. Her open arms beckoned like the expansive wings of a guardian angel. Her soft, brown complexion glowed like a teenaged girl's, while her dancing eyes sparkled like gems from the heavens. Eddie was flooded with a sense of peace and wellbeing as he heard her voice, as sweet and pure as the soloist in a glorious choir, inviting him into the beyond. "Come home, son." A rush of warmth rolled over him, melting the chains of the cruel present. Reaching out to her, he felt like a lost five-year-old who had just been found.

Eddie rose and floated from his thin, worn, prison mattress, then drifted through the stone walls and razor wire, watching the cons, guards, crazies, and corrupted fade away, like bad memories better forgotten. In the shifting shadows of his dream, Eddie saw the faces of his brother, sisters, friends, kind neighbors, long-forgotten childhood playmates, high school renegades, and smiling service buddies. The people of his past were dressed in fine, new clothes, forming a welcoming line of beaming smiles and hearty laughter.

In the hazy distance, he saw her. She was beautiful. She was vibrant. She was young. Erin Lambert was the very essence of life. Erin Lambert was healed.

"I love you, Erin," he said.

"I love you, Eddie," she replied.

Falling deeper into the dream, Eddie switched to standing on a green hillside, overlooking a lush valley. He gazed up into the forgiving eyes of Reverend Richard Garret, the towering minister from the church he'd attended with his mom as a child. Eddie touched the man of God's golden, silk robe, grasped his immense, powerful hand, and took in his words: "You have risen. It's a miracle. Hallelujah!"

"Hallelujah!" Eddie responded. "Hallelujah."

"You've been resurrected," the minister went on. "Your time of grace begins now. Hallelujah!"

Then, he heard a distant proclamation:

"He saved us, not on the basis of deeds which we have done in righteousness, but according to His mercy, by the washing of regeneration and renewing by the Holy Spirit."

"Yes."

"And we all, who with unveiled faces contemplate the Lord's glory, are being transformed into His image with ever-increasing glory, which comes from the Lord, who is the Spirit."

The dream was real. The dream was right. His suffering was gone. The Word had been true all along.

Eddie Nash had found the light.

56

THE LIGHT WENT OUT.

Eddie was cold and alone. Lost in darkness. Eddie was not back in the darkness of his cell. He had been cast into an endless space of nothingness. His mother was gone. His friends were gone. Reverend Garret was gone. Had his dream transformed into a nightmare? Or had he been swallowed up by Hell? Had the love turned to hate? Or had it never existed? Had madness taken over? Or had it had its grip on him all along? Had the devil himself come to claim his black heart? Did the beast know his secrets? Had Satan sentenced him to an eternal life sentence in the most horrible prison of all?

A voice called out to him: "Eddie. I know you." It had to be him. The Evil One. The self-indulgent, fallen angel with a vendetta against his Creator. The voice whispered, "I know the truth."

Then, Eddie saw her face—her skull. It was lifeless and insect-ravaged. Erin Lambert smiled at him from the grave.

More grotesque faces peered out from shifting shadows. Shrill voices howled from unseen places.

"God did not spare those who sinned but cast them down to chains of darkness..."

"Those who committed evil deeds will pay the penalty of eternal destruction."

"Has Eddie Nash changed the garments of his imprisonment?"

Eddie saw the cop who set him up. Demario spat in his face. "You killed her, nigger."

He saw the prosecutor who savaged him in court. "You want to kill again."

He saw the jurors who convicted him. "Guilty. Guilty. Guilty."

And the judge who had sentenced him. "Life without parole."

The TV reporters. "The Hangman of Eden is behind bars."

Far off in the darkness, Eddie saw a pinprick of light, coming toward him. The tiny circle expanded, until it repelled the darkness. It was not a heavenly light. It was the light of day. In the light, Eddie saw a friend. Yes. He saw Fridge. The benevolent guard. The sage of D-Block. He heard his deep, soothing voice call to him. "Eddie. It's all okay." Fridge began singing in sweet, low tones. "Go to sleep and goodnight." Fridge's copper eyes danced with delight as he whispered into Eddie's ear, "I always tell the truth, Eddie."

"You do," Eddie replied. "You are the truth."

"Listen to me, Eddie. I have something to tell you."

Eddie put his ear to the guard's lips and heard those words of wisdom, the ones that struck at his heart, the ones that tore at his soul:

"Every con to ever enter this prison was guilty of something."

57

CHARLES STEEL LOOKED UP AT THE NEON SIGN THAT BLINKED A GARISH invitation to the Bottoms Up Gentleman's Club. Under the words *"Hottest Strip Club in Eden"* flashed the silhouette of a nude woman, snaking around a stripper's pole.

Charles strolled through the pockmarked parking lot to the windowless stucco building that housed the club. He pushed through twin glass doors, embossed with matching silhouetted dancers, and stepped into the unattended lobby, then pushed aside strips of satin fabric to enter the lounge.

Charles edged along an elevated runway, studded with footlights, making his way to a long, hardwood bar against the back wall.

There were no customers sipping beer and ogling nude dancers. For that matter, there were no strippers swirling onstage or swinging from poles. It was four in the afternoon, and the fun was still to come. Charles spotted a short, balding man in a red, polyester shirt and khakis behind the bar, standing on his tiptoes to stock liquor on the shelves along the mirrored wall. The man pushed fifths of Jack Daniels into place, while humming an off-key rendition of "New York, New York."

This dealer in babes and booze—framed by a sign for *"$20 Lap Dances"*—looked familiar. Who did this short, balding denizen of a dive bar, this middle-aged caricature in red polyester, look like? A movie star? That was it. The barman was a dead ringer for Danny DeVito.

Charles choked back a laugh. "Good afternoon. How are you, sir?"

The barman eyed Charles' reflection in the mirror. "You're early. The show doesn't start until five. How about a drink?"

Charles pulled out his wallet, extracted a hundred-dollar bill, showed it to the barman, and laid it on the bar. "I'll have a Genie. Keep the change."

The DeVito-lookalike served up the beer and palmed the hundred. "Benjamin Franklin." He planted the bill in his front pocket. "My favorite president."

"Charles Steel." He extended a hand across the bar. "Private investigator."

The bartender shook it. "Frank Valentine. I own the place."

"Frank. I'm looking for a former employee of yours. She used to work here. Her name was Erin Lambert."

"Erin Lambert?" Valentine looked up at the ceiling. "Not ringing a bell. I just can't…"

Charles laid down another hundred.

The proprietor swiped it and found his memory. "Erin Lambert. Been a long time… ten years, maybe? We called her by her stage name, Breeze."

"Breeze?"

"Sweet kid. What a shame."

"She was murdered, yes."

"Hanged."

"Tell me about her," Charles said.

"What about her?"

"She had a drug problem?" Charles asked.

"Who doesn't?" Valentine replied.

"She dated your bouncer." Charles delivered the statement as a matter of fact. "Jimmy Dean Bernadi."

Valentine screwed up his face like he'd just tasted rancid meat. "Bernadi. I fired his ass. Good riddance to bad rubbish."

"Why?"

"Two reasons." Valentine's face turned as red as his polyester. "Two reasons."

"Yeah?"

"Jimmy got his rocks off hurting women."

"Oh."

"I don't tolerate anybody roughing up my girls."

"He roughed up Erin?" Charles asked. "I mean, Breeze?"

"Bad."

"The other reason?"

"The bastard was lifting twenties from the till."

"Got it." Charles nodded, unsurprised. "Where is Bernadi now?"

Valentine swiped a rag over the bar, shaking his head and laughing out loud. "Jimmy Dean Bernadi is the biggest heroin dealer in the four-county region. He spends most of his time babysitting his addicts down at the abandoned looney bin."

"Angel's Gate?"

"Yep."

"West of town?" Charles asked. "On Old Route 5?"

"You got it. There's only one."

"Thanks." Charles drained his Genie. "Got to run."

"Don't go there, man." Valentine threw the rag into a bin and put his hands on his hips. "Do *not* go to Angel's Gate. It ain't safe. The devil's in that place."

Charles Steel smiled at Frank Valentine. "It's cool. I'm not going there."

58

LOU STUMBLED DOWN THE PATHWAY THAT LED TO THE SKELETAL RUINS of the Angel's Gate Asylum for the Permanently Insane. Seventy-five years in the past, the twenty six rooms of the four-story structure had housed men, women, and children deemed to be incurable lunatics. The years had reduced the old estate to piles of rotting wood, twisted steel, and scattered stones.

Lou approached with unsteady steps, weaving back and forth on the rock-strewn path, humming the tune to Bob Dylan's "Mr. Tambourine Man." He kept his hands in the front pouch of his grease-stained New York Giants sweatshirt. He stomped on the tattered hems of his oversized jeans. Just one more junkie, looking for a fix in the gathering twilight.

Lou closed in on the main building. The once-grand holding pen for the disturbed and deranged was now a gathering spot for hardcore addicts who bought their drugs and consumed them on the spot. Lou wondered why this particular place seemed to lure such desperate souls.

Lou stopped and scanned the grounds. He gazed at the pillared house. It was as if decades of pain had seeped into it, like a ruptured gas line that never stops spewing poisonous vapor. He imagined what the scene must have been like back in the '40s and '50s. He could almost see gowned residents gazing out the tall windows or wandering, zombie-like, through the gardens. He could almost hear the buzz of the electroshock clinic, and the cries of the patients on the neurosurgeon's table. Lou knew that troubled souls had lived and died in this place, and believed their ghosts didn't want company.

He stumbled up crumbled stone steps and passed through the unhinged door, emerging into the gloomy room that had once served as an impressive intake center for arriving patients. His gaze gravitated to the skeleton of a central spiral staircase, and the remains of a grand piano that had once soothed afflicted minds with sweet melodies. Staggering through mounds of food wrappers, empty bottles, spent syringes, and used condoms, he sidestepped the sprawled bodies of a half-dozen stoners, curled up on ratty blankets, filthy rags, and bare floorboards. The smell of burnt opium and piss wafted in the dead air. A fat man in the far corner performed a sex act on an anemic woman. Undoubtedly, a trade—sex for drugs.

Lou settled into a heap on an open patch of floor against the back wall. Feigning the demeanor of a stupefied addict, he spread out on the damp boards, close to a door that led to a connecting room. He reached up and turned the knob, opening the door just a crack.

Peering into the shadows, Lou realized that this room had once served as the madhouse's kitchen. A sturdy-looking wooden table and five wooden chairs stood in the center. A wood-burning stove pushed heat across the open space. In contrast to the junkies' lair, the old kitchen had been cleared of debris and swept clean. In the far corner, a set of batteries, linked by a tangle of cables, served as a makeshift power source. A half-empty body of Jack Daniels sat on the table.

Lou braced himself for a long night. He let his mind drift into a semi-conscious state. He waited and waited. Minutes ticked by. Hours rolled by. The stoners' moans carried on wind pushing through rotting walls. The stench grew worse.

Then, he heard it. Sounds emerged from the kitchen. A door opening. The mingling of men's voices. Lou peered through the crack. Five men had entered from the back door and settled into the chairs at the table.

Jackpot, Lou thought. *Jimmy Dean Bernadi.*

Lou recognized those intense, dark eyes and brown hair from surveillance photos. The former bouncer from the Bottoms Up was now reigning over his opioid empire.

Lou didn't recognize the two rough-looking characters flanking Bernadi. The thugs had to be hired muscle, tasked with protecting the self-made drug lord. This was dangerous work. Threats were posed by desperate addicts, competing dealers, and cops who hadn't gotten the word this enterprise was off-limits.

Lou could only see the backs of the two remaining men. Once they turned to scan the room, he lit up inside. *Pay dirt.* The man with the rugged good looks, broad shoulders, and thick arms was Detective Peter Demario. The cop who'd beaten the confession out of Nash and framed him. The man sitting to his right—with the crisp, blue sports coat and short-trimmed, blond hair—was Mike Gorman, the cop who'd stalked Laura and attacked her on that secluded country road.

The gang was all here.

59

Lou edged closer to the door to pick up their conversation.

"This place is a dump," Demario snapped at Bernadi. "How can you stand it? Surrounded by trash, shit, and puking junkies."

"It *is* a dump," Bernadi replied with a what-the-fuck shrug. "A very *profitable* dump. It's served us both well over the years. It continues to serve us well. The gift that keeps on giving."

"You have a point." Demario flexed his shoulders. "In fact, it's time for your mortgage payment."

Bernadi nodded to the henchman to his right. The paid muscle rose and stepped to the counter. He opened a drawer and retrieved an overstuffed envelope. Returning to the table, he slid it to Demario.

Bernadi flashed a broad smile at the plainclothes officer. "Payment in full. Ten grand. All yours. Business is good. That last shipment of H put us over the top."

The Erie County Chief of Detectives sneered as he tore open the envelope, withdrew a wad of bills, and began counting. "All mine, Jimmy? Get real. Don't forget, we have partners. All of those respectable people have to get their cut."

Bernadi nodded. "The rich get richer."

Gorman piped in. "Shut the fuck up, Bernadi. Show a little respect."

Demario returned the cash to the envelope and slipped it into his jacket pocket. "We have another matter to discuss." His voice cut like a broken Coke bottle. "A very important matter that can't wait. One that involves you, Jimmy."

"What?" Bernadi sat straight in his chair and leaned in. "What about me?"

"This fucking trial," Demario snarled. "Or should I say, this fucking retrial?"

"The fucking retrial," Gorman echoed. "We have concerns about your testimony."

"No worries." Bernadi threw his hands up in an I've-got-this-covered gesture. "Eddie Nash is going down—again."

"Don't be so sure," Demario snarled. The edge of his voice was even sharper. "We can't afford to be smug. We can't afford to be arrogant. This is serious shit; it has to be handled with care."

Bernadi leaned toward Demario and Gorman. "Eddie Nash will be convicted of hanging Erin Lambert all over again. The poor bastard will go back to Attica to serve out his life sentence. He'll die in prison, and no one will care. That will be that. We have nothing to worry about."

"Stop." Demario slammed a closed fist on the table. "Your fucking arrogance is dangerous, and your assumptions are bullshit. We have to be certain that Nash goes down and stays down. Look, my ass is on the line here. I am not going down because you—Jimmy Dean Bernadi—said the wrong thing in court."

Gorman nodded in yes-man fashion.

Bernadi bowed his head. "Going down? Because of me?"

"Do you know how many brainless suckers I've packaged up and shipped off to prison? Dozens. Pathetic patsies, proclaiming their innocence all the way to the slammer. Now, what happens if the guilty verdict in the

Nash case is reversed? I'll tell you what. All those convictions come into question. All those losers get new trials. We can't let the first domino fall. We've got to end it here, once and for all."

"Yeah, sure." Bernadi held two hands up in surrender. "We'll make sure Nash goes down and stays down."

Demario peered through squinted eyes. "Let me be clear. We will dictate every word of your testimony in advance. You will memorize the script and recite it on the stand—verbatim. Is that clear? Word-for-fucking-word. Syllable-for-fucking-syllable. Like a goddamned parrot. Got it?"

"Yeah. Sure." Bernadi nodded quickly. He looked like a bobblehead doll. "Word-for-word. Verbatim."

"You will take the jury back to the hours before the murder. You will testify that Nash came to the Bottoms Up looking for the bitch. Except she'd gone out to the bridge to get high. Nash lost it. He threatened to kill her. To make her suffer. Then, he took off after her."

"Got it."

"There's more." Demario stood, leaning forward. "The people representing Nash present a danger. The bitch lawyer is smart as hell. The nigger PI is fucking relentless. This wrongful convictions outfit wants to do more than just free its client—it wants to splash our shit across the front page of *The New York Times*. You are not—repeat, *not*—under any circumstance to speak to those people before the trial. Avoid all contact. Run in the other direction. Keep your mouth shut. If they approach you, refer them to the written deposition you've already provided to the court. Understood?"

"Yes. The written deposition. The one that you wrote for me."

"Good. Now, don't blow it."

Bernadi exhaled. "I won't."

"Just one more item." Demario's smile bordered on the demonic. "In the event that Nash walks, we will be forced to reopen the Erin Lambert murder investigation. We will be forced to find the man who *really* murdered that poor confused girl. Now, let me see. Who could that be? Who else could have strung up that twisted little stripper? Who else had the motive? Who else had the opportunity? Oh. Wait a minute. *You* worked with her in that sleazy strip club. *You* dated her. *You* fucked her. You know, Jimmy, we can break your pathetic alibi. We can put you at the murder scene. Who knows? We might even recover a piece of lost evidence."

Lou closed his eyes and thought, *We have to find that towel.*

60

EDDIE NASH TOSSED AND TURNED IN HIS BUNK. HE WAS UNABLE TO sleep. His nightmares kept waking him up. Plus, there was too much noise. The sound of tin cups scraping against iron bars burrowed into his brain, like a tick digging into soft flesh. The D-Block inmates were raising hell in protest of the latest water shortage. The cacophony of voices was as relentless as the migraine circling in Eddie's head.

The cons chanted, "Water. Water. Water."

An electronic buzz filled the cell. The grinding sound of metal on metal grated in his mind. Eddie jumped to his feet as his door opened. He saw two blue-shirted guards, flanking a prisoner. In tandem, the guards flung the man into the cell.

The guard on the right laughed. "Nash, meet Evan Collier."

The guard on the left chimed in. "Your new cellmate."

As the door slammed closed, one of the guards hollered, "You two lovebirds have a lovely evening!"

Eddie had been expecting this. He'd feared that his single-occupancy status would be coming to an end. Earlier in the week, workmen had come into his cell to bolt a new bunk above his. The men told him that the maximum security penal farm in Plainfield was closing, and its four hundred inmates were being distributed to any facilities with even a little space. "Attica's taking two-hundred of 'em," one of the workmen said. "Get ready for company."

The thought of sharing his cell made Eddie cringe. He'd had many cellmates through the years, and he'd hated every one; it never worked out. Between the punks, perverts, black separatists, and white supremacists, the circumstances for cultivating friendships had been less than ideal.

Now, there was this: Evan Collier. Eddie sized him up. The man was built like an ox on steroids. His jaw was stubbled, his head was shaved, and his nose was bent in at least three places, so he was a fighter. Collier's face was defined by wild, bulging eyes, a wide, crooked smile, and spiderweb tats that ran down his neck. Dry, white spittle encircled his crusty lips.

Pig.

Collier had that unmistakable look of a lifer. It was obvious he'd been hardened by years behind bars. He looked like the kind of con who had nothing to lose and lived liked nothing mattered. Undoubtedly, he loved breaking the rules and hurting people.

The guards' push had sent Collier stumbling into the center of the cell. After regaining his balance, he straightened his back, locked eyes with Eddie, and spat on the floor. "Go to hell, motherfucker." Collier coughed phlegm onto the cement. "Fuck you."

Eddie cringed at the prospect of living, sleeping, eating, pissing, and shitting with this wild man. Certain that the worst was still to come, he maintained eye contact and braced for a fight.

Collier jumped at him and howled, "I'm coming for you! I'm gonna get you, motherfucker!"

Eddie curled his hands into fists. He knew the fight was coming. He had to counter the next charge. He had to kick the living shit out of this aggressive son of a bitch in convincing fashion. He couldn't let the newcomer establish dominance—or even equality. Eddie had to put him down hard.

For Eddie, the realization of the potential consequences hit harder than any punch the moron could throw. Eddie would not fight. No way. A fight — even in self defense — would get him disciplined. He would be confined to keep-lock or sent to the Box. The superintendent and guards would turn against him. His case for exoneration would be set back.

"Where's the shitter?" Collier demanded.

Eddie looked at the steel toilet.

Collier walked to it, stepped out of his clothes, sat down, and defecated. "Ahhhh," he moaned.

Eddie closed his eyes and turned away. The sight was unbearable, the stench stomach-turning. It moved through the dead air like poison gas. Eddie bent over and dry-heaved.

Collier roared, "Oh, baby! That was good! Was it good for you?"

The men in the next cell began retching in unison. "Jesus Christ!" one yelled. "We're dying in here!"

The irate cellmates banged on the door and called for a guard. "Get this fucking pig outta here! Get him the hell out!"

No response. The prison staff had been ignoring the water shortage complaints for hours. It would be another thirty minutes before a CO made his next round.

Eddie had a brain flash. Collier didn't know when the next check would be; he could take advantage of it. "The guard makes his next round in five minutes," Eddie lied. "I suggest you sit down and shut your fucking mouth."

"Or what?" Collier taunted, pulling his pants up. "Whatcha gonna do?"

"I'll demand that the guards remove you from this cell and lock your ass in the Box."

"No room in solitary, ain't you heard? Overcrowding."

"Look." Eddie changed his tone in an effort to reason with him. "Just take a seat on the bunk. Let's make the best of this. We both have to survive."

"I heard about you," Collier boasted, a wicked smile crossing his lips.

"Yeah?" What'd you hear?"

"Eddie Nash. Mr Innocent. Mr. Zoneration. Shit. You ain't goin' nowhere."

61

EDDIE LOOKED HIS NEW CELLMATE UP AND DOWN. COLLIER HAD BEEN outfitted in the standard green shirt and pants. To be expected. Then, Eddie noticed his shoes. For some reason, Collier still wore his thick, leather, lace-up boots from the prison farm. Eddie figured that the intake staff was slipping these days, what with all the overcrowding.

He stood his ground as Collier came face-to-face with him. God, the man's breath would peel the gray paint from the cinderblock walls.

Collier lowered his voice and said, "You ain't goin' free, Mr. Innocence Man." Collier looked down and spat at Eddie's feet. "You're gonna die a guilty man. Right here in this cell."

Eddie flexed his arms, expanding his chest as he glared. "Get outta my face."

Collier laughed, turned away, took two long strides back, and leapt onto the top bunk. "I'll be on top." Collier turned onto his side and buried his head in the pillow.

Eddie remained in the far corner, arms spread, legs braced, mind focused, ready to repel the raging madman. To his surprise, Collier seemed to be settling down, maybe even fading off to sleep.

Collier spoke from the top bunk with his back turned. "I'm just messing with you, celly. I'm just teasing in a good-natured way. We'll get along just fine." Still lying on the bunk with his back to Eddie, Collier began to hum. It took a few moments for him to fade into silence.

Eddie took a deep breath. The stench was still noxious, but fading. Maybe the worst was over. Maybe this strange man had made his statement and would now settle down. Maybe he would make an effort to get along. Eddie would go to the block warden in the morning and ask that Collier be moved—no, he would *demand* that Collier be moved; it was a safety issue.

Eddie crossed the cell and slid into the bottom bunk. He heard light snoring coming from above. *Thank God,* he thought. Eddie tried to put the disgusting creature out of his mind. How dare anyone ruin his run up to emancipation?

Stay cool, man. It's just a matter of time. Just hold on.

Eddie closed his eyes and shut out the world, hoping to drift to sleep. He envisioned the parade in his honor, the food at his homecoming party, and the headlines in the paper: *Innocent Man Set Free. Prison Ordeal Over.*

* * *

On the top bunk, Evan Collier was wide awake and as still as a corpse, his bloodshot eyes fixated on the ceiling. He lifted his feet, took off his boots, and rested them on his chest. He removed the leather laces and placed the boots by his side. Tying two laces together, he formed one long, taut strand. Giving a final tug to lock the knot, he smiled. Collier stretched the cord above his head, pulling both ends. It was strong enough; it would serve the purpose he had in mind to fulfill his mission.

* * *

Eddie Nash was oblivious on the lower bunk. He had fallen into a deep sleep and was a million miles from Evan Collier and the Attica Correctional

Facility. Eddie was lost in a Technicolor extravaganza. The marching band wore brilliant red uniforms; the trumpets flashed silver and gold.

Eddie turned onto his side, away from the wall and toward the cell. Feeling putrid breath on his face, Eddie opened his eyes. There he was: Evan Collier. Eddie saw the madman squatting on the floor next to the bunk, leaning over him, wild eyes gleaming with joyous hate, rancid breath rushing out in excited bursts. Eddie felt Collier's grimy hands dig into his shoulders as his muscled arms dragged Eddie's groggy body to the concrete.

Eddie felt himself being pulled to the right. He strained to free himself but couldn't move. Eddie pulled to the left. He still couldn't move. He felt weighed down by a boulder—Collier had his knees planted on his chest, pinning him to the dark, damp floor. Eddie watched the lunatic clench his right fist and swing his arm back, and he felt it slam into his jaw, delivering a shock of pain to his head.

Eddie opened his eyes wide as Collier wrapped his noose around his neck and pulled on the two ends of the tethered leather. The loop tightened hard around Eddie's larynx, the pressure choking off his faint cries for help. Eddie's eyes bulged, his chest heaved, his brain burned, and his breathing stopped. He could feel his lungs collapsing. This couldn't be happening, not now, not before the trial.

Eddie's face had turned a dark purple, his veins erupting, tendons bulging. He choked out one more gasp before his body seized. Eddie's eyeballs rolled into the back of his head as darkness closed down his inner world. Every muscle in his body went limp.

62

"NO! STOP!"

The command came from CO Jerry Florence—Fridge. The 240-pound guard raced into the cell like a fullback rushing the line, dug two hands into the loose fabric of Collier's shirt, flexed two powerful arms, and pulled the maniac off Eddie's motionless body. With a fierce whipping motion, Fridge flung Collier across the cell, sending him sprawling into a heap on the far side. The whoops and hollers of inmates echoed through the cellblock as Collier crumbled into a motionless heap. Fridge looked down at Eddie's unconscious body, as more guards raced to the rescue.

As Fridge started mouth-to-mouth, a second CO rushed into the cell and made a beeline for the fallen Collier. He shoved a polished, black boot against his throat, keeping him pinned to the cement floor.

A third CO raced into the cell, pushing a portable respirator. He pushed the compact machine to the side of the bunk and placed the mask on Eddie's face. The forced airflow re-inflated his lungs, causing a violent jerk and a loud cough.

"You're gonna make it," Fridge said, as Eddie returned from the brink. "You gonna make it out of this fucking hellhole."

63

THE PRISON MEDICAL WING HOUSED A TWENTY-EIGHT-BED INFIRMARY, and six examination rooms. Two full-time doctors, two part-time physicians, two physician assistants, and seventeen registered nurses conducted routine check-ups, tracked chronic conditions, and responded to life-threatening emergencies for two-thousand inmates. New medical equipment had been installed in the past year, prior to an inspection by state accreditation agents. Now, the repetitive beep of high-tech monitors careened off the stone walls and cement floors.

"I demand to see the doctor in charge," Laura railed at the medical aide manning the reception desk. "I demand to know the condition of my client. I'm his attorney. I've been waiting for two hours." Laura threw a second card on the aide's desk.

"I don't care if you're the Chief Justice of the Supreme Court." The clean-cut young man in the white clinician's coat put the second card in his desk drawer with the first one. "No civilians are allowed past this point when we're short-staffed. We have our protocols. Security first."

"Security before the wellbeing of your patients?" Laura asked with exasperation. "Or their rights?"

"Security first," the gatekeeper repeated, before casting his eyes down to a pile of paperwork.

A booming voice filled the grim waiting area. "GET THE DOCTOR! AS IN, NOW!"

Laura spun a one-eighty to see the source of the command. She stared at the massive CO standing behind her as the arrogant receptionist bolted from the desk and raced through the metal door that lead to the actual infirmary.

"Jerry Florence." The CO flashed her a knowing smile. "The guys call me 'Fridge.'"

Eddie had told her about the mammoth prison sage. "I know you, Fridge."

"I know you, too," Fridge replied. "The Innocence chick."

As the two traded smiles over the coincidence of meeting under such bizarre circumstances, a tall, thin man in his late thirties entered the room. His white coat fluttered in his wake.

"Dr. Jacob Barr," he said. "Sorry for the hassle."

Laura and Fridge nodded in unison.

"Listen. I apologize for the mix-up," Barr said. "This hepatitis C is kicking our asses. Ten percent of the inmate population is infected. We're just not staffed to keep up."

"Forget about it," Laura replied. "How's Nash? D-Block."

"He's on the mend," Barr said. "Follow me. I'll take you to him."

64

EDDIE LOOKED FROM LAURA TO FRIDGE FROM HIS PRONE POSITION ON the hospital bed. Bandages were wrapped around his neck and throat; he spoke with a strained voice. "What took you so long to get here?" Eddie held a remote-control device in his right hand. He hit a button, and the bed inclined to a modified sitting position. "I love this bed. My bunk can't do that."

Eddie's room resembled a typical hospital room in the outside world. Tubes and wires ran from various ports in his arms and chest to various medical monitoring machines around his bed. His neck and throat were bandaged, while the bruises on his face were healing in the open air.

"What *took* me so long?" Laura answered his original question in mock defensiveness. "I've been waiting for more than two hours to see you."

Fridge piled on. "I had to bust the door down to get her in here. You know, I don't like to wait."

"Yeah." Eddie shifted under a thick blanket. "I hear you busted into my cell and tore that lunatic off me. Thanks, Fridge. I owe you, man."

"Forget it, Brother Nash." Fridge waved his right hand in a dismissive gesture. "Just get yourself back up and running. Then, get yourself out of Attica. We don't need no innocent people taking up valuable cell space."

"I will." Eddie raised a clenched fist and shook it like a radical from the '71 riot. "Attica! Attica! Remember Attica."

"Collier is in the Box," Fridge reported. "He'll sweat it out for ninety days, before we ship him out to another facility."

"Can't say I'll miss him." Eddie ran a hand over his bandaged throat. "Son of a bitch."

Laura turned to face the doctor, who was standing near the door. "Doctor Barr, the patient appears to be making acceptable progress. Can you share your diagnosis and venture a prognosis?"

Barr stepped forward. "Sure. Eddie's sustained serious head contusions, a midgrade concussion, and severe injuries to his throat from being almost choked to death. And he's right. If Officer Florence hadn't gotten there when he did, I'm quite certain Eddie would have died from his injuries."

Eddie and Fridge exchanged glances.

Dr. Barr continued, "His prognosis is favorable. The injuries caused by the assault aren't permanent. We'll keep him here for three or four days to promote healing, hydration, and nutrition. We'll keep an eye on the dilation of the esophageal tube; however, it should improve within the same timeframe."

Laura turned to Eddie. "The trial date is ten days out. The prep has to start ASAP. I'm going to ask the judge for a continuance. You can use the time to regain your strength. I want you to be at one-hundred-percent when we walk into that courtroom. I want the whole world to hear you summon a strong voice and say, 'Not guilty.'"

65

THE EXONERATION ALLIANCE
THE INNOCENCE BLOG

BREAKING NEWS:

Retrial to Start

    In New York State v Edward Thomas Nash, *the long-awaited retrial of the first-degree murder case begins tomorrow at the Erie County Courthouse in upstate New York. Having secured the order for a new trial from a federal appeals court, the Council Against Wrongful Convictions will represent the defendant in this phase. The entire legal community—dozens of organizations and hundreds of attorneys—is watching this case with keen interest. A not-guilty finding will strike a powerful blow for the cause and send a powerful message to the critics. It will also raise a crucial question: How many more innocent people languish in our jails and prisons?*

REMINDER:

    Our annual conference will be held from January 10-13 at the Honorable G. William and Ariadne Miller Institute for Global Challenges and the Law, on the campus of the University of California at Berkeley. The conference is entitled "Unlocking the Prison Doors: Freeing the Imprisoned Innocent."

66

"WE NEED THAT TOWEL."

With that line, Laura ended a check-in call with Charles. She wanted that missing piece of evidence. Where was it?

She pushed the question out of her mind and headed to the courthouse.

The Erie County Courthouse was a three-story building with an elegant, pillared colonnade, leading to the arch of a grand, oak doorway. Constructed of red brick and poured concrete in 1901, it emanated a historic aura, despite a recent renovation that modernized the interior. The shoveled walkway was flanked by foot-high snowbanks. Above the steps flew flags of the United States and the State of New York. Laura took long strides, passing snow-dusted shrubs on her right, and a Revolutionary War cannon on her left.

She came upon a gaggle of reporters and picked up her pace.

"There she is." A tall, blonde reporter in a red sweater and black leather skirt navigated the icy walkway in spiked, black heels. The seductress of the six o'clock news extended a microphone into Laura's face. "Ms. Tobias, Ms. Tobias. Janie Mars, WABC. Just one question, please."

Laura put her head down and pushed on, leaving the scribes sliding in her wake. Their questions trailed her like relentless stalkers.

"Ms. Tobias, why should a convicted killer get a new trial?"

"Ms. Tobias, do you have new evidence? Can you prove his innocence?"

"Ms. Tobias, Ms. Tobias, how do you feel? How does your client feel? Ms. Tobias?"

Laura had put distance between herself and the trailing herd when another reporter stepped out of nowhere and blocked her path. "How do you feel about your chances?" He lifted a pen and prepared to scribble in his notebook.

"No comment." Laura sidestepped him like a baserunner skirting a shortstop's tag. "Maybe later."

Back in the clear, she continued her trek, noting that the media was out in full-force for Day One of *Hangman of Eden II*. The boring prelims were out of the way, and opening arguments were about to begin. TV ratings were about to spike.

In front of the oak doors, a familiar TV anchor was reporting live for the morning news. Laura slowed her gait enough to catch a couple of lines, hoping to get a feel for the media slant.

"The second trial of convicted murderer Edward Nash was delayed for two weeks, as the defendant recovered from injuries suffered in a prison fight," the anchor inaccurately reported. It was not a fight—it was an unprovoked attack. "Now, the atmosphere is tense, as his retrial in the brutal hanging of young Erin Lambert is about to begin."

The media circus promised to be even more spectacular than the one that set up its tents at this very courthouse ten years and seven months before.

Laura pushed through the oak doors and into the portico. She angled her way along the mahogany-paneled east wall, climbed the back staircase to the second floor, and hustled to a door blocked by an armed guard.

Presenting her ID, Laura stepped past the guard and into a windowless space, defined by wooden benches and slouching men. This was the holding room for prisoners awaiting trial. Laura stopped in her tracks at the sight of the clean-shaven man on a bench, hands folded on his lap, back leaning against the wall. Eddie? He was hard to recognize in the casual blue sports coat, white dress shirt, and red-and-white tie knotted at the neck. This was the first time, she realized, that she'd seen him in clothes that had not been issued by the New York State Department of Corrections and Community Supervision.

"Eddie." Laura beamed as she slid onto the bench next to him. "You look great."

"Thanks." Eddie checked out her brand-new, opening-day attire. "You look like the first day of school."

"Ready for this?" Laura's upbeat tone hid her nerves. She was here to allay her client's fears, not add to them. "All set to go?"

"Do I have a choice?" Eddie shrugged in his store-bought clothes. "Okay. Yeah. I'm ready."

Laura pushed aside her inner jitters and placed a hand on his. Squeezing hard, she whispered, "It's fine. You're supposed to be scared."

Eddie lowered his head and stared at the hardwood. "I don't know…"

"Look." Laura broke the short silence. "You can't show your fear. We're both going to have to keep our emotions in check."

"I know." Eddie straightened up on the bench and glanced at the bailiff against the far wall. "I'll be strong."

"Be prepared for anything," Laura counseled. "Show no reaction."

"Reaction?" Eddie asked. "To what?"

"The prosecutor is going to find ways to throw all those horrible words at you: Monster; murderer; inhuman; Hangman…"

"I know."

"The jurors are going to look at you with hate in their eyes."

"I know."

"The witnesses are going to repeat the same old lies: 'I saw him going to the bridge.' 'He threatened to kill her.' 'He couldn't wait to confess.'"

"I can handle it."

"The prison shrink is going to diagnose you as both a madman, and a cold, calculated killer."

"Fuck him. He's crazy."

"Eddie, you have to stay cool. Your job is to keep it under control."

"I will." Eddie pumped confidence into his voice. "I know what to expect. Remember, I've seen this movie before."

"This time, we're rewriting the ending." Laura chuckled as she expanded the metaphor. "This version ends with your acquittal. This version ends with justice flowing like a mighty river."

Eddie cleared his throat. "Look. You said it. We both know it ain't gonna be easy. Laura, you've gotta be straight with me. What worries you the most? What's the one thing that's eating at you?"

"The urine deposits," Laura replied in the fraction of a heartbeat. "Those damn urine deposits on the victim's body worry me the most. They tested positive for traces of your DNA. Those traces are the hardest evidence that links you to the crime scene."

Laura thought about the words of the original prosecutor, who surmised that the killer guzzled a beer before showering the corpse with piss: *"The defendant consumed a twelve-ounce bottle of Genesee beer and defiled the body with human waste. How else did those urine traces get on the corpse?"*

"Planted," Eddie said. "The cops planted that urine on her somehow."

"Don't worry," Laura said. "I'll make the argument."

Eddie turned away. "Fucking piss."

She laid her hands on his face and guided his eyes back to hers. "I've got this."

Eddie took her hand. "You know how I survived in prison, Laura? I pushed negative thoughts out of my head. The stomach-turning food. The brutal guards. The predators in the showers. I imagined all those things as pieces of trash, piled up in a huge garbage heap. I imagined a big, yellow bulldozer pushing all that trash out of my head. That's what I'm gonna do for this trial. The lies. The fake evidence. The judgement. I'm gonna imagine it as worthless pieces of trash. I'm gonna imagine *you* as the bulldozer."

67

LAURA ENTERED COURTROOM FOUR LIKE A GLADIATOR ENTERING THE Coliseum. The egotistic thoughts of career and fame were gone. Righting this miscarriage of justice was not. It was all that mattered.

The room was just beginning to fill with lawyers, court personnel, journalists, and spectators. Laura was halfway down the center aisle that split the two banks of church-pew-style benches, when she spotted Martha Barrack, staked out at the defense table, dressed to the nines.

"Hi, Laura." Martha waved. "Set to go?"

Martha leaned against the defense table with arms folded, tapping the heel of her handcrafted, Italian leather ankle boot on the hardwood, looking like a million bucks in her signature pique-knit black dress. The courtroom veteran cast a striking figure, from the revealing V-neck right down to the lace-embroidered hem.

Martha sized up Laura's modest gray cardigan, white, ruffled blouse, and black skirt. Laura had picked out the clothes while buying Eddie's new suit at the mall. "You look fantastic," Martha said, obviously lying. "Like a hard-working attorney. Brilliant. The jury will relate." She tilted her head to one side and let a broad smile cross her made-up face. "The future starts now."

Laura smiled back. "I'm feeling good."

She had come a long way toward accepting Martha as second chair. In the weeks leading up to the trial, Martha had helped craft a well-balanced legal strategy. Knowing the prosecutor's witness list from discovery, Laura and Martha would counterpunch each one. Knowing the full scope of the police frame-up, the defense would let the prosecution step into the holes they'd dug for themselves. Then, they would bounce off the ropes and land the big blows. Eddie Nash would not testify—unless the outcome was in severe doubt.

In the dull prelims, Martha had also excelled at *voir dire*—the pains-taking process of selecting jurors. Martha had conducted exhaustive research on the final batch of prospective jurors, rating each on their openness to the defense's case. For example, prospective juror Angela Hernandez was a married, thirty-six-year-old, Latino woman from nearby Genesee, New York. Two years back, Mrs. Hernandez's eighteen-year-old son, Miguel, had been arrested for stealing a car. He had been remanded to the county jail, pend-ing trial. The charges were dropped after the family spent $5,000 on a pri-vate defense lawyer, who proved that Miguel was innocent. There was a good chance, Martha told Laura, that Mrs. Hernandez would be sympathetic to a defendant. Agreeing with the logic, Laura pushed to make sure that Mrs. Hernandez was empaneled. Martha also discovered that prospective juror Harvey Keen—a white gentleman in his mid-forties—once headed a citizens' group favoring the restoration of the death penalty. Using a preemptive chal-lenge, Laura excluded Keen from the panel.

As the courtroom filled, Martha smiled at her junior colleague. "Don't forget; I'm here to back you up. You have first chair, and I have second. Use me as you see fit. Just remember, I know my stuff. I can critique your arguments, clarify points of law, cross-examine witnesses, and dig up prece-dent-setting cases. Besides, this judge has a thing for me; it can't hurt."

Whew, Laura thought. What will I do? Cheer you on from the sidelines?

Out of the corner of her eye, Laura saw the prosecutor enter the courtroom. She watched him stride down the center aisle with focused eyes, confident steps, and a briefcase that was undoubtedly full of ammunition. Laura felt a chill crawl down her spine at the prospect of taking on the state of New York. She was in for the fight of her life. Maybe it was good that Martha had her back.

68

"All rise."

Superior Court Judge James Peter Striker emerged from his chambers with his black robe trailing behind him. The distinguished jurist with wavy, white hair, a square jaw, and piercing blue eyes settled into the leather swivel chair behind the carved oak bench. Looming above the defense and prosecution tables, Striker scanned the packed courtroom, gaveling a few renegade whispers into silence.

"The clerk may swear in the jury."

Five men and seven women filed into the jury box, recited the oath, and settled in for the duration.

"For the state?" Striker barked. "Whom do we have?"

"Good morning, Your Honor." The smooth voice filled the room. "Bartholomew Ward, Deputy State Attorney. May I say, sir, it's an honor to be in your courtroom."

Bart Ward was a formidable stalwart of the state prosecutor's office. He looked impeccable in his blue, Brooks Brothers suit, newly coiffed black hair, and manicured black beard. In his forties, with ten years as a prosecuting attorney under his belt, Ward was known for his booming voice, dramatic flair, animated theatrics, and well-honed arguments. Defense attorneys had nicknamed him "Ward the Wizard" for performing magic tricks with judges and juries.

The Wizard was a winner. He scorned the milquetoast role of the prosecutor spelled out by the Supreme Court and canon of ethics of the American Bar Association guidelines that dictated the prosecutor—the representative of the people—must strive for justice, rather than just convictions. He should never stoop to underhanded means to convict an innocent defendant. Bart Ward was about notching convictions by any means possible. His twenty-five wins in felony murder cases proved it.

Putting Ward in charge of the prosecution also provided cover for County Prosecutor Mel Radowitz, whose methods in the original trial were certain to come under fire this time around. Radowitz would be second chair to Ward in the retrial.

"Defense counsel," Striker barked. "Stand."

Laura and Martha stood in unison and introduced themselves.

"Ah." Striker grinned. "Nice to have you back in my courtroom, Ms. Barrack."

"Thank you, Your Honor. The pleasure is mine."

The judge rapped his gavel. "Counselors, approach."

The four attorneys stepped to the bench to hear the judge lay out the ground rules. "Prosecutors, I want your case to be based on the facts. Not sensational accusations. Let's leave the sensationalism to the experts, the media."

The co-prosecutors nodded and stepped back.

"Defense," Striker growled, "the county police and prosecutor are not on trial here. You are to stick to the facts. Tread with care on claims of official misconduct. These proceedings are not going to be turned into a referendum on the police. Do I make myself clear?"

"Yes, Your Honor." Laura and Martha spoke as one.

"Now, step back," Striker ordered. "Let's get to opening arguments. The reporters in the gallery haven't been fed for days."

Prosecutor Ward approached the jury. Did he have a magic trick in his back pocket?

"Your Honor, and ladies and gentlemen of the jury." Ward gripped the podium with two hands and nodded at each juror. "The defendant is charged with an unspeakable crime. Edward Thomas Nash is accused of the brutal, premeditated hanging of a troubled young woman, Erin Lambert. Erin Jane Lambert was a human being who met her fate at the end of a knotted rope, strung from a pedestrian bridge outside the small town of Eden.

"Yes, this is a sensational case. Yes, the details are horrific. We will not ask the jury to ignore the monstrous nature of the crime. No one can ignore the grotesque nature of the act, or the monstrous depravity of the perpetrator; no decent human being could be expected to consider this crime without feeling repulsed.

"However, the state will refrain from stirring the passions of the jury by rehashing the vivid details of the rope, the noose, and the breaking of the neck. Instead, we will present cold, hard evidence—*irrefutable* evidence—that will prove the defendant's guilt beyond a reasonable doubt. We will present evidence—*undeniable* evidence—that will prove that this defendant planned and committed this abomination. I implore you to pay attention to this evidence. Listen to this testimony. It will prove that Mr. Nash is guilty beyond a reasonable doubt. Beyond a *shred* of doubt. Edward Thomas Nash *is* the Hangman of Eden."

Ward returned to the prosecution table with a smug half-smile that said *mission accomplished*. The skilled prosecutor had made the jury cringe with his gruesome description of the crime, while promising to stress the facts over sensationalism. Masterful.

Laura hoped to bring the jurors back to reality. She released her grip on Eddie's hand and approached the podium that stood in front of the twelve blank faces in the jury box.

"Your Honor, and ladies and gentlemen of the jury. Unspeakable. Hideous. Gruesome. Monstrous. Grotesque. The prosecutor used these emotional superlatives in the first minute of his opening remarks, remarks in which he pledged to place the evidence, the testimony, and the facts above the sensational details. I watched as many of you cringed at his reference to the slip of the knot and breaking of the neck.

"The fact is, the prosecution *has* to stir those passions because its theory of the crime is wrong, its eyewitnesses are mistaken, its evidence is paper-thin, and its conclusion is false. We will show you the gaping holes in their case. We will show you the faulty testimony and bad evidence. We will show you that Edward Thomas Nash did not commit this crime. You will see that Edward Thomas Nash is an innocent man.

"The law intends reasonable doubt to be a high bar for the prosecution to scale. Think about it. Proof beyond a reasonable doubt. We will shed more than reasonable doubt on the prosecution's so-called 'evidence,' and their so-called 'testimony.' We will shed more than reasonable doubt on the claim that Mr. Nash was—or still is—prone to violence.

"Of course, one thing is true: This was an unspeakable crime. All the more reason to make certain that an innocent person does not pay for it, while a guilty one—and there *is* a guilty one out there—goes free."

69

WHISPERS AND MURMURS ROSE IN ANTICIPATION.

"I call Detective Peter Demario to the stand," Prosecutor Ward boomed.

Demario lowered himself into the witness chair and relaxed, running a hand through his thick black hair. Wearing a light-green sport coat and pow-der-blue golf shirt, he looked like a man with a fast-approaching tee-time. The ruggedly handsome investigator made eye contact with each juror.

"Chief Detective Demario." Ward spoke with a tone of reverence. "Did you have occasion to take a confession from the defendant?"

"Yes. He admitted to killing the victim—hanging her from a walking bridge. He was anxious to get it off his chest. He told me the whole story, and then repeated it on video. Every detail. It was obvious that he was our man."

Ward had the bailiff roll the two-minute video clip for the jury. Eddie looked exhausted as he recited the words. "Then, I threw her off the bridge." Still, the chilling details made the jurors squirm.

Ward looked pleased. "Now, Detective, did you have an occasion to examine the evidence gathered at the crime scene?"

"Yes. The tire tracks and hair fibers led back to Mr. Nash. Two empty beer bottles found at the scene contained his DNA. Urine deposits taken from the victim's upper torso also matched Mr. Nash's DNA. The evidence all traced back to the defendant. It all pointed to Mr. Nash."

"Detective, do the police have a technical term for this kind of case?"

"Yes." Demario zeroed in on the eyes of the jurors. "'Open and shut.'"

Laughter trickled through the courtroom.

Laura sprang to her feet. "Objection."

"Sustained." Judge Striker groaned. "Save the sarcasm for the squad room, Detective."

Demario assured the jury that the investigation was flawless. Of course, he'd followed standard police procedure to elicit the confession. Of course, he'd followed standard police procedure to gather the evidence. No, he would never exceed standard procedure to tilt the scale against any defendant. "I play by the book. I have to be a role model to younger officers."

After Ward the Wizard thanked him for his outstanding service to the community and praised his openness on the stand, Demario straightened his back and shrugged his shoulders. He was clearly looking forward to being cross-examined.

"Chief Detective Demario." Laura moved between him and the jury. "Do you know what this is?"

He looked at her prop and smirked. "It's a phone book."

"Detective Demario, isn't it true that you used a phone book just like this to elicit the confession from Mr. Nash? Isn't it true you struck my client over the head multiple times with a phone book and demanded that he confess?"

"No, not true."

"Isn't it true that you cuffed the defendant to a water pipe in the interview room? Isn't it true that you pointed your service revolver at his head and ordered him to confess?"

"No. False. Wrong. Ridiculous. I followed procedure. I asked questions."

"Objection. Objection. Objection." Ward's voice thundered liked cannon fire. "No basis in evidence. Prejudicial. The police are not on trial here."

"Ms. Tobias," Judge Striker intervened. "Tread carefully."

Laura was not surprised to hit the stone wall. In fact, she'd charged into it on purpose. Her research had revealed a clear three-phase pattern in the detective's testimony in previous trial appearances and depositions.

Phase One: Demario denied each allegation of misconduct.

Phase Two: Demario accused the interviewer of impugning his integrity.

Phase Three: Demario boiled over with wild and unpredictable statements.

"I suppose you placing a plastic bag over his head is standard procedure."

Right on cue, Demario rushed into Phase Two: "You insult me, and police everywhere, with your baseless statement." He snarled like a narcotics dog who'd cornered a drug dealer with pockets full of coke. "I followed the rules and regulations when questioning the suspect and leading the investigation. Like I do in all my cases."

"You never bend the rules to put a bad guy away?"

"Don't you accuse me of being a bad cop. Police officers are a thin blue line between the decent people and the monsters."

Prosecutor Ward twitched in his Brooks Brothers suit and stood to object. "Your Honor, Defense Council is badgering the witness."

"Ms. Tobias." The judge studied her with a don't-defy-me stare. "What part of 'tread carefully' didn't you hear?"

Laura continued to rattle Demario without accusing him. "What are expedited cases? Have you been to the Bottoms Up? Did you know Miss Lambert? Why not pursue other suspects?"

"Nash killed her. It was obvious from the get-go. Hell, a retard could see it."

Ward the Wizard clearly wished he had a magic spell to shut up his witness.

Demario tightened his fists. His brain was as hot as a five-alarm arson fire. This bitch lawyer was making him out to be a thug. *I wish I had my fucking nightstick,* he thought. *I'd pummel the bitch to a bloody pulp. Like that spic kid in the projects last week. No. No. No. Got to keep control. She's playing me.*

Demario took a deep breath. "Let me spell it out. Number One: Nash was screwing her—no, he was *romantically involved* with her. Number Two: Nash was furious at her stripping and pill-popping. Number Three: Nash knew she hung out at the bridge—sorry. Poor choice of words. He knew she frequented that bridge. So, he got his tire iron, and he got his rope and went there to make her pay. And he confessed. What more do you want?"

"You cleared his mental block for him."

"Objection."

"Withdrawn."

Right on cue, Demario hit the next phase. "Look, I risk my life on the streets every day. I'm the only one standing between you and the monsters."

"Your Honor," Ward objected, "this is getting out of hand."

"I agree. Ms. Tobias, get back to the facts. Or sit down."

Demario was proving himself to be the narcissist she'd pegged him for. Now that he was in his most fired-up stage, it was time to apply shock therapy. She had been holding back one piece of research for this moment.

"Chief Detective Demario. Do I have this right? As a corporal in the U.S. Army, you served as a battlefield interrogator?"

"Yes." Demario inhaled and exhaled. He firmed his posture and calmed his voice. "My job was to extract information from Iraqi prisoners, to extract intel to save our soldiers' lives."

"Did you use enhanced interrogation techniques? Waterboarding? Light deprivation?"

"I was operating on the field of battle. I was interrogating enemy combatants."

"So, you used enhanced interrogation techniques?"

"I got results. I got the truth. Those methods were approved at the time. Came right out of the interrogation handbook."

"Given your expertise, you've also trained police cadets in interrogation techniques?"

"Yes. I trained police cadets in standard police interrogation methods."

"And you've written about your training methods in the *New Police Academy* magazine?"

"Um... well... I believe I wrote one article..."

Laura held up a copy of the magazine and flipped to a two-page spread entitled, "Extracting Truth." She asked Demario to read a portion—highlighted in yellow—of his own work.

"'*Police officers can learn a great deal from military interrogation methods—both physical and psychological.*'" Demario sneered at his own prose. "'*These techniques should be used to elicit confessions from uncooperative criminal suspects. The modern police officer must realize that he is at war with the criminal element, and enhanced interrogation is a vital weapon in the fight for the streets. The police are the only ones standing between the public and the monsters.*'"

Laura sneered at his sneer, then smiled as he twitched. "Does this include slamming phone books over the heads of suspects? Dropping plastic bags over the heads of suspects? Pointing a pistol at suspects?"

"Objection!" Ward howled. "Argumentative!"

"No," Striker said. "Given the witness' own words, I'll allow it."

Demario straightened in his chair, eyes blazing like hellfire. "All I can say is it works."

70

ERIE COUNTY MEDICAL EXAMINER MARVIN WARRINGTON SERVED AS the perfect setup man for the prosecution. Each time the ME cited a medical phrase to describe the crime, Prosecutor Ward turned to the jury and repeated the term. The Wizard had a way of questioning a witness and testifying at the same time.

"Contusions caused by blunt force. Death caused by a severed vertebra."

Ward then distributed gruesome crime scene photos to the jury that added emotional fire to the scientific jargon. "Please examine the marks on the thorax... I call your attention to the cranial contusion... you can see the mark from where the hangman yanked the knot."

Laura was glued to each word of the ME's testimony, even though she knew that she would not cross-examine him. The night before, Martha had asked to handle the cross on Warrington, and—after an hour of back and forth—Laura had agreed. The fact was that Laura had gained a cautious degree of respect for her senior colleague. She was beginning to see the strengths of her well-dressed rival. Martha had made a real difference during jury selection, while offering a steady stream of useful insights and advice in the testimony phase. On top of that, Martha was in good standing with the judge. She could use that to gain the leeway she'd need to undercut the ME's testimony.

"Thank you, Dr. Warrington." Prosecutor Ward turned away from the stand and retreated to the prosecution table. "Your witness."

Martha rose from her chair, strode to the witness stand, and smiled up at the judge. "Good morning, Your Honor. I'll be handling cross for the defense."

"Good morning, Counselor. Good to see you. Please, proceed."

Martha loosened her eye-lock on the judge and moved her gaze to the witness. "Good morning, Dr. Warrington." She widened her smile and sweetened her voice. "Just a few questions, sir."

"Morning." Warrington, a thin, wiry man who came across as the nervous type, shifted in the witness chair and straightened his tie. "Go ahead."

"Now, Dr. Warrington." Martha turned her back on him to face the jury. "In the simplest possible terms, can you explain the cause of death? For the benefit of those of us who do not have your impressive and extensive medical and scientific expertise?"

"Certainly." The ME tried to look around Martha at the jury but just managed to look awkward instead. "The victim suffered a fractured cervical vertebra, due to the rapid speed of the fall, and the long distance of the drop." The ME placed his right forefinger to the front of his own throat. "The rope left a deep, distinct, inverted-V-shaped furrow on the victim's throat that matched the braid pattern of a rope."

Martha turned to face the witness. "So, to put it in layman's terms, Dr. Warrington, the victim suffered a broken neck."

"Well. Yes. To put in layman's terms. Yes. The impact of the drop broke her neck."

"Is this common in hanging deaths?

"No. Not at all." Warrington adjusted his wire-framed glasses and flexed the shoulders of his oversized suit coat. "The vast majority of hanging deaths result from constriction of the airways and compression of the arteries."

"Constriction of the airways." Martha again turned to face the jury, while repeating each word a second time. "Again, to put it in layman's terms, Doctor. Most of the time, the victim strangles to death?"

"Well, in essence, that is true. The fall interrupts the supply of blood to the brain and restricts the breathing process. As you put it, the victim strangles to death. Within a matter of minutes."

"And as you pointed out, Doctor, death by strangulation is far more common in hanging cases than death by a broken neck. In fact, had you ever seen a hanging death that caused a broken neck prior to this case?"

"Well, no. As a matter of fact, I had not. This case has been a first. I hope it's the last." Warrington smiled at the jury. Grim, serious faces stared back at him.

"Hmmm. You have never seen a hanging death caused by a broken neck like this before? In all your years of experience? Why do you suppose that is, Doctor?"

"All hanging deaths are rare. This kind of hanging is *very* rare. This hanging was meticulously planned and flawlessly executed. It resembled a judicial hanging. Very rare. Very rare, indeed."

"A judicial hanging? You mean an execution?"

"Yes."

"Like executions centuries ago?"

"Yes."

"Because of the skill of the hangman?"

"Yes. The killer knew the speed of the fall and the length of the drop would create adequate torque to fracture the vertebra."

Martha looked to the ceiling. "The precision of the technique was exceptional?"

"Yes."

"The choice of the rope and precision of the knot also suggest that?"

"Yes."

"Dr. Warrington, based on your testimony, the average person could not have committed this cold and calculated crime. This act was committed by a person with a great deal of knowledge, expertise, and preparation. This act was committed by an expert."

"I suppose."

"Wouldn't it have taken an expert to choose the ideal rope?"

"Yes."

"To tie the perfect knot?"

"Yes."

"To set the right fall?"

"Yes."

"To calculate the torque?"

"True."

"Can we also conclude that there is nothing in the experience of the average person that would prepare them to perpetrate such a calculated act?"

"I suppose."

"It seems to follow that the average person would have no idea how to carry out such a precise undertaking?"

"True."

"Not the average schoolteacher?"

"Of course not." Warrington chuckled at the suggestion. "*Certainly not.*"

"Or the average chef?"

"Of course not."

"Or the average automobile mechanic?"

"Well. I suppose not. That is true, but—"

"Thank you, Dr. Warrington. I agree. There is nothing in the experience of the average automobile mechanic that would prepare him to carry out such an act. Not an automobile mechanic like the defendant, Edward Nash."

Ward flew to his feet. "Objection! Objection! Counsel is testifying."

"Withdrawn," Martha said. "No more questions."

71

Laura waited to leave the courtroom to give the herd time to migrate out. Her goal was to get to her car without being besieged by reporters. Or being encircled by rowdy protestors, clamoring for a guilty verdict. She got up from the defense table, dropped her legal pad into her briefcase, and started down the center aisle of the empty courtroom. She pushed through the twin oak doors, emerged into the narrow hallway, and headed toward the staircase that wound down to the exit. Ten or twelve feet from the stairs, she stopped in her tracks, her path blocked by a glowering, middle-aged man and a dour, middle-aged woman. Laura recognized the couple as Erin Lambert's parents.

"Mr. and Mrs. Lambert." Feeling ambushed, she struggled to find the right words. "How are you?"

Those were not the right words.

"How *are* we?" Paul Lambert hissed like a snake coiling for the strike. The six-foot-two, two-hundred-pound man in the crisp flannel shirt and blue jeans glared at her with eyes that told her to go fuck herself. "We're reliving a nightmare. We're reentering hell. Why are you bringing this all back? Why are you defending this monster? Why doesn't this state have capital punishment? He should be dead. Like our little girl. Why does she rot in the grave, while he gets a new trial?"

"Please. Just stop this insanity," Josie Lambert piled on. The petite woman in the white, cotton dress stood one step behind her husband. "Don't destroy us all over again. Don't send this killer back into the world. Don't put another family through the pain that we've been through. I want my little girl back. How can you do this to us?"

Laura held up two palms. "Hold on." She looked over her shoulder and spotted a court bailiff stationed at the courtroom door. Laura caught his eye and, with a toss of her head, signaled him to come over. She turned to face the irate couple. "We can't have this conversation." She took a long backward stride. "I'm sorry. This is not going to happen. It's inappropriate."

The Lamberts took a step closer to her, eyeing the bailiff, hustling in their direction.

At that moment, the transcript from the sentencing phase of the first trial flashed through Laura's mind. Paul Lambert had been the first to take the stand to put a human face to the case by delivering a family impact statement. In tears, he'd explained to the judge how he'd been devastated by the loss of his beautiful, young daughter. Erin had been pulling her life together before she was "strung up by that self-made executioner." Paul Lambert pleaded with the judge to impose the maximum sentence on Nash, whom he called, "a cold-blooded murderer with the mind of a jackal and conscience of a snake." The victim's father had seen "evil in Nash's eyes" when Eddie visited their home a couple weeks before the murder. At that time, Mr. Lambert thanked Eddie for looking out for his little girl—encouraging her to give up drugs and quit the strip club—but, in between sips of beer, he could see the evil lurking inside Eddie. *Now, I will live the rest of my life knowing that I did not do enough to save my little girl from this cold-blooded killer.* The grieving father concluded his remarks to the original jury with the lament, *"With her gone, my life is over, too. My wife's life is over. We exist to keep the memory of our little girl alive. Period."*

Josie Lambert's testimony had reflected the same searing pain, with less anger. "I see a mother and daughter walking down the street, and I fall to the sidewalk in tears," she said in the penalty phase. "I see a young woman coming out of the hair salon with a cut like Erin's, and I have to stop myself from calling out her name. I miss her sweet smile. I miss her mischievous laugh. I miss having her in my life."

Laura could not imagine their pain. The loss was unfathomable. Of course, they wanted justice. All the defense research had shown the Lamberts to be good, decent people who did their best to raise their daughter right and rescue her when she veered off-track. Paul Lambert was a longtime and highly decorated military man, now working as a foreman at the regional recycling plant. Josie Lambert was a registered nurse at the Eden Community Clinic and had even walked Eddie through his check-ups. "I kept the man healthy, so he could murder my daughter," she had sobbed to the first trial judge. It was no surprise that their loss still hurt all these years later. That kind of pain never went away. Still, Laura couldn't let herself get drawn into a conversation about it.

Placing himself in Laura's path, Paul Lambert went on. "You can't ignore us forever," he snarled at her, grabbing his wife by the arm and yanking her toward the stairs. He looked back and yelled, "You'll hear from our attorney!"

Laura exhaled. She gave the bailiff the all-clear. He stopped in his tracks and headed back to his post. Laura stood alone in the empty hallway for a long moment, trying to make sense of the encounter.

One of the most profound changes in the criminal justice system, she knew, had been the escalating participation of victims and victims' families in trials. Responding to the understandable pleas of the victims' rights lobby, all fifty states had passed laws allowing "victim impact statements" at sentencing.

Laura supported the victims' rights movement—until it infringed upon the rights of the accused. Although she sympathized with the Lamberts, her preparation for the new trial had shown that they could pose a threat to her client. After their daughter's death, the grieving couple had turned to a victims' rights advocate to navigate the complex terrain of the police investigation and trial. The Lamberts also hired a local attorney to handle inquiries from the police and medical examiner, and to make sure the prosecutor *"dotted his i's and crossed his t's."* The Lamberts even tapped a public relations professional to craft their victim impact statements.

Laura hoped that this time, it would not come to that.

* * *

Laura was still reeling from the encounter when she climbed into the Mustang. Paul Lambert's words reverberated inside her. *"We're reliving a nightmare."* Josie Lambert's words made her eyes tear up. *"I miss my little girl."* Laura was searching for her car keys when her phone buzzed. It was Nick, and this time, she wanted to talk to him.

"Nick. Hi."

"Just checking in. You okay?"

"Your timing is impeccable."

"What's wrong?"

Laura filled him in on the clash with the victim's parents.

"I can't imagine their pain," she told him through tears. "To lose a daughter is beyond horrible. To lose a daughter in such a violent way is unbearable. I hate putting them through this all over again. They've suffered enough."

The line was silent for a long moment.

"Laura." Nick spoke softly. "You can't take the responsibility for their loss. You have to keep your eyes on the prize. The life of an innocent man is in your hands. Only you can set this right. Just keep pushing forward. You're doing the right thing. You're the difference between justice and injustice."

"Yeah, I guess you're right, Nick."

"I have one more point to make." Nick paused, as if searching for the right words. "It's going to sound cruel and crass and totally uncaring. I apologize in advance."

"What is it?"

"It's about the Lamberts."

"Okay."

"Well, their daughter was a stripper, a drug addict, and an alcoholic. Their daughter was killing herself."

"Yeah."

"Where were their tears when she was alive?"

72

FORMER-STRIP-CLUB-BOUNCER-TURNED-DRUG-DEALER, JIMMY Dean Bernadi, knew that once he took the oath to tell the whole truth, he would lie his ass off. Bernadi had memorized the script prepared for him by friends in high places and was ready to recite the words in open court. In response to a set-up question posed by Prosecutor Ward, Bernadi pointed to the defendant, swearing that Nash had stormed into the Bottoms Up Gentleman's Club the afternoon before the murder.

"Nash sat at the bar and demanded a beer. I served him. I wanted to calm him down. He seemed all agitated and nervous. To tell you the truth, he seemed out of control."

"What happened after that?" Ward lobbed the softball questions before stepping back to admire Bernadi's swing. "What did the defendant do?"

"He started peppering me with questions about Erin: Where was she going after work? Was she still on the pills? I told him the truth: She'd been going out to that bridge to get high. Eddie went nuts. He threatened to go out there and make her pay for all her lies. Let me put it this way: Eddie said—and I quote—'I'll kill the bitch.'"

As for his own whereabouts at the time of the murder, Bernadi presented the jury with what appeared to be a solid alibi. He had taken time off from the Bottoms Up to attend a rock concert in Buffalo. According to

Bernadi, when Erin Lambert was hanged from that bridge, he was a hundred-and-fifty miles away, swaying to a rock-and-roll beat with ten-thousand other music lovers.

"The police corroborated my alibi. I was nowhere near that bridge."

* * *

As the prosecutor returned to his table, Laura studied her legal pad. On the top page, she had scrawled six words: *Genesee. Two. Planted. Pink Floyd. Alibi.*

She'd made the notes after a phone call with Delilah, who'd been researching the life and times of Jimmy Dean Bernadi. Laura also had memorized the report from Lou, summarizing the backroom conversation between Bernadi and Demario at Angel's Gate. She knew the creep was testifying from a prepared script, and she had to push him off it. Jimmy Dean Bernadi was none too smart, she thought, and he could be manipulated on the stand.

"Mr. Bernadi." Laura blocked his view of the jury. "You testified that Mr. Nash ordered a beer from the bar at the Bottoms Up. Is that right?"

"Yeah."

"What kind of beer?"

"What?" Bernadi laughed at the question. "Look, this happened ten years ago. I don't remember who ordered what back in 2009. Do you remember what kind of beer you drank on a specific date ten years ago? Give me a break."

Laura turned to the judge. "Your Honor. Permission to treat the witness as hostile?"

Judge Striker looked down at Bernadi's slicked-back hair and leather jacket. "Granted."

"Mr. Bernadi. Did Mr. Nash have just one beer? In point of fact, didn't he have *two* beers?"

"Hmmm." Jimmy seemed nervous. "Now that you mention it. Yeah. It was two beers. Big deal."

"What kind of beer? Eddie always favored Genesee."

"Yeah. That was it. He had two Genies. In those green bottles."

"Makes sense," Laura said. "Genie is a local favorite. Brewed right up the road in Rochester."

"Good beer," Bernadi said. "We sold a lot of it."

"Thank you, Mr. Bernadi. Now…"

Laura paused for a moment to watch him squirm. Silence had that effect on bad liars. She had to keep him off-balance. She recalled a Mets game her dad took her to as a kid. The Mets pitcher threw hundred-mile-an-hour fastballs that the Dodger hitters pasted all over the park. The Dodger pitcher threw slow curves the Mets batters whiffed at and popped up. Laura was going to feed Bernadi a steady diet of slow curves.

"You testified that you had an alibi. You claimed to be attending a music concert in Buffalo the night of the murder."

"I didn't *claim* it," Bernadi snapped. "I was *there*. Love a good concert. I'm a hard rock connoisseur."

"Did you go with a friend?"

"No."

"Did you save the ticket stub?"

"No."

"Did you use a credit card at the venue?"

"No."

"So, you can't prove you were there."

"The cops checked it out. They verified it. I was there."

"Like they verified the tire track evidence?"

The prosecutor shot to his feet. "Objection."

"Withdrawn. Mr. Bernadi. What band headlined the concert?"

"What?"

"Who was the headliner? The main act?"

"Um, damn… I know this… don't tell me… hell, I don't recall at the moment."

"You don't recall the headline group?"

"Nope. It was a long time ago."

"Pink Floyd headlined the concert. Who forgets Pink Floyd? Even ten years later? You call yourself a rock connoisseur?"

Bernadi shifted in his seat and tugged at his leather sleeves, then wiped beaded sweat from his forehead and coughed into his balled fist. "I forgot, okay? It happens."

"You saw Pink Floyd. One of the most famous rock bands of all time. And you don't remember it?"

Bernadi looked around the courtroom like a kid lost in a grocery store.

Laura scanned the courtroom pews. Detective Demario sat in the third row. The right side of his mouth was twitching, and his eyes flashed like hazard lights. PI Charles Steel stood against the back wall. He shook his head back and forth. No. He had not found the towel.

"Mr. Bernadi. Jimmy Dean." Laura was setting him up for the fall. "Were you really at that concert?"

"Yes."

"Okay. Let's recap your testimony. Just to make sure we understand. Prior to the murder, you served Mr. Nash two bottles of Genesee beer at the Bottoms Up. It follows that you collected two empty Genie beer bottles from the bar after he left. It also follows that Mr. Nash's fingerprints and DNA were on those bottles, which were in your possession the afternoon before the murder."

"Umm. I guess."

"Were those the two bottles that ended up at the crime scene? The ones seized by the police? The ones with the defendant's DNA?"

"No. No way. I know nothing about that."

"Now, Mr. Bernadi. Jimmy Dean. You also testified that you left the club that afternoon and drove to Buffalo. You were going to attend a rock concert. Except you have no ticket stub, no credit card receipt, no one saw you there, and you don't remember the headline act: The unforgettable Pink Floyd."

"I guess so. Listen. It is what it is."

"Isn't it true you never attended the concert?"

"No. I mean, I did. I mean, yes. I did go to the concert."

"Isn't it true you went out to the bridge to meet Erin?"

"No."

"You were angry with her. For breaking up with you. You committed this crime and planted the empty beer bottles to incriminate Mr. Nash."

Bernadi sat dumbfounded, stupefied, and mute, a deep shade of red washing over his face.

"Objection! Objection! Objection!"

"Thank you, Mr. Bernadi. No further questions."

73

THE EXONERATION ALLIANCE
INNOCENCE BLOG

BREAKING NEWS:

Exonerations Hit Record High

    For the fourth year in a row, the number of exonerations in the United States hit a record high. Two-hundred-and-seventy-two men and women across the country were added to the National Registry of Exonerations. This brings the total number in the national database to 2,568. The registry has captured detailed information on all known exonerations in the U.S. since its founding in 1989. Each person in the database was convicted of a major crime and later cleared as a result of new evidence of actual innocence. Registry Founder, Professor James Samuelson of UCLA Law School, said the growing numbers prove that wrongful convictions are more common than ever believed:

    "Many prosecutors, police officers, and judges continue to insist that wrongful convictions are rare exceptions—the price we pay for a civil society. We now know just how wrong they are. In fact, imprisoning an innocent person is an all-too-common occurrence."

74

"THE COUNCIL AGAINST WRONGFUL CONVICTIONS" WAS ETCHED ON A temporary sign on the foggy glass door of the rental office at 124 Main Street in Eden. A winding staircase led to the sparse, second-floor workspace. Laura sat at a thrift-store desk, crafting questions for the state's expert psychiatric witness, who was set to take the stand when court reconvened on Monday. Feeling a need to stretch her legs, she clutched her half-full coffee mug and strolled to the plate-glass window that overlooked the street. She'd spent much of the night talking to Nick on the phone. He had become a supportive listener. His calls had helped her through the rough patches.

Laura watched the storm pummel pedestrians at the intersection of Main and Church. The brave souls pushed against a gusting wind that blew sheets of ice and snow into their faces. Ice crystals clung to telephone wires, and the branches of oaks and birches bent toward the sidewalk in the plaza across the way. Beyond the buildings, in the distant hills, the sun wove in and out of the inky clouds rolling in from Lake Erie.

Laura reflected on the case in the silence of the moment. For the most part, the defense of Eddie Nash was off to a good start. The strategy of counter-punching the prosecution witnesses was damaging the state's case. Detective Demario's cross-examination had pried loose an important cornerstone of the prosecution's narrative: The confession. The rattled detective's arrogant embrace of military-style interrogation techniques confirmed that the confession was coerced in violation of police standards and common decency. The county medical examiner's cross-examination had loosened another pillar in the case against Nash. The ME's description of the hanging cast doubt on Nash's ability to even commit such a precise and complex act. This crime reflected the skill of a cold, calculated executioner with knowledge and experience in the grim hangman's art. Then, there was the cross-examination of the former strip club bouncer. The bumbling and stumbling Jimmy Dean Bernadi had handed the jury a viable alternative to the prosecution's theory. Did Bernadi lie about his alibi? Did he drive out to that bridge? Did he kill his ex-girlfriend? It seemed, Laura thought, that the defense was building reasonable doubt. Was it enough to motivate the jurors to acquit? Not yet.

Despite the small victories, Laura guarded against overconfidence. Those narrow courtroom successes, those skillful manipulations of bad witnesses and weak evidence, were not enough. Short of a breakthrough, *State of New York v. Edward Thomas Nash II* would be decided by a second jury verdict.

Laura looked down at a legal pad and lifted a ballpoint pen. She had a thought to incorporate into the final statement to the jury.

> *Imagine this: You turn on the news to learn that a close friend has been murdered. You're reeling from the shock, when the police knock on your door. You're eager to help them find the killer, until you realize the shocking truth: You are their target. You're arrested. You're chained to a wall. You're beaten with a phone book. Threatened with a gun. Suffocated into falsely confessing. You're dragged into court, dressed in an electrocution belt, and called "a monster." You're found guilty and sent to prison for the rest of your life. And you're innocent.*

She put down the pen. She was getting ahead of herself. She needed a breakthrough.

The only game changer in sight was the bloodstained towel—the likely source of exculpatory DNA evidence—and it was nowhere. Charles and Lou had cultivated sources to scour the Erie County evidence room, to no avail.

They had cultivated another source to search the state police lab, to no avail. Where was it? Given the monstrous nature of the crime, and the unpredictability of human nature, without that evidence, those twelve mortal men and women might do anything, including convict an innocent man for the second time. She needed that bloodstained towel. Charles and Lou had to find it. Where were they?

Buzz. Buzz. Buzz.

The front door buzzer snapped her back to the here and now. *Who could that be?* She hustled down the narrow staircase, opened the door, and gasped with delight.

"Dad!" she said. "Tripod!"

75

John Tobias brushed snow off his blue-and-white ski parka before opening his arms in an eagle spread.

Laura stepped out the door and into his arms before bending to embrace the shivering, three-legged Border collie.

"What are you doing here?" She looked up at her dad's wind-reddened face and snow-flecked stocking hat. Laura scooped up Tripod and headed back upstairs. "Come in," she urged, looking over her shoulder. "You must be freezing."

John stomped his black snow boots on the ground before following upstairs. "Winter picked a hell of a day to make a show of force."

Laura stored his coat, hat, and gloves in the closet at the top of the stairs, then carried the collie to the threadbare couch. Settling on the worn cushions and holding Tripod in her lap, she asked her father the obvious questions: "Why are you here? What's going on?"

John pulled up a wooden chair and sat opposite her. The smile on his face gave way to a serious glower. Reaching into his red-and-white flannel shirt, he withdrew a set of papers, a half-inch-thick stapled sheaf, folded down the middle. After straightening out the fold, he held out the cover page, revealing the emblem of the New York State Police.

Laura strained to read the title:

NEW YORK STATE POLICE COMMISSION ON CORRUPTION
DRAFT
CONFIDENTIAL

"What is this?" Laura asked. "It looks official."

John opened to the first page. "Remember how I told you I'd been tapped to serve on a special commission to examine police corruption in New York State?"

"Yeah." She nodded. "Thanks to your rep as the prosecutor of crooked cops."

"Well, the chairman just distributed this memo. It summarizes the results of a major investigation into police misconduct in western New York State."

"Hush-hush? And you're showing me?"

"Look, kid. I have to be straight. I am crossing an ethical line. I'm making a conscious choice to cross that line. You have to know what's happening around you. You have to understand the people you're dealing with. The danger you're in. You're my daughter, for God's sake. Ethics be damned."

Laura nodded. "I get it. So, I'm making the conscious choice to cross my own line. I want to know what's in it. What I'm up against. I want to know just how bad these people are."

John flipped to Page Two and starting reading. *"This memo summarizes the findings of a two-year joint investigation by the New York State Police and the FBI into suspected law enforcement corruption in four counties in western New York State. The probe found that a network of rogue police officers took bribes and payoffs from legitimate businesses in exchange for protection, and skimmed drugs and money from major narcotics dealers. The police conspired to arrest, convict, and imprison suspects without regard for guilt or innocence to build their reputations as 'super-cops.' Certain prosecutors, judges, and prison administrators either took part in the scheme or turned a blind eye to the corruption."*

"Holy—!" Laura gasped. "What a scam."

"An unprecedented breach of duty."

"How did it work?"

"You've heard of 'heater' cases?"

"Heater cases?"

"Okay. County prosecutors had the option of designating high-profile investigations as 'heater' cases. Each case was funded to the hilt and fast-tracked to expedite an arrest and swift conviction. The cases were routed to the detectives with the highest arrest rates, and judges with the highest conviction rates and most severe prison sentences."

"A straight line to the slammer."

"Yes."

Laura tilted her head. "There's still nothing illegal about a program of efficient prosecutions and convictions."

"Until a band of rogue cops formed a secretive network—codenamed 'Vigilance'—to supercharge the process. The Vigilance cops routinely manufactured evidence and lied on the witness stand to make sure suspects went down fast and went away for long stretches. Vigilance prosecutors kept a steady line of convicted defendants flowing into the state prison system, while prison administrators made it hard for those inmates to meet with lawyers or file appeals. The pipeline just went on and on. Justice ran amuck."

Laura pictured the face of Attica Superintendent Leon Wilkes, and the swirling red-and-blue lights of a prison patrol car. She recalled all the bureaucratic barriers, designed to block her face-to-face meetings with her client. Was Wilkes part of the scheme?

She returned her focus to her dad. "Why would the cops go to the trouble of framing innocent people?"

"The detectives became gods in blue uniforms. The highest conviction rates. The biggest cases. In the shortest amount of time. No one wanted to question the success of cops who were taking bad guys off the street. Their reps as arrest and conviction machines insulated them from scrutiny from Internal Affairs and state police inspectors. These 'super-cops' were making the streets safe from crime, so they did as they pleased."

"Invincible."

"Free to run wild. The 'super-cops' turned the Vigilance Network into their own criminal network. They operated protection rackets for drug traffickers. They charged the biggest drug dealers a 'tax,' and in exchange, shielded them from arrest. They even harassed their competing dealers. In one case, the cops supplied a major trafficker with guns, bulletproof vests, and police radios."

"Oh, my God." Laura cringed. "Total abandon."

"Vigilance officers carried spare weapons in their 'war chests' to plant at crime scenes. New recruits were required to plant a weapon on a suspect as a show of loyalty. The top cops even doled out awards and plaques for recruits who framed civilians, coached false witnesses, planted evidence, stole drugs, and covered up their tracks."

"No doubt, Detective Demario was front and center," Laura said. "He had to be a ringleader."

"Demario lorded over a supporting cast of dirty detectives and crooked uniforms. He distributed the shakedown loot up and down the network. The corruption thrived because honest officers, prosecutors, and judges looked the other way. No one raised a red flag, because the cops in question were arresting bad guys and reducing crime. As whispers of the scam spread, law-abiding officers transferred out of the region, while corrupt ones moved in. The whole thing just fed on itself. It grew into a monster."

"When did the investigation start?"

"The state police and FBI launched the investigation two years ago. No one outside a trusted core knew about it. The secrecy was needed to keep from tipping off the bad guys."

"What's next?"

"The shit will hit the fan in two or three weeks. There will be an announcement at a joint state police and FBI press conference. The state and feds plan to indict up to eight cops and two prosecutors right out of the box. Demario and company have no clue of the hell that's about to rain down on them."

"What then?"

"At that point, the state attorneys will have to determine how many cases were tainted. Prison doors will swing open for hundreds—maybe thousands—of convicts who were denied their rights. I guess you Innocence Project types will be busy."

76

THE EXPERT PSYCHIATRIC WITNESS IS AN ESSENTIAL ACTOR IN THE MOD-
ern courtroom drama. The clash between prosecution and defense expert psychiatrists is a common inflection point in each trial. As *New York v. Nash II*
resumed, the battle of the shrinks took center stage.

Deputy State's Attorney Bart Ward nodded from the podium to consulting prison psychiatrist Edward J. Peters.

"Now, Dr. Peters, do I have this right? You are both a medical doctor
and a psychiatrist?"

"Objection." Laura rolled her eyes toward the high ceiling. *"All* psychiatrists are medical doctors. It's a prerequisite."

"Sustained," Striker ruled. "You know better, Mr. Ward."

"Yes, Your Honor." Ward glanced at a paper on the lectern. "Let me
ask this, Dr. Peters. You are a graduate of the respected Commonwealth
Medical School?"

"Yes."

"Objection." Laura rose halfway to her feet. "Calls for supposition."

Striker appeared annoyed as he turned to Ward. "Get on with it,
Mr. Prosecutor."

"Your Honor, I'm trying to establish the high level of credibility of this witness."

"Make it fast."

"Dr. Peters, did you receive an award from your medical school's alumni association?"

"Yes. I was honored with the Herald R. Knight Community Service Award for my work in both the prison and a community clinic. I work at the prison two days a week, and the clinic three days a week. It's not lucrative work, but it is rewarding."

"Very admirable, Dr. Peters. In fact, wouldn't you agree that your appearance here is a form of community service? I mean, you're not an over-paid expert witness who goes from trial to trial, charging exorbitant fees to testify for the highest bidder. You're a community servant, doing your duty."

"I suppose." Peters shrugged. "We all have a responsibility to give back."

"Now, Dr. Peters. Did you have an occasion to conduct an extensive examination of the defendant?"

"Yes. I examined Mr. Nash on twenty-four separate occasions, over a two-year period. I spoke with the patient at length in my role as a certified psychotherapist, and I administered a battery of tests that revealed certain traits."

"Traits?" Ward eyed the jurors as Dr. Peters continued.

"Mr. Nash exhibits a rare form of antisocial personality disorder that blends the traits of a psychopath with those of a sociopath. He exhibits the cunning manipulation of the psychopath, and the moral detachment of the sociopath. Nash is prone to grandiose acts of violence that are brutal, sadistic, and symbolic."

Ward looked from juror to juror, while repeating the words for emphasis. "Brutal. Sadistic. Symbolic." The prosecutor turned back to the witness. "Dr. Peters, would hanging a person qualify as brutal, sadistic, and symbolic?"

"Yes."

"No further questions."

77

Laura laid her notes on the lectern. She hid her elation behind a poker face. The prison shrink had opened himself up to a decimating cross. She planned to impeach his credibility, undercut his diagnosis, scorch his veracity, and—with any luck—make him cry. Given his self-importance, and lack of experience as an expert witness, she wanted to watch him squirm. Juries never believed squirmers.

"Dr. Peters, you testified that your diagnosis of the defendant was based on twenty-four separate sessions."

"Yes. Twenty-four is the standard for an assessment in such a complex case. Anything less would not provide the requisite data and insight on which to base a diagnosis. Twenty-four two-hour sessions over a two-year period were required at a minimum."

"Sufficient? Do you mean that anything less would be insufficient?"

"Yes."

"Anything less could lead to an incorrect diagnosis? An invalid result?"

Laura watched as Peters' expression turned grim. His internal danger alarm was sounding. He stuttered. "Umm… well, yes, it could."

"Your Honor, may I approach the witness?"

"You may."

Laura carried a folder to the stand, withdrew a sheet of paper, and handed it to the witness. "Dr. Peters, this is a list of dates of your sessions with Nash. Prepared by you. Signed by you."

"Yes. Twenty-four dates."

She took back the list and handed him a spreadsheet. "This is your daily sign-in log from the prison's mental health wing."

"It is."

"Prepared by you?"

"Yes."

"Signed by you?"

"Yes."

"Sir, tell me this: Why are eight dates cited in the exam list not listed in your daily sign-in log?"

Peters fumbled with the spreadsheet. He put one leg over the other. Then, there it was: He squirmed.

Laura had him. "The dates of eight sessions are not reflected in your sign-in log, because you were not at the prison on those days. You were a hundred miles away at the community clinic. The clinic where you work on your days out of the prison. We have those records, too."

"I can't explain it," Peters stammered. "There must be a mistake."

Ward rose to object but stopped halfway. He knew he had no grounds.

Laura smelled the kill. "You couldn't examine Mr. Nash on those eight days, because you weren't there. Meaning that the maximum number of sessions you could have conducted with Mr. Nash was sixteen."

Peters' face was ashen. "I guess that's the case."

"You guess?"

Peters glared at her. "Yes. That *is* the case."

"Yet, moments ago, you testified that a minimum of twenty-four examinations are needed to establish a credible diagnosis. Less than twenty-four would lead to an invalid diagnosis. Your words, Doctor."

Peters' hands began to shake. His neck twitched. Sweat beaded on his forehead and ran into his eyes. He took out a tissue and wiped the fogged lenses of his Clark Kent glasses.

"Well. Hold on. Let me see. I'm sure I can explain it." His voice wavered. "Wait a minute," he muttered. "Maybe this explains it. Umm. Yeah. Okay. Sixteen. Sixteen sessions. That's all it took. The case wasn't that complex. Yeah. These kinds of cases can be straightforward. This one was *very* straightforward. The man was a psychopath and a sociopath at the same time. I knew it right away."

"Except you testified that the case was 'complex.'" Laura knew she was stretching it when she turned to Striker. "Your Honor. You may wish to explain perjury law to the witness."

Striker smirked, but Peters didn't see him. He looked at Laura, as if pleading for mercy.

She struck again. "Isn't it true that the twenty-four sessions are the minimum proscribed by medical guidelines?"

"Yes. I dropped the ball. I apologize to the court."

"So, your diagnosis is invalid. Your own words, sir."

"Well. Yes."

Laura smiled. She needed him to lighten up. "I see. Thank you for being truthful. Let's take a breather. Would you like a glass of water?"

"Yes, thank you."

The bailiff brought it, and Peters gulped it down. His crimson face lightened in color.

"Is that better?" Laura asked with feigned compassion. "Are you more relaxed now?"

"Yes. Much better. Thank you."

Laura changed course. "Let's turn back to your impeccable credentials. Let's talk about your recent community service award. Congratulations."

"Thank you."

"You made a speech at the award ceremony. You received a standing ovation."

"Yes. I was honored. It was too much. I mean, I'm no public speaker but—"

"You're too modest. I'm sure you deserved it."

"Thank you."

"Did you know the speech was recorded?"

"No. I wasn't aware."

"I have a word-for-word transcript."

"You do?"

Laura handed him the transcript and asked him to read the highlighted paragraph.

The waver returned to his voice as he read. *"As psychiatrists, we have a profound obligation to exceed standard guidelines when diagnosing patients for serious mental disorders. These cases are never straightforward. A shortcut can lead to untrustworthy findings. The human mind is a complex organ, and our diagnoses are just approximations—oftentimes, we just don't know. The consequences for the people we are supposed to help can be dire."*

78

Defense psychiatric expert Charlotte Meyers spoke with quiet confidence. Her credentials from Harvard and BU were as impressive as her clear, understandable explanation of the psychiatric facts. She also drove the final sword into Peters' testimony.

"Mr. Nash is neither a psychopath nor a sociopath, let alone a combination of the two. Combination psychopath-sociopaths do not exist, except in the mind of the prison psychiatrist who spoke today. The two medical terms have distinct meanings. There is no such case in professional literature. There is no such case in the history of psychiatry."

A juror scanned the gallery, but Dr. Peters had left the building.

"I base my findings on my own assessment of Mr. Nash." Dr. Meyers made eye contact with each juror before continuing, "I can assure you that his responses and test results were one-hundred-percent consistent with a normal person faced with a difficult situation. He is in control of his faculties and shows empathy to his family, friends, lawyers, and fellow inmates. He does not harbor excessive bitterness or show any violent tendencies toward others. In my opinion, Mr. Nash's mental health is quite good, considering he's serving life without parole for a crime he did not commit."

Laura approached the witness. "Dr. Meyers, please explain the slide on the monitor."

The image on the flat screen showed a human brain with yellow markings around an almond-shaped area in the center.

"The slide shows the brain of a person diagnosed with severe antisocial personality disorder. The yellow area shows significant volume reduction in the part of the brain called the 'amygdala.'"

"This condition in common in people with antisocial personality disorder?"

"Yes."

"And this slide?"

The imaged switched to a new brain scan, this time with a larger area in yellow.

"This image shows the brain of a normal adult. The yellow markings show a full-sized, healthy amygdala."

"This is common for normal individuals?"

"Yes."

"And this slide?"

"This is a slide showing the brain of Edward Thomas Nash."

"The defendant?"

"Yes."

"Your assessment?"

"Edward Thomas Nash has a perfectly healthy human brain."

* * *

After the trial adjourned for the day, Laura returned to the office to meet with Charles and Lou. There had to be a way to locate the bloodstained towel.

"It's in here somewhere," Laura said. She spread her hands over pages of the original investigative file on the conference table.

"Check this out." Charles held up a transcript of the Eden police dispatcher calling in the troops after the discovery of Erin's body.

He read:

"*DISPATCH: All units respond to sighting of a female body at the West End Pedestrian Bridge on Utility Road F. Be warned, people. Bring your puke sacks. The victim is hanging from the bridge. Repeat—hanging victim at West End Pedestrian Bridge. Proceed with caution.*

"*EDEN UNIT SIX: Eden Six to Dispatch. Did you say, 'hanging victim?'*

"*DISPATCH: Confirmed. Hanging. Female victim.*

"*EDEN UNIT TWO: Eden Two responding. Two miles out.*

"*DISPATCH: Confirmed.*

"*EDEN UNIT FOUR: Eden Four responding. Four miles out.*

"*DISPATCH: Confirmed.*

"*EDEN UNIT SEVEN: Eden Seven responding. Five miles out.*

"*DISPATCH: Confirmed.*

"*GENESEE UNIT ONE: Genie One here.*

"*DISPATCH: Come in, Genie One.*

"*GENESEE ONE: Approaching scene. Shit. There is a girl hanging from that bridge. Holy shit. Will secure the scene and preserve evidence.*

"*DISPATCH: Genie One, listen up. Eden has jurisdiction. Repeat. Eden has jurisdiction. Hands off the scene. Our units are en route.*

"*GENESEE ONE: We have jurisdiction. This is on our side of the boundary line. Securing evidence. Repeat. Securing evidence now.*"

Charles slapped down the transcript. "There it is. The Genesee Police Department were the first to respond, and they considered it their crime scene."

Lou picked up the narrative. "The Genesee cops mistakenly believed they had jurisdiction. That bridge is right on the line between Eden and

Genesee. The Genesee first responder began collecting evidence before the Eden cops arrived!"

Charles slammed his hand on the table. "I think we know what happened to that bloodstained towel."

79

THE NORMALLY IMMACULATE PROSECUTOR WORE A WRINKLED SUIT. HIS tie was spattered with wine drippings. Puffed-up flesh formed purple mountains around his bloodshot eyes. Sharp, horizontal creases furrowed his forehead, and his hair was a mess. Bart Ward looked like a tired man—tired of faltering witnesses, sketchy evidence, and mounting signs of police and prosecutor misconduct.

Bart Ward was tired of the anger on the judge's face, and the doubt in the jurors' eyes. The defense, it seemed to him, was closing in on reasonable doubt. *This is not going well.* The retrial of Eddie Nash was becoming a showcase of police and prosecution misstatements, mishaps, and misdeeds. The headlines were gnawing at his reputation and disrupting his sleep. The defense had even cast doubt on the urine traces recovered from the victim's body. Laura had the samples tested with more advanced techniques, which showed the DNA was not Nash's. Ward was on the ropes. It was time to distance himself from lying cops and crooked prosecutors. He had played no role in the original investigation and trial. Why should he—with his stellar reputation on the line, and his bosses in Albany on his back— pay the price for these two-bit ham-and-eggers?

So, the seasoned prosecutor invited the green defense attorney to meet him in the private attorney room on the third floor of the old courthouse after the trial adjourned for the day.

Ward looked across the walnut conference table to his young adversary. The Wizard sighed like a war-weary soldier. "This case is keeping me up at night."

Laura feigned disbelief. *"You?* I've been working on it for months. I haven't had a good night's sleep since spring." *What is he doing? What is he up to?*

"First, Laura." Ward hit her with his tired-as-an-old-dog blue eyes. "May I call you Laura?"

She nodded.

"Laura. Let me compliment you on the way you've handled yourself, both in and out of court. You are a formidable adversary—unstoppable with Martha at your side. You've brought out certain irregularities in the original trial that are—I must confess—rather troubling."

"'Rather troubling,'" Laura repeated. "Your talent for understatement remains stellar."

"I plead guilty to that." Ward winked through his mountain of eye flesh. "These irregularities may have—and I repeat, *may* have—compromised the fairness of the original trial. Perhaps—I stress the word *perhaps*—your client was denied a fair trial. I want you to know this: The State of New York does not condone the use of false evidence or dishonest testimony to convict innocent defendants of major felonies. The State of New York does not seek to put innocent people in prison. The State of New York does not accept wrongful convictions."

"Good to know." Laura lost the smile. "I would hope locking up innocent people is not a state priority."

Laura recalled what her father once told her on a fishing trip. Let the fish take the line out as far as it can. Once he's tired himself out, it's a lot easier to reel him in."

"What are you getting at, Mr. Ward?"

"Please, Laura. Call me Bart."

"What are you getting at, Bart?"

The deputy prosecutor raised an eyebrow like it was all he had the strength to do. "May I be blunt?"

"Please." Laura leaned back in the antique armchair in the book-lined meeting room. "Blunt is good. I need more blunt in my life."

"The position of the prosecution," he said, "has evolved. Our view of your client has evolved."

Laura narrowed her eyes. "You call that blunt?"

"Okay. Fine." Ward flexed the shoulders. "Let me ask you one simple question: How would your client like to avoid the agony of a jury verdict?"

"'Agony of a jury verdict?'" Laura looked to the floor and chuckled. "My client is looking forward to it. He believes the jury is relating to our case. That the jury is siding with him. He's feeling good about his chances."

"Maybe." Ward adopted a poker face. "Maybe not."

"Bart, my client is not guilty. The guilty party is still at large. The real killer is threatening the public. On the other hand, the Erie County police and prosecutor are guilty of their own crimes. Perjury. Obstructing justice. False imprisonment. Look. I had nothing to do with the original trial. *You* had nothing to do with the original trial. I know the reality. *You* know the reality. How do we put an end to this insanity?"

"Let me put it this way," Ward barked. "How would your client like to walk out of prison a free man?"

"Specifics, please."

"By the end of the week." Ward pounded a fist on the desk and leaned in closer. "How would he like to be home by the weekend?"

"Can you get him tickets to the Jets game? Maybe throw in a Broadway show? Now, come on, man. Spell out the details."

"Goddamn it," Ward snapped. "Don't you—" He caught himself. He held out his hands, palms up, in a show of surrender. "I'm offering you a plea deal."

Laura assessed the situation. This was a critical moment. This was a potential turning point in this whole saga. Ward was tendering an Alford Plea—one of the most curious and contradictory conventions in modern jurisprudence. Stemming from the 1989 Supreme Court ruling in *Alford v. North Carolina,* the agreement allows a defendant to plead guilty—or no contest—while maintaining his claim of actual innocence. In essence, the defendant admits that the state has enough evidence to convict him beyond a reasonable doubt, while maintaining that they did not commit the crime.

"Terms?" Laura reached down, opened her briefcase, and withdrew a pen and pad of paper. "One at a time."

80

PUT YOURSELF IN HIS PLACE. WHAT IS HE THINKING?

She tried to see it from the prosecutor's point of view. Ward's narrative of the crime had been damaged in open court. His witnesses had been picked apart during cross-examination and shot down by more respected and believable experts. His chances of winning were growing dimmer, and the specter of a loss was gaining clarity. A loss would be devastating to the State of New York. A not-guilty verdict would mean that the state had robbed ten years of an innocent man's life. It would open the door to a barrage of bad press and trigger a massive wrongful conviction lawsuit. A not-guilty verdict would also expose the police frame-up and highlight the fact that the cops had never even *looked* for the real killer.

The *real* Hangman of Eden had been out there the whole time, and the unsuspecting public had been at risk of more gruesome murders. The Hangman may have even killed other women, while Nash was in stir. Right under the noses of the smug cops and clueless prosecutors. The defeat would let down the victim's family and friends, as well as the whole community. Laura pictured Mr. and Mrs. Lambert's faces, lined with the pain of their unimaginable loss. No, Bart Ward was not going to risk all of that on the off-chance that he could turn his case around.

"Thank you for the offer." Laura's voice had gone robotic. "Now, please, for the last time, the terms."

Ward leaned back and cleared his throat. Laura positioned her pen above the pad of paper.

"Very well." Ward opened the leather-bound notebook and withdrew a single page. "It's straightforward. Rather simple."

"Good. Simple is smart. Go ahead."

"One: The State of New York and/or Erie County admits to no wrong-doing in the original investigation or trial of Mr. Edward Thomas Nash."

"Got it."

"Two: The State will be held harmless from any wrongful conviction or false incarceration claims brought by Mr. Edward Thomas Nash."

"Got it."

"Three: The original guilty verdict remains on the books as the official outcome of *State of New York v. Edward Thomas Nash.*"

"That, too."

"Now. This is important. The state recognizes that Mr. Nash has spent ten years and seven months in prison for the crime of murder in the first degree. The time served fulfills his entire obligation to the state."

"I understand."

"Do you? We're guaranteeing his immediate release from prison with the execution of this agreement. Mr. Nash will face no danger of a new conviction on this charge. Prior to his release, Mr. Nash may state in open court that he is innocent of the charge. He can explain that he's accepting the plea as a means of gaining his freedom. All Mr. Nash has to do is sign on the dotted line. I have taken the liberty of drafting the actual document." Ward handed the paper to Laura, adding, "That's the beauty of the Alford Plea. Everybody wins."

Laura studied the document for a long moment.

"So, let me get this straight, Mr. Ward." She looked into his eyes. "On the books, Eddie Nash remains a guilty man. A convicted killer in the eyes of the law. His opportunity for exoneration is gone—forever. Mr. Nash goes into the parole system and can be sent back to prison at any time. Meantime, Demario and company go on to frame the next unsuspecting victim. Case closed. Do I have that about right?"

"Except for one small point: Nash walks. Your man goes free."

"I'll bring him the offer." Laura placed the one-page document in her briefcase. She snapped it shut and rose to her feet. "I'll also recommend he trash it."

81

EDDIE HAD SETTLED INTO HIS NEW DIGS AT THE REFURBISHED COUNTY jail, a three-story brick building connected to the courthouse. His morning commute consisted of an escorted stroll—in jumpsuit and shackles—through an underground tunnel, to the holding room in the courthouse. There, he changed into street clothes supplied by his legal team and waited to be led into the courtroom. After a day of keeping his mouth shut, while Laura and Martha attacked the prosecution case, he took the reverse trip back to his cell on the second floor of the jail.

In his newly painted cell, Eddie waited for a guard to slip a plastic tray through the slot in his door. The cafeteria made pork chops or chicken breasts that tasted like gourmet fare, compared to the swill doled out back in the slime line in Attica.

The biggest difference between the jail and the prison, though, was the nature of the inmate population. The jail prisoners—a mix of white, black, and Latino—were called "detainees." Most had been convicted of nothing. They were awaiting trial on minor drug beefs, low-level B&E raps, and even trumped-up traffic charges. Eddie had met an eighteen-year-old Latino boy awaiting trial for leaving the scene of a minor car accident. Eddie counseled him—and all the rest he met—against living a life at cross-purposes with the legal system.

"You won't win," he insisted. "Don't waste your life."

Most listened. A few thanked him. These guys were different from the hardcore cons back in Attica. In jail, Eddie hadn't come across a single white guy who bore the Aryan Nation mark, or a single black dude who wore the colors of the Black Panthers. These were kids, and Eddie liked them.

On this night, Eddie paced back and forth in his twelve-by-fourteen-foot cell. What the fuck was he supposed to do? Regaining his freedom was no longer a hazy fantasy or a shadowy dream. Regaining his freedom was now a stark probability that could come to pass at any time. Cold, hard questions circled in his head like starving vultures: *Where will I go? How will I live? Where will I work? Will I be embraced as an innocent man? Will I be shunned as a killer who got off?*

His world had changed since he'd first heard the prison door slam shut. His father had passed away of cancer. His mother had grown old. His two sisters had moved from their small town to the big city. Most of his friends had fled, too—without so much as a goodbye visit or forwarding address. Eddie had never used an iPad, carried a cell phone, or shopped at Walmart. What the hell was he supposed to do when he got out?

Eddie Nash was haunted by the choice. To take the Alford Plea. To reject the Alford Plea. To go free. To roll the dice.

He asked himself over and over: *Should I accept what is, in point of fact, a veiled guilty plea? Should I walk out of prison as a first-degree murderer on parole? Should I roll the dice with twelve people I don't know and hope for the best?* He wanted to grab the deal—*any* deal—to get his freedom. He wanted to end this nightmare and walk away a free man.

I have to take it. I'm crazy not to.

There was a second voice in head, though. Quiet. Confident. Reasonable. This voice urged him to reject the plea—to stand strong. Regardless of his token claim of innocence in court, copping to the plea would be an admission of guilt. Back in the real world, he'd be branded a convicted first-degree murderer who just happened to catch a lucky break. He'd be saddled with a felony record, and a parole officer itching to send him back. In fact, he'd be one parole violation away from a return trip to slammer world.

Don't do it, man. Don't be fooled again. Don't trust the fucking system.

Eddie pictured the face of Laura Tobias in his mind's eye. He could see her beautiful smile. Full of compassion. He could hear her beautiful voice. Full of passion. He could almost reach out and touch her in the shadows of his cell. The idealistic young woman had believed in him. She'd knocked down every barrier in their path. Over the months, through the highs and lows, she'd gained his trust and admiration.

No. He had come to respect her. Hell, he had to face it. In a certain way, he had come to love her.

She's been right all along. How can I turn away now?

Laura had made her position known. *"Don't take the plea,"* she'd advised Eddie as he left the holding room that day. *"We're going to win this. You will be exonerated."*

* * *

Nash's tortured decision to turn down the plea forced the trial into its final stage.

The next morning, the prosecutor strode into the courtroom a new man. Bart Ward sported a new suit, perfectly fitted and pressed. His smiling face emitted a confident glow.

What's going on now? Laura wondered. *What happened to his wrinkled coat and stained tie? What about his bloodshot and flesh-shrouded eyes?* Ward looked rejuvenated, as if he'd slept like a baby. *Oh, no!* Had Ward the Wizard faked exhaustion to give the defense a sense of false confidence? What did he have up his cufflinked sleeve?

"Your Honor. The prosecution calls Mr. Samuel Newman."

Laura turned to Eddie and whispered, "No worries. It's just the prison snitch. We saw this coming."

The entrance to the courtroom swung open and a tall, well-proportioned man with coiffed gray hair strode down the center aisle. Head up. Clear eyes. Even stride. The witness wore a conservative three-piece suit that rivaled the prosecutor's and carried a large, black book at his side. His own Bible. He was allowed to use it to take the oath.

This was not your ordinary snitch.

"Do you know him?" Laura whispered to Nash at the defense table. "Have you talked to him?"

"Met him once or twice. He never looked like that. Never told him nothing."

Prosecutor Ward smiled at the witness. "Mr. Newman. Where do you reside?"

"The Attica Correctional Facility."

"I see. Why are you there?"

"I made a mistake. As a young man. I robbed a bank."

"You've served seven years of a fifteen-year sentence."

"Yes."

"I understand you're a model prisoner."

"Yes. I serve as a prison trustee. I mentor young prisoners. I've completed the prison ministry program. I teach Sunday School and chair the religious studies group. I've received numerous commendations from the staff for modeling the behavior of a rehabilitated inmate. I am striving to return to society as a new man."

"Do you know the defendant, Edward Nash?"

"Yes. We've spoken many times. In the mess. In the canteen. In the yard. He confided in me. He confessed to me."

Newman went on to describe the murder in gruesome detail. He claimed that Nash told him everything: How he'd studied the hangman's art. How he'd purchased the perfect rope. How he tied the classic knot. How he beat the victim with a tire iron. How he made a couple of mistakes while committing the crime. Getting slashed in the leg with a broken vodka bottle. Leaving behind a white towel stained with his own blood.

The jury was spellbound.

The prosecutor leaned against the witness box. "How can you recall these details?"

"Because I wrote them down."

"You're telling me you wrote down Mr. Nash's confession?"

"Yes. I keep a journal."

Laura and Martha flew to their feet. "Objection."

The judge growled, "Approach."

The attorneys raced to the bench.

"Your Honor," Laura fumed. "We know nothing of this journal. It was not listed in discovery."

"Your Honor," the Wizard countered, "Mr. Newman made the journal known to us in our pre-trial meeting yesterday. He had concealed it to spare Mr. Nash a blow-by-blow account of his confession. However, he had a last-minute change of heart, and here it is."

Striker eyed Ward. "You knew nothing of it until yesterday?"

"Yes, sir."

"I am loath to allow evidence like this at this late stage."

"Your Honor, to us, this is new evidence. New and *critical* evidence."

"Very well. I'll allow it."

82

Laura sat in the empty courtroom, staring into space. The prosecutor had blindsided her. Had he worn that wrinkled suit just to give her a false impression? Had he spent a sleepless night just to look exhausted? Did he know all along that Nash would reject the plea offer? At this point, the journal was damning. The jury would believe every word. Eddie Nash would go down for the second time.

Laura picked up her phone. Hit the number for Ward the Wizard. She'd take the plea. If it was still on the table.

She waited for him to answer.

Charles burst into the room at that moment and rushed down the aisle to the defense table. He grinned and said three glorious words: "I found it."

Laura disconnected the call. "The bloodstained towel?"

"Yep."

"Where?"

"Turned out it had been confiscated by the Genesee Police Department and stored in its evidence bin all this time. Remember, at first, the Genesee cops thought they had jurisdiction, before conceding the case to Demario and the Eden police. The Genesee police chief agreed to hand it over, rather than face a contempt of court charge. I'm stunned; he obliged."

"He may have seen the downside of protecting Demario. No one wants to go down with a dirty cop."

"Turns out that a detective with the Genesee Police Department—no Sherlock Holmes—was the first responder to the scene of the murder. Thinking the crime had been committed in Genesee, the detective seized the towel and stored it in the evidence locker at the Genesee police station. He tagged it, *'Lambert Homicide Evidence Item #1.'* All nice and proper. Then, he left it to collect dust. It's just been sitting there all these years without anyone realizing that it was the key to the case. I guess Demario and company figured it was secure and out of sight with their friends in Genesee. So, why bother with it—unless they needed it at some point?"

"What condition is it in?"

"Good condition," Charles reported. "Very little degradation."

"Then, it can be tested for DNA. We should get it to the lab ASAP."

"I'll drive it to the lab in Rochester tonight. With a state police escort and monitor. I'll arrange for an expedited test." Charles was a man with a plan. "We should have a complete DNA profile within forty-eight hours."

Laura's spirits brightened. "Once we have the DNA profile, we can have it run through the FBI database. We can check it against DNA samples of hundreds of thousands of criminal suspects. A match will give us the identity of the real killer."

83

THE JUDGE'S CHAMBERS HAD BEEN TRANSFORMED FROM A MAHOGANY and leather-bound den for the contemplation of legal nuance to a modern workspace for producing important legal opinions and holding private meetings with counsel. An ergonomic workstation with a high-speed computer stood next to a bookcase in the far corner. A large, plate-glass window allowed natural light to flood the space. A sparkling, glass-topped conference table with five cushioned swivel chairs occupied the center of the room.

A bit like the chambers, Superior Court Judge Peter J. Striker had transformed himself over his years on the bench. The rugged, handsome, white-maned jurist had been a private litigator, defense lawyer, and prosecutor before ascending to the judiciary. Over the years, he had gone from a stickler for the letter of the law to a more open-minded arbiter of the legal process. At this point of his career, Striker had one goal: To oversee fair trials that were not vulnerable on appeal. He was respected for giving ample leeway to both sides, while weighing legal disputes and rendering fair opinions. It was also rumored—whispered in the corridors of the courthouse, and the local lawyer hangouts—that the good judge had a temper. If cornered, the pissed-off Striker could skewer wayward barristers.

Facing counsel and co-counsel for the defense and prosecution at the glass conference table, he looked over his wire-framed glasses to chief prosecutor Bart Ward.

"Mr. Ward."

"Yes, Your Honor?"

"Are you aware that I've been practicing law in courtrooms for more than a half-century? Attorney-for-hire. Defender. Prosecutor. Judge."

"Yes, sir."

"Mr. Ward."

"Yes, Your Honor?"

"Do you to know that I've spent the past fourteen years presiding over cases in this courtroom? I've handled cases ranging from parking tickets to murder."

"You record is well-known, sir," Ward groveled, "and respected by all."

"I've ruled on cases ranging from dog bites and domestic disputes to hit-and-runs and homicides."

"Yes, Your Honor. You have an outstanding record. A fine—"

"Now, Mr. Ward."

"Yes, sir."

Laura nudged Martha's elbow as Striker crooked his neck.

"Over all those years, I thought I'd seen it all." The judge narrowed his eyes and curled his upper lip.

"Sir?" Bart Ward squirmed a bit. "What do you—?"

"Until now," Striker snapped. "Until this case."

"Sir?"

"Mr. Ward, explain something to me. How is it that I hear of new evidence at this late stage—as the case goes to the jury? Why am I sitting in chamber with lawyers from both sides, examining evidence, while the jury prepares to deliberate? How is it that I'm being asked to rule on the admittance of a potentially explosive piece of exculpatory evidence at the eleventh hour?"

"Your Honor, I can't—"

"It's not a complicated question. Certainly not for a learned attorney such as yourself. Why the hell am I learning of a significant source of DNA evidence at end of the trial? How was this central sample of DNA kept out of the trial up until now? Why wasn't it brought forward in the first trial? How did this happen?"

Stammering, Ward tried to explain. He told the judge that the towel had been placed in the wrong police department's evidence bin by accident. It had been left there for more than a decade without anyone realizing its importance. Hell, no one even knew of its existence. Stumbling over his words, the chief prosecutor moved his gaze from the irate judge to his co-counsel, who was wiping sweat from his bald head one chair over.

Striker moved his blue lasers from Ward to Mel Radowitz. "Ahhh. Mr. Radowitz. The Honorable County Prosecutor. The brilliant legal mind behind *State of New York v. Edward Thomas Nash I.* The architect of a first-degree murder conviction that was based on no evidence or valid testimony. How do you explain this last-minute piece of discovery, sir? What's your story?"

Radowitz was crimson from his sweat-covered dome to his wrinkled neckline. "It was a mistake, Your Honor. An honest mistake."

"A *mistake?*" Striker roared as all four lawyers stiffened their posture. "An honest mistake? Like paying the witness? Like fudging the tire evidence? Like botching the psychiatric analysis? Like coercing the confession? Honest mistake after honest mistake. Gentleman, I have lost patience with all these mistakes. I view these mistakes as grounds for dismissing the indictment and handing this entire mess over to the Board of Legal Ethics and Responsibility. The Board can spend the next year determining who was at fault. Gentleman, I may be a simple country lawyer, but I ain't stupid. How dare you bring this foul-smelling pile of legal dung into my courtroom?"

Ward started to rise but stopped halfway as Striker snapped, "Sit down."

The judge closed his eyes and took a series of slow breaths. He turned to Laura and Martha. "Counsel for the defense." Striker seemed to have forced a degree of calm back into his roiling temper. "Tell me about this towel."

"Your Honor, the exhibit tagged 'Lambert Homicide #1' was supplied to the defense three days ago, pursuant to an order of this court issued to the Genesee Police Department. The exhibit—a white towel with visible blood splatter—was tested at the I-Gene Diagnostic DNA Testing Laboratory in Buffalo. I-Gene is certified by the American Association of Crime Laboratories and the College of American Pathologists."

"The findings?" Striker asked. "What did we learn?"

"The DNA extracted from the blood on the towel did not match the DNA sample taken from Edward Thomas Nash. This non-match was presented by the lab with a degree of certainty of 99.96%. Your Honor, Mr. Nash did not leave that bloodstained towel at the murder scene."

"Who did?" Striker boomed. "Who the hell did?"

"No one knows. Working with our law enforcement counterparts, the Center Against Wrongful Convictions ran the DNA profile through national, state, and local databases for the storage and exchange of DNA profiles. The Combined DNA Index System—CODIS—did not contain a sample from a criminal offender who matched this DNA profile."

Martha said, "Your Honor, it appears the man who killed Erin Lambert does not have an arrest or criminal conviction, so there's no DNA on file that matches the DNA on the towel. The actual perpetrator is still at large and poses an immediate risk to the community. The sooner this case is disposed of, the sooner the police can begin looking for the real killer."

Judge Striker stared into space. He let the room go silent. He repositioned his glasses, shifted in his chair, and glanced at the DNA report. He removed his glasses and turned to the chief prosecutor.

"Mr. Ward?"

"The state acknowledges the validity of the test results."

Striker rose to his feet, towering. His mere presence emitted a palpable force. He left his place at the table and walked up to Bart Ward. The good judge placed a hand on the shoulder of the good prosecutor. "I expect you to do the right thing."

84

THE EXONERATION ALLIANCE
INNOCENCE BLOG

BREAKING NEWS:

Convicted Murderer Proved Innocent

NEW YORK CONVICT EXONERATED

TEN-YEAR PRISON ORDEAL ENDS

The Council Against Wrongful Convictions has exonerated an innocent man more than ten years after his first-degree murder conviction.

Edward Thomas Nash is expected to leave the courtroom a free man tomorrow, after Superior Court Judge Peter J. Striker rules in a vacating hearing at the Erie County Courthouse. In his original trial, Nash was convicted of first-degree murder in the hanging death of a young woman in rural New York State.

Sentenced to life without parole, Nash served ten years and seven months at the Attica Correctional Facility. His jailers testified that he was both a psychopath and a sociopath—a charged refuted by expert defense witnesses and common sense.

Nash was not available for comment.

His attorney, Laura Tobias, spoke to reporters on the courthouse steps with this comment: "This is a banner day for the innocence movement. An innocent man has achieved justice. He is going home. At the same time, we know there are thousands more men and women unjustly imprisoned across this country. We will celebrate this, then get back to work."

85

Superior Court Judge Peter J. Striker looked down from the bench at Edward Thomas Nash.

Striker pounded the gavel and proclaimed, "You are free to go."

Eddie Nash dropped his head, tears of joy flowing.

Cassie Nash raised two hands to praise God.

Laura exhaled. Another prisoner was freed from the tomb of the innocent.

86

Sponsored By:

The Council Against Wrongful Convictions

The sign welcomed guests to the spacious Adirondack Room at the Empire Gardens Hotel in Buffalo. The crowd was in the mood to party. Luminaries from the national innocence movement mingled with public defenders, private attorneys, and even a few prosecutors. The guests chatted about the case around a chiseled ice sculpture of a blindfolded woman, holding the scales of justice. A half-dozen state representatives and local politicians mingled with guests and fielded questions from reporters, armed with audio recorders and notebooks. Three former prison inmates—exonerated of felony charges after serving long sentences—captivated the curious with their trials, tribulations, and transformations.

"I spent twenty-seven years in Folsom State Prison—the worst pen in California—for a murder I did not commit," one told a circle of onlookers. "The Innocence Project lawyer had to prove my innocence and point police to the actual killer. Sound familiar?"

Eddie Nash beamed into the lens of the photographer's Nikon 8310 Single Lens Reflex and—in sync with the beaming woman next to him— pronounced the word of the moment: "Freedom!" The flash assured a perfect exposure and signaled the next in line to step up for a picture with the guest of honor.

A recording of "The Redemption Song" by Bob Marley and the Wailers clashed with the clink of crystal stemware, and the voices of seventy-five guests.

A voice boomed over the speakers. "May I have your attention, please?"

All eyes turned to the center of the room.

In the center of the crowded space, the charismatic CEO of the Council Against Wrongful Convictions stood with a microphone in hand. Josh Linder raised a sparkling glass in the direction of the guest of honor.

"A toast to an innocent man. Best wishes, my friend. Your future starts now, Eddie."

The crowd cheered.

Josh looked toward Laura and hoisted his glass again.

"To his amazing attorney—the unstoppable Laura Tobias. A shout-out to the entire legal team. Great work!"

More cheers.

Josh turned to his left. A cameraman from a local TV station was focusing on him. "You know," Josh said to the camera, "our perception of wrongful conviction has changed over the years. We used to believe that sending an innocent man or woman to prison was a rare exception. We accepted this once-in-a-generation anomaly as the price we pay for living in a society of laws and courts. Now, we see that innocent people are imprisoned—even executed—in far greater numbers than anyone ever imagined. Ladies and gentleman, Eddie Nash is a living reminder of that grim reality. He sacrificed more than ten years of his life to teach us an invaluable lesson: We can never stop fighting for the incarcerated innocent."

Cheers rolled and glasses met.

A voice called from the crowd. "How does it feel to be out, Eddie?"

Someone thrust a microphone in Eddie's face.

"I haven't breathed clean air, eaten good food, or been hugged like this for so long," he said. "I'm just happy that this horrible nightmare is over."

87

THREE MONTHS LATER

Laura cruised down the country road. The top of the Mustang was down. The radio was up. Bruce Springsteen's "Born to Run" flow from the Bose speakers, the drumbeat pounding to the passing of the white lines under the tires. Laura felt the cool air flowed into her face. Her hair—longer now—whipped in the wind. The passing scenery made her smile. Lush pastures. Green hills. Trickling streams. Springtime—rebirth. Longer days, and evening thundershowers. Warmer temperatures, and new leaves. She saw the sign:

Eden

21 Miles

Left Lane

Laura did not plan to stop to see Eddie and Cassie on this visit. She took heart, though, in Eddie's good fortune. She knew that after the trial, Eddie flew home on the wings of press reports of his total exoneration: *"Innocent Man Home Free. Eden Man Found Innocent. Ten-Year Prison Ordeal Over."* She also knew that the cards and balloons at his welcome home party made him feel great. Knowing his taste for fried chicken, a local businessman presented him with a thousand-dollar gift certificate to Bojangles.

Laura continued down the highway. Eyes focused on the lane dividers, she thought about Eddie's good fortune. Two weeks after his return, Eddie accepted a six-thousand-dollar check from the state's modest inmate compensation fund. Eddie had the good form to wait a few days to lodge his $10 million lawsuit against the State of New York. Wrongful imprisonment. Malicious prosecution. A million for each full year spent at Attica.

He let the additional seven months slide.

With one hand on the steering wheel, Laura smiled at Eddie's courage. She'd accompanied him to two legal conferences for The Prison Project—a group fighting mass incarceration. At the end of Eddie's speech, he raised a fist and yelled, *"Attica! Attica! Remember Attica!"*

Otherwise, Laura advised him to keep a low profile, and he complied. He lived in a modest apartment at Eden Arms and worked as a mechanic at Jo Jo's Truck Repair. He took his mom out to dinner at the Riverside Diner every Wednesday and escorted her church every Sunday. They'd told Laura that the world looked big and beautiful from that new, gleaming, glass chapel on Heaven Hill. Reverend Garrett always delivered a good sermon, and the choir was heaven-sent. The sermon about the return of the Prodigal Son was their favorite. Eddie had stopped making fun of God. Just in case.

Laura returned her focus to the highway. Five miles from the turnoff for Eden, Laura glanced down at the newspaper on the passenger seat. *The New York Times* was open on the blue vinyl, like a friend riding shotgun. The headline above the fold called out like a gunshot blast. *"Police Corruption Scheme Triggers Multiple Arrests."* There was a smaller headline under it. *"Ten Indicted on Corruption Charges."*

Laura thought, The New York Times *is one hell of a newspaper.* Laura had read the whole article before setting out that morning. *The Times* reported that Eden County Chief of Detectives Peter Demario was a central figure in a shadowy network of corrupt cops and crooked prosecutors. Demario was indicted on counts ranging from corruption and conspiracy to using excessive force and filing false reports. He remained free on bail, while awaiting trial on charges that could land him in prison for twenty-five years.

I hope they stick him in Attica. I hear there's an open cell in D-Block.

Erie County Prosecutor Mel Radowitz was indicted on one count of corruption for his misdeeds in the original trial. Plus, a legal ethics board was on track to disbar him for malpractice. He never should have flirted with the Big Lie. In the end, the Big Lie always takes you down.

Attica Superintendent Leon Wilkes—Laura's biggest fan—was not indicted. At least, not in the first wave. However, Wilkes was under investigation by the state's Prison Review Board for mismanaging funds. How the powerful fall. Like a wall. One brick at a time.

Laura saw the sign for Eden. She leaned the Mustang into the exit and turned onto Burnt Mansion Road. She passed the old Angel's Gate Mental Asylum, recalling how Lou masqueraded as a stoner to get inside those crumbling walls. How he stole those secrets and triggered the search for the bloodstained towel. The exonerating evidence. Laura gazed out at the ruins. There were no dopers wandering through the overgrown gardens or burnouts sprawled on the crumbling porch. Their neighborhood dealer was gone.

Jimmy Dean Bernadi was no longer in a position to supply heroin and opioids to the addicted. He was ensconced in the county jail, awaiting trial on felony drug distribution charges. The strip-club-bouncer-turned-opioid-king was busted just three weeks after the end of the Nash trial. Laura smiled at the memory of his pathetic testimony. His bumbling web of lies and contradictions. How she revealed him for the liar that he was. How she raised the possibility that he was the bad guy. The essence of third-party guilt. In the wake of Nash's exoneration, Bernadi was—for a short time—a key suspect in the reopened Erin Lambert murder investigation. It turned out, though, that he really had attended that rock concert. Jimmy's alibi was for real. He was nowhere near the crime scene. He just had a bad memory. *Who forgets Pink Floyd?* Be that as it may, Laura's bluff had served its purpose. After the trial, a number of jurors told reporters that they believed Bernadi was the Hangman of Eden.

Alas, no. The search went on.

Laura considered how her life had been transformed since the trial. Over the Christmas break, she and her dad drove up to the Adirondacks. Surrounded by snowcapped mountains and icy streams, they shared memories of Janet Tobias. His wife. Her mom. They hiked up the mountain trail and looked out over the grand vistas. They felt closer to her than they had in years. They also promised to return to that spot every year. Laura had finally forgiven herself, and the eight-year-old girl who couldn't stand to see her mother go.

"I get it now," Laura told her father. *"Mom didn't leave me. She lives inside me."*

Her deathbed temper tantrum was nothing more than the normal expression of a terrified little girl. She'd always known that. Mom must have known it, too. Laura just had to embrace it.

At long last, Laura had exonerated herself.

Laura turned onto Meadow Lark Lane. Big houses. Nice part of town.

She smiled at one more piece of personal news. She no longer worked for the Council Against Wrongful Convictions. With all the press coverage from the case, she'd gained quite the rep within the legal community. The head of an important advocacy group in Albany—the state capital—had tracked her down. He praised her work and offered her a job. It was a proposition Laura couldn't pass up. Working for the Center for Legal Reform would enable her to push for new laws to help the incarcerated innocent even more. It would help prevent future innocent defendants from being convicted and locked up in tombs of the innocent. The reforms would help people across the legal spectrum. Fewer innocents would go to prison. Police would focus on actual criminals. Victims and survivors would see the real perpetrators punished. The public would have more confidence in the laws and the courts.

Laura looked forward to the challenge—once her hiatus was over. She wouldn't start the new job for another month. So, right now, she was a free agent—open to doing whatever.

88

LAURA PULLED UP TO THE THREE-STORY, BRICK HOUSE AT 122 MEADOW Lark Lane. It had what real estate agents call curb appeal. Three stories, freshly painted. Large, shining windows flanked by black shutters. A wooden swing on the wrap-around porch. Shrubs flanking the brick walkway.

Laura climbed out of the Mustang and strolled up the walk. The azaleas were blooming, the red bushes on fire. She bounded up the porch steps to the red oak door. The woman who'd invited her was waiting there. The woman who'd tracked her down and asked her to pay a visit. The woman who'd said it was vital that they meet.

"Mrs. Lambert." Laura smiled. "How are you?"

"Thank you for coming, Laura," Mrs. Lambert said. "Please come in and sit, and call me Josie."

For some reason, Josie Lambert looked up and down the street as Laura stepped past her.

The two women sat in antique armchairs in the well-appointed living room. Josie wore a white, cotton dress. Much nicer than Laura's loose-fitting, flannel shirt and faded jeans. What did she care? She wasn't on duty. She didn't have a job yet.

Laura pointed to a framed photo of a young girl on the coffee table. "Is that Erin?" The girl in the picture was playing the piano, her eyes riveted on the keys. She was maybe ten years old.

"Yes," Josie Lambert confirmed in a voice that threatened to break. "It's my little girl. My beautiful little girl."

Erin wondered, *Is it a permanent shrine or a prop for my visit?*

Josie Lambert cleared her throat. "You must be wondering why I asked you to come down."

"Well, I was surprised to get your call. I know the trial was very upsetting to you and your husband."

"Yes. It was."

"I'm sorry. I didn't know how to spare you the pain."

"No. You did the right thing."

Laura tilted her head. "What do you mean?"

"Let me explain." Mrs. Lambert leaned forward. "My husband and I want to tell you something. We want to tell you something about our little girl."

Laura nodded and asked, "Where is Mr. Lambert?"

Mrs. Lambert lifted a water glass from the coffee table and took a sip. "I'm afraid Paul got called into work. There was an emergency down at the recycling plant. He's a very high-level foreman and has to respond to all the crises. He's out there now. He wanted to be here."

"Oh. I'm sorry I missed him."

Laura knew that Paul Lambert was an important man at the Erie County Recycling Center, overseeing metal reclamation. Laura had wanted to meet with him. She wanted to make a new start. Their encounter in the hallway of the courthouse was so unfortunate.

Laura smiled at Josie. "I understand why he can't be here. He has responsibilities to tend to."

"Miss Tobias," Josie Lambert said, "I have to tell you how sorry we are. Paul and I both believed that Eddie killed our precious daughter. We were so distraught over the loss that we lost track of the truth. The evidence just seemed so overwhelming against him, and we were desperate for justice. In the sentencing part of that first trial, we urged the judge to impose the maximum sentence. We are so sorry. We were wrong. When I—"

Laura interrupted. "Why apologize to me?"

Mrs. Lambert took another sip and looked out the window. "You brought out the truth. You righted the wrong. We owe you our thanks. Perhaps you can pass along our apology to Eddie. I'm sure he has no interest in hearing from us. We wouldn't presume to contact him. How is he?"

"He's good. He's adjusting. He harbors no bad feelings." Laura reached over the coffee table to take the woman's trembling hand. "You are a compassionate person, Mrs. Lambert. Are you still working as an RN?"

"Yes. At the Eden Community Clinic. Doing my part."

Laura paused before treading on new ground: "Mrs. Lambert, I have to ask you this: Have you given any thought to who may have killed Erin? Now that you know it was not Eddie Nash?"

"My husband has been turning it over in his mind," she replied. "He wants to tell you what he thinks. He believes he knows who did it. He'd love to get your opinion. He respects you so much."

Laura hesitated for a brief moment before speaking. "Maybe I should drive out to see him."

89

As Laura pulled away from the curb, she left Josie Lambert standing at the door, looking up and down the tree-lined street. Laura drove out of the neighborhood and turned onto Industrial Drive. Auto-parts stores, machine shops, and used car dealerships whizzed by. She checked her rear-view mirror. A black SUV was behind her.

Laura turned onto the curving entrance road to the Erie County Recycling Center. She passed a huge dumpster, overflowing with yard waste. A man was heaving a bag of lawn clippings into the bin. She passed the glass recycling center and cringed at the sound of bottles being ground into sparkling shards. She watched an industrial trash compactor flatten mounds of trash.

She parked outside Building C. Paul Lambert ran the scrap metal reclamation operation in the sprawling, yellow, corrugated tin structure.

Laura walked toward the southwest corner of the building. She followed signs pointing to the office. She passed stripped cars, rusted refrigerators, broken air conditioners, and stacks of copper pipe. She saw Mr. Lambert waiting at the office entrance, holding open the door, smiling out like an old friend.

"My wife called and told me you were coming." He ushered her in— his long, muscular right arm stretched out in a grand gesture. "After you."

Such a gentleman.

Laura glanced at his rugged face, thick neck, broad shoulders, and salt-and-pepper hair. The man was one of those young sixty-somethings—the ones you saw in TV travel ads. The physically-fit ones who pissed off overweight thirty-year-olds.

Lambert extended a calloused right hand. Laura grasped it and shook. *Hell of a handshake*, she thought. Laura widened her smile to hide her skepticism. "How can I help you, sir? Your wife told me you have information to share. She said you have an idea about who may have killed Erin."

"I have something to show you."

"Oh?"

He opened a steel door that led into the plant, where useless throwaways were shredded, twisted, and melted for rebirth. He motioned her through with another sweeping gesture. "Step right in. It's right here."

Laura stalled at the sight of the stripping and crushing machines.

"After you," he said. "I insist."

She thanked him and passed by him.

The automatic lock self-activated behind them. No employees were at work. It was just the two of them. Alone together. With the scrap metal and grinding machines.

Laura scanned the interior of the building. Twisted steel and mangled aluminum overflowed from large, green bins. Dismembered cars and kitchen appliances that had been trashed by their owners awaited mangling. Destruction before resurrection. The automated crushing and shearing machines—idle for the moment—were set to flatten, cut, and spew out reclaimed iron, steel, nickel, and copper.

Laura coughed into her sleeve. The air was toxic. It dripped with chemicals used to strip rust. She looked from the concrete floor to the high ceiling. Four hardened steel rafters ran from north to south. She clutched her cell phone like it was a weapon, even though she knew there was no service in this tin coffin.

"Congratulations, Laura." Paul Lambert's voice was low and firm. "You performed well at the trial. You proved your client's innocence. You exonerated him. You won the day."

"The facts were on my side." Laura fought back the waver in her voice. "All I did was let the truth reveal itself."

"We had Eddie Nash all wrong. We persecuted an innocent man. We made a terrible mistake. We owe him so much."

"It's history now." Laura forced a smile. "Time to move on."

"Is it?" Lambert retorted. "A killer is still out there."

"The police are on it. They're closing in on him. The Hangman of Eden is going down. Justice will be done."

"I know who did it." Lambert smiled with wide eyes. "I know who killed my little girl."

90

"How do you know?" Laura feigned surprise. "How *can* you know?"

"Come on, Laura." Lambert's inflection was as flat as the aluminum sheet under the industrial press. His eyes gleamed like the bright sun, reflecting on polished steel. An odd smile was fixed on his face. "Tell me, Laura, what do you know about me?"

Laura shrugged. "Just the basics. Paul Michael Lambert. Born in The Bronx, 1962. Served in the U.S. Marines. Special Intel Officer for twenty years. High-level, elite service. Top-secret work in Afghanistan. So secret, your military record was sealed. For a time."

"Very good."

"Retired in 2000. Settled in Eden with your wife and young daughter. You went to work here. Bought that nice big house. Erin was your only child."

"She was." He looked to the oil-stained floor. "I lost my only child. I guess I was a good soldier, and a bad father."

"I'm sorry, Mr. Lambert, for your loss."

He paused. His smile widened and waned, then widened and waned again. "Let me share a simple truth: What you know will save you. What you don't know will kill you. You know I was in the military. You know my service was secret. Congratulations. You don't know what I *did* in the military."

Laura smiled back at him. *Damn,* she thought, *I hate to be underestimated.*

She saw Delilah Cole in her mind's eye, the sweet and brilliant paralegal from the Council Against Wrongful Convictions. Her former assistant and protégé. What a friend. She was so nice to conduct all that research as a parting gift to her old boss.

"Well, Mr. Lambert, you're wrong about that. I know quite a bit about you. I know you served in Special Forces in Afghanistan. You were secretly attached to the Afghan armed forces. The military records for those missions were declassified last year. Fascinating reading. Despite the redactions."

Surprise registered on his face. He stared at her in silence.

Laura pictured Charles Steel, the master investigator. Charles was so nice to tap his military connections to secure the records. Charles had also tracked down Lambert's old commanding officer. Now retired. Their talk was revealing.

Lambert's upper lip curled. "Very good, Laura. Excellent work. The innocence lawyer has done her homework. Most impressive—as always."

"You were an observer at the Afghan National Prison, Pol-E-Charkhi. A hellhole east of Kabul. Surrounded by crumbling walls, razor wire, and mass graves."

"How did you—?"

"It was the one prison sanctioned by the Afghan government to carry out executions. Taliban prisoners were put to death as terrorists. Hundreds of them."

"True. Put to death for good reason."

Laura locked her eyes with his. Cold as ice. "All the executions were carried out by the traditional method: Death by hanging."

Lambert grinned. "I witnessed the hangings. From high scaffolds. Sixteen-foot drops. Neck-snapping death."

Lambert stepped to a work bench and picked up a device. It looked like an industrial remote control. He hit a button. A buzzer blasted. The harsh noise was followed by the hum of polished steel, gliding on greased runners. Laura tracked the sound to the ceiling. She looked up at the source. She saw the steel ceiling beam with the greased runners. A three-foot iron hook was mounted on the beam. From the iron hook hung a rope.

At the end of the rope was a noose.

She showed no emotion as the hook, rope, and noose glided along the runners in her direction. She watched as it stopped in the space between herself and Lambert. The makeshift gallows was in place. She tried to count the loops above the knot but couldn't. It didn't matter. She knew there were thirteen.

She stared into the soulless black holes that were Lambert's eyes. He was still at the workbench. Twenty feet away. She saw those black holes narrow. She heard him mutter a curse. She felt hate emanating from deep inside of him.

"Bitch," he spewed. "You're too fucking smart for your own good."

The hangman's rope stood between them, the noose swinging back and forth, maybe six feet off the oil-soaked floor.

Laura straightened as Lambert walked toward her. She retreated until her back hit the wall. She watched as he closed in and asked, "What else do you know?"

She stared. Not so much as a blink. "I know about your sister, Charlene. Her suicide was so tragic. Hanging herself like that. Nice of her to name you her beneficiary."

Lambert grinned as she continued, "I know about the life insurance policy."

"Oh?"

"The one you took out for Erin. The piano prodigy."

He sneered.

"I know about the fifty grand you collected."

"I needed the money for a boat," he admitted.

"What about Nash?"

"Nash was an easy scapegoat. A patsy made-to-order."

"So, a couple weeks before the murder, you invited Nash to your house. You give him a couple beers and talked about Erin. You thanked him for trying to save your poor, misguided daughter. And you saved the empty bottles."

"Go on, Counselor. You have the floor. For a moment."

"After you beat Erin with an iron pipe and strung her up, you planted the empties at the crime scene. Empty bottles with Nash's DNA. Nice touch."

"I thought so."

"For the longest time, I struggled with the urine evidence. How did you pull that off? How did Eddie's urine get on Erin's body? Then, I remembered your wife. Sweet little Josie. Your accomplice. The registered nurse at the Eden Community Clinic. The clinic where Eddie got his physicals. It was so easy for her to swipe a urine sample, freeze it, and give to you to drip onto the body. The Big Lie was born."

Paul Lambert turned as crimson as blood. "You know too much."

"Of course, you never bet on Erin slashing you with that broken bottle the night of the murder. Inflicting a gouge and drawing blood. You never expected to have to go back to your truck—the one you rented with cash under a fake name—to retrieve the towel. You were so careless to leave the towel behind. With your bloodstains on it."

"Laura Tobias. The brilliant lawyer."

"Paul Lambert. The Hangman of Eden."

Lambert laughed. "I'll tell you this much: I learned a great deal at Pol-E-Charkhi. Made the executioner my best friend. He was such a good teacher. He showed me all his secrets. How to choose the rope. How to set the fall. How to tie the knot."

"Thirteen loops?" she asked.

"That was my touch," Lambert sneered. "My signature."

"Why Erin?"

"My daughter. The drugged up stripper. The shameless whore. Whores deserve death."

"You're a killer."

"I'm an executioner. There's a difference."

Laura clutched her phone.

"Your phone can't save you." Lambert laughed. "No service in here. You can't call 911. Sorry. Too late."

Laura held it up like a prize. "It's not just a phone."

Lambert stared with smug arrogance. "What is it?"

"It's a transmitter."

At that moment, the door from the office crashed open, and Laura's accomplices joined the party. The man in the blue suit was a state police investigator. The two men in body armor carried automatic weapons. Charles and Lou were right alongside them.

"Erin Lambert's father," Charles said. "The Hangman of Eden."

Lou grunted. "Fucking murderer."

Laura moved closer to the deranged executioner. She looked into his eyes. She waited for the handcuffs to click.

"You're going to need a good lawyer," she said.

He looked back with impotent fury.

"And," she added, "it won't be me."

THE END

Special Thanks

John J. Lennon

Currently:

Sing Sing Correctional Facility

Previously:

Attica Correctional Facility

More Thanks

Readers

Neva Bowers

Lisa Klingburg

Helen Bowers

Bob Esselburn

Denise Esselburn

Natalie Esselburn

Steve Schwadron

Wynn Witthans